PRISONERS of HATE

AF556319

C.V. Murali

Published by:

Cedar books

An Imprint of

Pustak Mahal®, Delhi

J-3/16, Daryaganj, New Delhi-110002

☎ 23276539, 23272783, 23272784 • *Fax:* 011-23260518

E-mail: info@pustakmahal.com • *Website:* www.pustakmahal.com

Sales Centre

■ 10-B, Netaji Subhash Marg, Daryaganj, New Delhi-110002

☎ 23268292, 23268293, 23279900 • *Fax:* 011-23280567

E-mail: rapidexdelhi@indiatimes.com

■ Hind Pustak Bhawan

6686, Khari Baoli, Delhi-110006

☎ 23944314, 23911979

Branch Offices

Bengaluru: ☎ 22234025 • *Telefax:* 22240209

E-mail: pustak@airtelmail.in • pustak@sancharnet.in

Mumbai: ☎ 22010941

E-mail: rapidex@bom5.vsnl.net.in

Patna: ☎ 3294193 • *Telefax:* 0612-2302719

E-mail: rapidexptn@rediffmail.com

Hyderabad: *Telefax:* 040-24737290

E-mail: pustakmahalhyd@yahoo.co.in

Disclaimer : The novel is entirely a work of fiction. The names, characters and incidents portrayed in it are the work of the author's imagination. Any resemblance to actual persons, living or dead, events or localities is entirely coincidental.

© Author

ISBN 978-81-223-1070-2

Edition 2009

All rights reserved. No part of this publication may be reproduced, stored in a retrieval system or transmitted, in any form or by any means, electronic, mechanical, photocopying, recording or otherwise, without the prior permission in writing from the author/publisher.

Printed at : Param Offsetters, Okhla, New Delhi-110020

Dedication

In memory of Patti –
my grandmother – a kind soul

Acknowledgements

I would like to express my gratitude to my family, friends, critics and readers who felt after reading my first book that all was not lost and there was a writer in me – after all.

It gave me the courage to venture again.

I would like to thank my family again for keeping my spirits up while I wrote this book and searched for a publisher.

And, finally my heartfelt appreciation for my publishing team for spending time, effort, money and reposing their trust in my work.

We shall overcome,
We shall overcome,
We shall overcome some day...
We shall live in peace,
We shall live in peace,
We shall live in peace some day...
We'll walk hand in hand,
We'll walk hand in hand,
We'll walk hand in hand some day...
Oh, deep in my heart I do believe,
We shall overcome some day...

Lyrics derived from Reverend Charles Tindley's gospel song "I'll Overcome Some Day"

Contents

Prologue

The heat and humidity was taking its toll. His pace was slackening and the sweat was running down his face in streams. Nevertheless, he was not the one to give up. This was the last stretch and he was willing himself to move on. He was gasping for oxygen and could feel his heart on an overdrive. He could feel the rush of blood; and for an instant, he thought it was all over. He closed his eyes and ran as he had never before. He stumbled and collapsed. He opened his eyes and smiled weakly. He had made it.

Shivaji Park is a vast expanse of greenery in the central Dadar area of Mumbai. Established by the British in 1925 and named after the 15th century Maratha warrior, it has over the ages acquired significant historical, cultural and sports value.

Historical, because it has been the venue for huge gatherings of freedom fighters prior to Independence, and for innumerable political gatherings and movements, post Independence.

Cultural, because it is a second home to many institutions which organise a wide variety of social activities round the year, like drawing competitions for children, lectures by eminent personalities, marriages, *pujas...*

Sports or rather cricket, since it has been the nursery for Indian cricket... producing among others, the two most prolific run-getters in Indian cricket annals – Gavaskar and Tendulkar.

The neighbourhood is also one of the few remaining strongholds of the original Maharashtrian way of living in Mumbai.

Farhan Rasool slowly got up with the smile still lurking on his tired face. He had finally managed to run ten laps around the park today – a distance of thirteen kilometres non-stop. He usually ran between seven to eight laps but had today pushed himself to the limit. He felt satisfied and happy. It was not often that he felt happy.

He looked at his watch, it was only seven, but the heat and humidity was sapping. He took a swig from the bottle of water that he carried, and looked around. He could see the group in khaki shorts still going about their morning drills, with their cries renting the air. Cries that had terrified him and had wanted him to run away. Nevertheless, he had stood his ground and now, he watched them with a feeling of contempt and hate.

Hate and revenge – these were the primary emotions that had kept him sane and helped him to survive. Hate for the country, for the society and its environs where he was born, brought up and where he worked. They had turned his world upside down and he was now having his vengeance. The best part about the entire thing was that they did not know; they only knew him as the Physics lecturer who taught at one of the leading colleges in Mumbai. The other face of Farhan, the mastermind behind recent terrorist attacks, remained unknown. Farhan smiled again; he was beginning to enjoy his dual role...

A few hundred metres away, Madhav Karve was also beginning to enjoy his dual life. He smiled as his wife Reena brought in his bed tea and the morning newspaper. He dismissed her with a wave and pored through the newspaper. His blood boiled as he read reports about the killing of tourists in Srinagar in broad daylight. Bastards, he thought; only a pogrom could eliminate these vermins. The country needed a Fuhrer to exterminate these descendants of Chengiz Khan. A hint of a smile crossed his face as he remembered the faces of the families he had butchered with his own hands. That was the other side of Madhav, quite at variance from the Madhav Karve, who was a successful builder. He got up from his bed... today was going to be an eventful day.

A couple of blocks away, Sanjay was getting ready for work. He had to rush to catch the train that would take him to the newspaper office where he worked as a journalist. He had been working for the past eight years now, and those eight years had seen him witness many gruesome events. However, those rare acts of courage, in face of adversity, still gave him hope... hope for the country, for the majority of his countrymen and for the future of his unborn child. He bade goodbye to his wife, who was on her maternity leave, and left.

A smile crossed Sanjay's face as the train pulled out of Dadar Station. Nafisa had come into his life like the monsoon rains of Mumbai and had rejuvenated him. He could smile now as he remembered the shock that he had seen on his parents and future in-laws' faces, when they had announced that they wanted to get married. It had been a long struggle to bring the Gujarati Brahmin and the Bohra Muslim families together. But all is well that ends well, he thought. His train of thoughts came to an abrupt end as the train came to a halt at the Churchgate station. Another day in office, but it could be an important day, he thought.

Ladies and gents, you have now had brief glimpses of the three protagonists in this story – Farhan, Madhav and Sanjay. Ordinary names, ordinary people...Only time will tell.

You seem to be puzzled by my sudden appearance, wondering where I fit into the scheme of things. No, I am not the one telling you the story, nor do I fit into the storyline anywhere. Perhaps, for want of any other word, you can call me the **Sutradhar** *and* **Vidushak** *rolled into one.*

The term Sutradhar literally translates as 'the one who holds the threads'. In classical Sanskrit theatre and in various regional folk theatres, he is a central figure who narrates and sometimes even manipulates the performance. The Vidushak, on the other hand, is the clown, who can take liberties with the narrative and act as a social critique.

I shall be the link between those three men, their lives and times and you...

❁❁❁

CHAPTER-I

Before

Farhan

Farhan Rasool was born in 1974 into a prosperous Sunni Muslim household which lived in a three-bedroom house in the Prabhadevi area of Mumbai. He was the youngest child and his birth, after three daughters, had brought a lot of joy and merriment into the family. His sisters were much older than him, the eldest being twenty years older and the youngest ten years. His father Ghulam Rasool had migrated to Mumbai from a small village near Meerut in search of a livelihood, to support his family.

The Quit India Movement was at its peak and Bombay, as it was known then, was the scene of demonstrations and violent protests. Young Ghulam was torn between the urge to join the demonstrations and to earn a living and provide succour to his parents. He chose the latter. He joined a small transport company as a clerk. He was a diligent boy and very soon impressed the owner, Ehtesham Ali, who suggested that he should join some night college and complete his graduation.

He soon joined one and thus began his years of learning, at work and in college. While he learnt and grew at work, the country was in total turmoil. Independence was round the corner and so was the talk of partition and formation of Pakistan. Riots had broken out in various parts of the country. Bombay remained peaceful, but there was tension prevalent in the air. Refugees started to arrive from Punjab and Sind and there were talks of Muslims moving en masse from various parts of India to the soon to be formed country of Pakistan.

Ehtesham Ali's family belonged to a village in Punjab near Ludhiana and Ghulam could see him getting agitated, day by day, as he received news of riots in those parts. Things came to a head when Ehtesham heard one day that their neighbours had massacred his uncle's family in cold blood and all the Muslims of the village had decided to migrate to Pakistan.

One morning when Ghulam went to work, he found the office shut. He stood at the door, and waited, and waited...

Finally, tired of waiting, he decided to go to Ehtesham's residence, which was a couple of streets down the office. Ghulam had gone there a couple of times on some errand. He went there and knocked at the door.

"Who is it?" cried a voice from inside.

"It's me, Ghulam Rasool. I work at Ehtesham *Saab's* office," replied Ghulam.

"Come in, the door is open," replied Ehtesham Ali's voice.

Ghulam opened the door gingerly and went inside. The room was dark; many of the belongings lay here and there and somebody packing, at the far end of the room, could be seen.

"Sit down," said Ehtesham. "We are leaving for Pakistan in a day or two. I am trying to get the best deal for my company. Many of the employees are also coming with me. Would you also like to join me?"

Ghulam was too shocked to react. Slowly he said, "But why?"

"There is no place for us in this country now. We will become second-class citizens here, that too, if they leave us alive," replied Ehtesham Ali.

Tears welled in his eyes.

"My uncle and his family were killed by their own neighbours. They had lived all along like family for generations and suddenly.... How can you now trust anybody, if you cannot trust your neighbour? I came to this city when I was like you. I never studied, but I built up this business from scratch. This is where I became a man and now..."

Saying so, he burst into tears. Ghulam did not know how to react.

"Ehtesham *Saab*," he said slowly. "Everything will become alright by the grace of God, have faith in Him."

"How can I trust anyone?" wailed Ehtesham. "I have spent the best part of my life here and I have no desire to leave. But, my children deserve a good future and I do not know what the future holds for them here. At least, they can live life without fear in Pakistan."

"But," said Ghulam, "How do you know what is in store for you there? How can you leave everything and run away? Nobody can drive us out from our own country."

"No, Ghulam," answered Ehtesham. "I have made up my mind; I can no longer live in a place where I need to live in fear. It is probably God's will; and who am I to question His will?"

There was a long period of silence.

"Ghulam, come with me," said Ehtesham, "and we will rebuild our lives in Pakistan."

"But," said Ghulam, "It is an unknown place and I do not want to go there."

"Bombay was unknown to you when you came here," replied Ehtesham, "but see, now you do not wish to leave this place. We are going to Lahore and I am sure you will like it."

"But I do not wish to leave this country," said Ghulam. "Muslims and Hindus have lived together for ages; yes they have fought with each other. But then which family does not fight? I am sure that this is also a passing phase and we have nothing to fear. With due respect, Ehtesham *Saab*, I am not coming."

A wry smile lit up Ehtesham Ali's face.

"You are right," he said. "But you are young and I am old. I do not have the courage or your faith to keep me going. Maybe when things become normal like you say, I will come back.... You are a brave and determined person, Ghulam; and I have a request for you. Can you take over my business and run it? Do not look surprised. I would rather entrust it with you than sell it off. I have built it from scratch and I am sure, you will be my worthy successor. Don't say no, Ghulam. I know you can do it."

And as India awoke to a new life and freedom, Ghulam Rasool, all of twenty-three years of age, became the proprietor of The New India Transport Company in Bombay. The sudden change of fortunes did not go into young Ghulam's head. He continued attending the night college and completed his graduation a year after. As the country slowly found its feet, so did Ghulam's business.

The business prospered and Ghulam felt happy with the decision he had made that afternoon in Ehtesham Ali's house. He got married. Soon, the first of his daughters was born. He named her Nargis, after the leading lady of the silver screen. His second daughter Waheeda followed in a couple of years.

He bought a new flat in Prabhadevi and a car; his children joined the local convent school. But Ghulam Rasool continued with his simple lifestyle. He was a pious person, not unduly religious, but one who kept his *Ramzan* fast. But Ghulam Rasool had one vice; he was addicted to the Hindi movies, which were churned out from Bombay. He was a die-hard fan of Raj Kapoor. He made it a point to see all his movies, on the first day of their release and then many more times after that. He could see a mirror of himself in the simpleton, down-to-earth roles that Raj Kapoor often played.

In all these years, Ghulam had kept in touch with Ehtesham Ali through letters that became more and more infrequent as relationship between India and its new neighbour started souring. Ehtesham Ali was happy in his new home. He had managed to start a new business which was doing well. His children were happily married. And then, Ehtesham Ali's world came crashing down.

The year was 1965; Ghulam Rasool's wife was pregnant with their third child and India and Pakistan were engaged in a full scale war in Kashmir and Punjab. On a sultry August evening, there was a knock at the door and Ehtesham Ali opened it to find three policemen. He had broken no law and was shocked to see them. The policemen were curt; they showed him a search warrant. As he and his family watched in amazement, the policemen turned his house upside down.

"Ah!" screamed one of the policemen.

Ehtesham saw that the policeman had his hand around some papers.

The policeman brought the papers and pointed at his face.

"Letters from India!" he said, "You bloody Indian spy..."

Before he knew what was happening, Ehtesham was bundled in the police van. He spent the next fifteen days in prison and came back a broken man – physically and mentally. Ghulam heard about this from a former colleague, who had followed Ehtesham to Lahore. He was pained; he wanted to send a response, call up his benefactor, but did not do so since he did not want to complicate matters further. That was the last time he heard about Ehtesham Ali.

Ghulam's daughters were growing up and his house was filled with joy and laughter. He was a happy man, but he still had one regret; he did not have a son. He wanted a son who would help him with the business as he grew older and who would carry the business forward. His regret slowly turned to frustration and he increasingly became very irritable.

The business had expanded and had reached new heights. Ghulam Rasool had opened offices in several towns and often had to travel to his various offices. On one such routine visit to Solapur, he found himself stranded in his hotel. Riots had suddenly broken out and there was curfew in many parts of the town. It was now late evening on his second day and he decided to go for a short walk because he felt cooped up sitting in his hotel room. He walked a couple of blocks; the roads were quite deserted and he started feeling uneasy. He was about to turn back when he heard a cry. He turned back and found a group of people chasing a single person at a distance. The person, or rather a boy was running and panting, and was coming straight towards him. The boy came running, caught hold of him and cowered behind him. Ghulam Rasool stood there between the boy and the mob running towards him.

Ghulam was not a coward, neither was he a brave man; he was in fact just like the vast majority of people. He went about his life not bothering anybody and not bothering to help others, if he could. That is not to say that he did not care; he cared very much for the people, who worked for him and took care of them and their families, and was always there to help them in times of need. However, when it came to strangers or society in general, he preferred to be a bystander. He was pained, frustrated to see poverty and hunger stalking the streets of Bombay. He hoped the government would do something about it sooner...

When does one reach breaking point? When does apathy, indifference, frustration translate itself into action? When will we break away from this collective apathy? I am sure sitting there in the comfort of our homes, we would have had many animated armchair discussions on what ails this country and what the government, the police, the administration should be doing? But, dear friend, what have we been doing about it? What would you have done had you been in Ghulam's place?

Ghulam could now see the mob clearly, there were about ten persons; all of them had swords, knives in their hands and looked terrifying. They were within fifteen feet of him and he could sense and feel his impending end. He felt a strong urge to throw the boy away from him and run, but he stood his ground. He could see the eyes of the leader now, blazing in rage and anger.

"Stop!" he shouted.

The mob was almost upon him. For a fraction of a second, the leader's eyes and his locked and in that moment, the leader shouted at the mob to stop. They stopped and surrounded him, barely an arm's length away.

"*Allah O Akbar!*" shouted a voice from the back and the cries were reverberated by the entire group.

"Let that boy go," shouted the leader to Ghulam, "or you too shall die."

"What has he done?" asked Ghulam calmly.

"He is a Hindu," replied the leader. "They have burnt our shops and houses, hundreds of our people have been killed since yesterday, he must die."

"The boy has done you no harm." replied Ghulam, "Let him go. I am old, I have lived my life; kill me if you want."

Ghulam would wonder later in his life, what made him say those words. Where did he get the courage to utter those words?

"Kill him also!" shouted somebody.

"Are you a Hindu or a Muslim?" shouted someone else.

"How does it matter?" replied Ghulam. "You want to kill; so kill me and spare the boy."

"No, we cannot kill our own," shouted another person.

"He must be a Hindu," screamed someone, "kill him; that is why he is trying to trick us."

"Shut up," said the leader and the noises died down.

Ghulam knew his life was hanging by a thread, but at that moment it did not seem to matter.

"What is your name?" asked the leader.

"Ghulam Rasool," he replied.

"Ghulam," he said, "one word from me and both you and the boy will be dead. You must be having a family; do you want your children to be orphaned? Go away. I don't want my hands bloodied by killing a fellow Muslim."

The crowd was getting restive now.

"Enough!" screamed a voice. "Let us kill them both and get on."

Suddenly, they heard the sound of a siren; a police siren and in the dying light of the day, they saw a police vehicle speeding towards them. As Ghulam and the boy watched rooted at their spot, the mob started running helter-skelter.

They could now hear shots; firing from the policemen, who seemed to be firing at them indiscriminately. They were now in grave danger of being shot by the policemen.

Ghulam quickly ducked along with the young boy and lay face down on the ground. The firing seemed to go on for eternity and Ghulam expected a bullet to hit him any moment. Then there was silence and a lot of shouting. He lay still, not knowing what to do. Suddenly, he felt somebody kicking him.

"Get up!" shouted somebody.

He rolled over to find a policeman standing over him. He got up to find a few bodies strewn around, including the leader of the mob. The boy had still not got up; Ghulam bent down and patted him. There was no movement.

"*Arrey*! What are you trying to do?" said the policeman; "he is dead."

Now he saw a bullet mark on the boys' temple. He cried in anguish; he had failed to save the boy, after all. Suddenly he found himself handcuffed and being pulled rudely towards the police jeep.

"What is happening?" Ghulam cried out.

"You were rioting," replied the policeman rudely.

"But, I was only trying to save the boy from the mob," replied Ghulam.

"Shut up and get in," said the policeman. "You cannot get away by telling me all that nonsense."

Ghulam was bundled into a small, dark cell in the police station. There were already a dozen or so persons in the place and he was barely able to sit. He could not understand why Allah was testing him like this. He had only been trying to save that boy, poor soul and here he was locked up for rioting.

The night wore on. He could barely see the faces of the others, but could feel their breath. There was not much conversation going on and he wondered how many more like him were there in the jail. Suddenly he felt panicky and started shouting, pleading and asking to be let out. There was loud cursing from the other inmates who seemed to be fast asleep. He continued shouting until something hit him hard on his head and he passed out.

He woke up to see some light filtering through a small opening. Now he could vaguely make out the faces of the people in the cell. Most of them were young boys and they all seemed to be fast asleep. He felt a throbbing on his head and noticed he had a big lump; somebody must have hit him real hard yesterday night, when he was shouting. Slowly, the motley crowd around him started stirring and soon they were all up and talking; they all seemed to know each other. Ghulam sat sullenly wondering at this twist of fate.

The day dragged on, suddenly a hefty Inspector along with a *Havaldar* marched in. He pointed at three boys who were then dragged by the *Havaldar* out of the cell. He was about to close the gate, when the inspector pointed to Ghulam, who was also forcibly taken out. All four were led into a larger room which had a table and a chair. The inspector went and sat on the table. All the four were made to stand in a line facing him.

"So," he said slowly, looking at them turn by turn; "How many people did you kill?"

"I did not kill anybody," shouted Ghulam, "I was only trying to save the boy when you came and arrested me."

The Inspector looked at him intently and said slowly, in a whisper, "It's me who does the shouting here, not you."

"But I am innocent," pleaded Ghulam, "I was only trying to save that boy."

"Where is the boy?" asked the Inspector.

"You, I mean the police killed him when they started shooting," replied Ghulam.

"So," said the Inspector his voice slowly rising, "you say that you tried to save the boy and we killed him."

Ghulam did not reply.

"Answer, my question!" shouted the Inspector.

"Yes, I mean the police must have accidentally killed him," he said. "We were lying on the ground to protect ourselves and a bullet must have hit him."

"Interesting," replied the Inspector. "But, why were you trying to protect the boy?"

"He was a small kid and the mob was after him," replied Ghulam. "How can one watch in silence..."

The Inspector nodded his head, got up slowly from the table, and suddenly gave a big slap to one of the boys standing on the line.

"So, what is your story? Did you also try to save some one? Come on tell me," he said, the voice again not rising above a whisper.

"We just threw stones, *Saab*," he cried out, "we did not kill anybody. Please let us go; we shall not do it again."

"Take these guys," he said to the *Havaldar*, pointing to the three boys, "and put them back in the jail. Let them be hungry for a day..."

He now turned back to Ghulam.

"You seem to be a decent man, then why were you instigating the mob to kill the boy," he said slowly.

Before he realised, Ghulam felt a heavy hand landing on his face and he fell down with a thud.

"Tell me the truth or I will blow your head out," said the Inspector and pointed his gun at Ghulam's head.

Ghulam could see death facing at him again. He looked at the Inspector calmly and said, "You, your men have already killed an innocent citizen; I suppose it will not matter if you kill one more."

Ghulam could see the rage on the Inspector's face as he said this. Abruptly, the Inspector turned away and went and sat on the table. He motioned Ghulam to come and sit on the chair.Ghulam got up and walked shakily and sat down.

"Get him a glass of water," the Inspector said to the *Havaldar*.

Ghulam drank the glass of water greedily.

"Now, tell me your story," said the Inspector.

The Inspector listened in silence as he heard the whole story.

"You are a brave man, Mr.Ghulam Rasool," he finally said. "I believe you. Rest assured that the guilty policeman, who shot the unarmed boy, will be punished and the boy's family would be compensated. You may go now; I am extremely sorry for all the trouble caused to you. My men will escort you back to your hotel."

Ghulam Rasool never told this story to anyone and carried on as if nothing had happened. He was to tell this story later but that was much later.

Ghulam's wife observed that he suddenly seemed different now. His fretfulness and irritation had gone as suddenly as it had come but he seemed to have become very remote, forlorn, and aged. His jet-black hair was slowly turning into grey. She wondered what was happening and tried to ask a couple of times but met with little success.

The years went by; Nargis was eighteen now and she had just entered college-Medical college.Ghulam and his wife were proud of her, but the happiest person was Ghulam's mother; Ameena. After loosing her husband a decade back, she had moved in with her son and had developed a strong attachment to the children. The children were in turn deeply attached to their grandmother. *Dadi jaan*, as she was known, also became immensely popular with the children of the locality.

Ameena Begum had never seen the inside of a school and was married off at the age of fifteen. Her husband Abdul was a kind and gentle person, but illiterate like her. He worked as a farmhand and did not know anything else. But, it was their resolve that their children should not suffer their fate.

Ghulam was born when she was seventeen. The local school was a broken down building where classes were not held regularly and was a centre for all vices at night. The nearest government school was seven kilometres away but it would be too tiring for the young Ghulam to walk the distance.Ameena went up to Mahendra Singh, the only teacher and asked for his help. In a place where most of the farmers where not willing to send their children because they were an additional hand in the field, this was most unusual.Mahendra Singh decided that he would teach Ghulam at his home till he was big enough to walk to the nearest school. So began Ghulam's formative years in schooling.Ghulam was an inquisitive and intelligent child and was quickly able to grasp whatever was taught to him. When he was nine years old, Mahendra felt that it was time for Ghulam to join the nearby school and start his formal schooling.Ghulam started to enjoy life at school, though it meant nearly an hour and half of walking in the morning and after school. His parents were thrilled at seeing their son learning and growing. However, their financial situation had turned from bad to worse. There had been excessive rains and floods followed by drought, and yield from the farms had drastically reduced.Ghulam had passed out from school and was desperate to help them out. His parents wanted him to join the college at Meerut; the school was ready to give him a scholarship. But Ghulam wanted to earn and support his family. He had heard from some of the other villagers that there were plenty of jobs in Bombay. So after bidding a tearful goodbye to his parents, he took a bus to Meerut and from there a train to Bombay.

Within a month, the first money order arrived at the Rasool household and things started looking better. But Abdul and Ameena were sad that their son could not join college and had to take up a job to support them. They were therefore thrilled when they received a message along with the money order that he had joined a night college.

Independence was in the air and so was the talk of Partition. Muslims constituted ten percent of the population of the village where Abdul and Ameena lived. Till now, there had been no animosity between the Hindus and the Muslims. Yet, as news of the riots and killings in the country broke out, they became worried. They were also worried for Ghulam.However, nothing happened. India became a free country and Ghulam became the owner of a company. They were overjoyed. Ghulam wanted them to come and live with him in Bombay, but they did not want to leave the comfort of their village. In one of his annual visits to the village, his parents suddenly informed him that they had selected a bride for him and he was getting married within a week.

Ghulam returned to Bombay with his newlywed wife Nausheen. She like Ghulam had been born and brought up in the same village, but her family was the most prosperous Muslim household in the village since her father had a rice mill unlike the other Muslims, who were mostly farmhands. But Nausheen had never left her village and Bombay was a big shock to her. However, she quickly adjusted to life in the city and served her husband, like she had done her father before. The children were born and they religiously went to their village annually.

Despite Ghulam's repeated requests, his parents refused to come down to Bombay. They were now living a comfortable life in the village but his father continued to work in the fields in spite of his weak health. And one day, he suddenly passed away while working on the land he loved.Ghulam's mother was heartbroken and lost the will to live.

Ghulam brought her forcibly to Bombay. For a month, she hovered between life and death and then gradually she was back on her feet. Nargis was her constant companion during that time, and soon a deep bond developed between them. She found a new meaning in life—her granddaughters. She started reliving her childhood through them. She was very happy that they did well in school like their father and it seemed the culmination of her dreams when Nargis entered Medical College. However, while all this was happening, she could sense the change happening in Ghulam over the last few years. She could not comprehend what was affecting him and felt concerned.

One evening as they sat for dinner, Ghulam announced that he had booked tickets for himself, Nausheen and his mother for embarking on a *Haj* pilgrimage. He looked at Nargis and asked her to take care of the younger children, while they were away. Ghulam's wife and mother were concerned about leaving their young children alone but Ghulam seemed to have made up his mind. A relative, who lived in Bombay, agreed to take care of the children in their absence. Preparations began in right earnest and soon it was time to leave. They were scheduled to depart by ship from Bombay port which would take them to Jeddah and thence to the holy city of Mecca.

The journey to Jeddah was uneventful, the seas were unusually calm and even though they suffered some bout of seasickness, they were in reasonably good condition when they finally arrived after ten days of sea travel. The subsequent days went off in a blur. Inspite of the enormous crowds and the heat and dust, Ghulam felt a sense of well being after a long time. They too had taken the path taken by millions of pilgrims over the ages; their journey had taken them to Mecca, Mina, Arafat—holy places which they had only heard before. Finally they were back at the port, ready to make the journey back. It was late in the evening and as they sat tired, but contented; they noticed an old man walking towards them. He had a long beard and unkempt hair; both were as white as the clothes he was wearing. As he came near, Ghulam had a feeling that he knew this person and knew him well. All of a sudden, it dawned on him and he rushed to the old man and grasped him with both hands. It was his benefactor,Ehtesham Ali.He led him slowly up to a seat; his wife and mother quickly understood who he was;Ghulam had told them countless number of times about Ehtesham Ali.

"You look well," said Ehtesham to Ghulam. "I heard there was a ship leaving for Bombay and I had a feeling that maybe you would be there." There were tears in the old man's eyes.

Ghulam could not control himself; he took the old man's palms and wept uncontrollably. The ladies looked on silently. After some time, they calmed down and then the words flowed. As Ehtesham told them the story of his arrest and being called an Indian spy, Ghulam cried in anguish.Ehtesham's story slowly unfolded before their eyes. His business had soon started floundering and his world started crumbling. Both his daughters and their entire family perished in a gruesome accident soon after, and his wife died heartbroken. His misery did not end therein. His son, who was yet to be married, had joined the Pakistani Army and was posted in East Pakistan. The war with India began in 1971 and one day, he received a message from Army headquarters that his son had become a martyr for the cause. They brought his body home and he buried the last member of his family with his own hands. He was now penniless; some kindly person took him to a destitute home and he lived there now. The same person who had taken pity on him had sent him for his *Haj* pilgrimage and here he was now ready to go back. The womenfolk wept as they heard the story.

Ghulam's mother lamented, "How can God be so cruel on such a noble person?"

Ehtesham consoled them. "It is said that God only tests those persons whom he has a liking; maybe he wants to see my endurance. But today, I am happy. I can die in peace. I have become a *Haji* and have met my long lost son, Ghulam."

"I will not let you go," said Ghulam. "You are coming with us; I will talk to the officials and take you with me."

"Let it be," replied Ehtesham; "this is how things have been willed to happen."

But Ghulam did not want Ehtesham to go. He went and met the Indian and Pakistani officials and pleaded with him. Relations between India and Pakistan were at the lowest and none of them were even willing to listen.

They sat together that night, not sleeping; wanting to hold on to those moments for ever. It was soon morning and time for Ghulam and his family to leave.

"As soon as I get to Bombay," he said, "I will contact the embassies and get you there, at the earliest."

Ehtesham smiled. "You are still very naive," he replied. "May God be with you!"

As their ship streamed away from the port, Ghulam could see the bent figure of Ehtesham Ali becoming smaller and smaller and then he could see only the horizon.

Ghulam and his family were overjoyed to be back home and meet their children. The children were very happy too.Nargis had assumed the mantle of an adult and had taken good care of the household. Soon after reaching Bombay,Ghulam went to the Pakistani consulate and pleaded with them to help him locate Ehtesham Ali.The officials were initially curt, but hearing the story, they said they would communicate with the destitute home in Lahore and asked him to come back after fifteen days. On the sixteenth day, Ghulam was back at the consulate.

"I am sorry," said the gentleman there. "You are too late."

Ghulam did not understand.

"Ehtesham Ali died on his way back from Jeddah and was buried at sea," said the official.

The world swayed before him and Ghulam had to grasp the chair to remain standing. He could hear somebody asking whether he was fine and needed a glass of water. He returned home in a haze. A chapter in his life was over.

How many friends and relatives have been torn apart by Partition? How many families have had their homes uprooted? How many men and women have lost their lives and their near and dear ones? I am sure the wise men would have had a justification for the pain and suffering.

But ask the businessman who became a pauper overnight? Ask the wife who saw her husband killed in front of her? Ask the husband who saw his wife carried away by unknown men, never to return? Ask those parents who saw their children lying lifeless? Ask those children who never had a childhood? Ask those ageing parents who saw their young valiant sons becoming martyrs in those so many wars and proxy wars?

Has it been worth it,Freedom--but at what price?

Farhan was born on a day when the heavens had opened out and it appeared as if the deluge would drown the city and its inhabitants. The rain and water could not dampen the high spirits in the household. There was laughter and joy. The celebrations went on for many days both in the house and in Ghulam's office.Ghulam asked his mother to name the child and she named him Farhan-The Happy One. He had brought back happiness to Ghulam and the entire family.

Farhan was a quiet child. He hardly cried and spent most of his time sleeping. A year went by fast. Farhan was able to crawl and take a few steps. His youngest sister Mumtaz stopped playing with her dolls since she had got a live one to play with her now. Farhan also enjoyed playing with her. The other sisters were too busy in their lives to be able to spend much time with their baby brother. The entire family – father and mother in the front with Farhan on his mother's lap and the three daughters along with their grandmother, at the back, would often go to the Chowpatty beach, crowded in their Ambassador car. There would be much giggling and pushing and pulling in the back and Farhan would watch with mild amusement. As he grew up, he continued to be a quiet and serious child, very unlike his boisterous sisters. He rarely gave any trouble to his parents and grandmother and Ghulam was secretly proud of him. He joined the same school that his sisters had studied.Nargis was now in her final year of Medical college and Waheeda had also followed in her footsteps and joined the same Medical college. It seemed like they were going to become a family of doctors.

Farhan was very studious. He liked nothing better than to read and spent long hours poring over books. Even before he could read, he used to look at the pictures intently .His grandmother used to tell him stories and the young Farhan would listen to them rapt in attention and keep asking questions until his grandmother would get enough of him and shoo him away. Ameena Begum had a great repertoire of stories; she told him stories which had been passed down for generations; stories from the Quran; stories of her childhood; stories about Ghulam. She also told him about the world, the country, Bombay—as she perceived.

So as Farhan grew, so did his knowledge of history and the world around him and also his bonds with his grandmother.

The year was 1984. Farhan was ten years old and in class five. Both his elder sisters had been married to doctors and had set up their own private practices along with their respective husbands.Mumtaz, unlike her elder sisters was studying arts.Ghulam had turned sixty and was still involved in managing the business on a daily basis. He sometimes took Farhan to his office, not only at Bombay but along with him when he went for some short tours to neighbouring towns. Farhan used to ask him all sorts of questions and Ghulam would be very happy answering them. He longed for the day when he could hand over his business to his son and retire.

Once, taking advantage of the school holidays, Ghulam had taken Farhan to Ratnagiri by overnight train. They arrived in the morning and were planning to stay for a couple of days. They were sitting in the office when news came that the Prime Minister had been assassinated. Further news started trickling in; the situation was becoming tense and businesses and shops were closing down and there were rumours of violence.Ghulam went back to the hotel with his son; he was reminded of the unfortunate incident so many years back and did not want anything similar happening. He wanted to get back to Bombay as fast as they could. He was able to arrange tickets by the afternoon train next day.

Ghulam heaved a sigh of relief only when the train pulled out from the station. Farhan had never seen his father so tense before; he tried to ask him a couple of times, but was brushed aside. Farhan was very perceptive and knew something was nagging Ghulam and decided to keep quiet. As the train moved along, Farhan could see Ghulam Rasool relaxing for the first time in the past twenty four hours.

He was now able to pick up some courage now and he asked, "*Abba*, what is the matter?"

"Nothing," replied Ghulam.

But he knew that Farhan was not satisfied with his answer.

"It was long ago," said Ghulam, "before you were born..." and for the first time Ghulam narrated the incident in Solapur.

Farhan listened to the whole story quietly. After what seemed a long time, he asked "Did they ever punish the policeman who shot the boy?"

"I do not know," replied Ghulam.

Ghulam felt better now that he had shared his story, albeit with his small son. But his son's question made him feel guilty. He had never bothered to find out...

It was evening now and the train was chugging along slowly. Suddenly, the train jerked strongly as if the driver had applied the brakes abruptly and the train started to come to a halt with a lot of groaning and screeching. For about five minutes there was silence, and then they could hear some noise. The noise was getting louder. Ghulam peeped out to see a group of people advancing towards the coaches. Some of them had entered the coaches at the front and others were running towards the coaches at the back. They were shouting and seemed to be armed. Ghulam was alarmed, he did not know what was happening. He took Farhan in his arms and held him closely. All the other passengers in the coach had also become afraid and were sitting as if in a trance, holding their children. Already there were rumours flying around that riots had broken out in the country and Sikhs were being targeted. There was a Sikh family sitting in the same compartment as that of Ghulam; an old lady, a boy of Farhan's age and a couple-the boy's parents. The family was already very tense and as they heard the sound of the people advancing, the old lady clasped the boy to her and started reciting from the *Gurbani* loudly. Although his father was holding him tightly, Farhan felt afraid for the first time in his life. He could hear the sound of people getting into the coach and their shouting and screaming. He could hear the intruders advancing towards their compartment. All of a sudden, they were there; three of them—armed with swords and knives. They gleamed when they saw the Sikh family and shouted obscenities. Two of them grabbed the Sikh gentleman, tore the turban from his head and rudely chopped his hair. The women were screaming and pleading for him to be left alone. The men then started to drag him away from the women. The women were now hitting the men and pleading for help from others. Farhan watched, in horror, the scene unfolding in front of them. One of the attackers suddenly turned back and pushed the women, who fell down. He now noticed the small boy, who was standing and crying. He laughed; the laughter of a maniac and in one stroke plunged the sword through the child's body. The boy's eyes widened for a second and then the lifeless body fell on top of the women. The women fell silent for a moment, but as the full impact of the situation dawned on them; they wailed in unison. Their heart rending screams rent the air as Farhan watched the scene in horror. The boy's father had been dragged out of the coach and he saw them pulling him away from the train into the trees. He closed his eyes and held onto his father tightly. The train suddenly started moving again, as if nothing had happened. By now, the other passengers had woken up from their state of inaction and were crowding around the two women and trying to comfort them. Some of the passengers were urging others to raise an alarm to stop the train again, while others wanted the train to move on and halt at the next station only. In the midst of all this confusion, lay the body of the child. Except for the wound on his chest, he lay as if in sleep.

One more statistic to add to so many others
Partition riots, 1947-Five lakh
1984 riots-Three thousand
Bombay riots, 1992/1993-Nine hundred
Gujarat riots, 2002-Two thousand

The orgy of violence continues ...Has anybody been convicted? No, we need to move on. So we appoint Commissions of inquiry and forget about the last riot till the next one hits us on the face. We move on for we need to fulfill our vision---the vision of 2020, a vision of developed India. Does that mean we will stop killing each other after 2020? Stop behaving like beasts?

No, no, no...Developed as in becoming an economic superpower; we will have eight lane highways connecting all our villages, all our villagers will have mobile phones, we will send men to the moon, we will be a great nuclear superpower, the Americans and Brits will come running into the country to pump in many more millions, every town will have back offices that service the western world. But we shall not stop killing. In this land, which has given us messiahs of non-violence---Mahavir, Gautam Buddha, Gandhi, we shall continue killing...killing each other.

The train had stopped at a station. People were running here and there. Farhan could see lots of policemen on the station. The dead child and the wailing women were offloaded from the train. The last Farhan saw of them was they being led away by a group of policemen.

The train reached Bombay at night. They had dinner and went to bed. Neither Ghulam nor Farhan mentioned the incident to each other or to the others. That night as he lay in bed, Farhan found sleep eluding him. The boy's face with the startled look kept coming again and again. It was going to be his recurrent dream for years to come, until much later.

Farhan was already a quiet boy, so nobody noticed when he became more quiet and reserved. The secret between father and son remained; and they would take it with them to their graves.Farhan had now moved to high school. His outstation trips with his father had stopped. He was doing well at school and his teachers were happy with him. So was his family. He continued to be a voracious reader and his room was now filled with books.

One night he was lying with his head on his grandmother's lap on the verandah and gazing up the stars, as she was telling him a story.

Suddenly he interrupted her and asked, "*Dadi*, what drives a man to kill another?"

He repeated the question, since she looked blankly at him, not understanding what he was trying to say.

"What is the matter, Farhan? Why are you asking me this?" she asked.

"Well, *Dadi*," he replied, "one finds in the papers, everywhere, people killing each other. Why?"

Ameena thought over it for a while.

"People kill for money, greed, power; sometimes in anger, desperation, revenge...Some others kill for upholding the countries' honour, their family honour. But, my child, you should not be bothered about these things," she replied.

School kept Farhan busy. There were exams and extra classes and assignments and tutions. He liked all the subjects, but there were two subjects that were dear to him- physics and history. Subjects which seemed to be as different as chalk and cheese.

Farhan was fascinated by physics; by the insight it brought into everyday facts. He was fascinated with the possibilities it brought about and he longed to become a physicist. One of the most captivating things which he read and reread again and thought about for long periods was the theories on the origin of the Universe. He was puzzled by the Big Bang theory, on how the universe emerged from an explosion of a single, dense and hot state and was continuously expanding. But where did that singular dense state appear from? And why did it appear? And what was there before? And where was all this expansion going to lead? These thoughts on physics, often lead him to think about God and religion. On where, God and the various religions figured in the scheme of things. He could not find answers to any of these questions; neither in the books he read nor from his teachers nor his grandmother.

Farhan turned to history in order to find those answers which could not be provided by physics. He delved into the origins of the various religions trying to find answers. He could find none. However, as he read more about history, he became more aware of the conflicts between various religions; more aware of his Islamic roots.Farhan had never felt himself any different from others, although he was the lone Muslim boy in his class. He studied in a missionary school where they read a couple of lines from the Bible every day morning; but he recited them as he did any of his subjects. He did not have many friends in his neighbourhood but his sisters had many, so he used to tag along with them when they visited the *Ganapati pandal* during *Ganesh Chaturthi* and burst crackers during Diwali. He recited the Quran religiously and also fasted during *Ramzan,* but that was because everybody else in his family did so. As Farhan probed further into history, he was also puzzled by the concept of nationhood.

Why were there so many countries in the world? If religion was a basis for formation of a nation, then there should be only a handful. If language was a criterion, then there should be many more. He wondered why Maharashtra could not be a separate country, if Nepal or Bangladesh could. What was so sacrosanct about nationhood? Why was patriotism such a noble word? Nations were but lands separated by imaginary lines; why this affinity or need for affinity to a nation. Why was there such a compulsion to be a patriotic citizen? Jingoism in the name of the nation is patriotism; the same in the name of the religion is communalism. How were the two different? How was the pilot in the aircraft, bombing a hundred houses in an enemy country different from that man in that train, who killed the Sikh boy in the name of religion? Why was Mahmud of Ghazni reviled while Alexander hailed? He did not find any answers, any explanations...

Farhan had appeared for his class ten exams and now had lot of time as he waited for the exam results. Preparations were on for the marriage of Mumtaz, who had completed her post graduation in Fine Arts and had decided that she had enough and wanted to get married. The groom was an army officer and he had been sent for an urgent posting to Aligarh where riots had broken out. He was expected back in a couple of days. Farhan's elder sisters had come along with their children and the house was once again filled with the noise and laughter of the children. There was only five more days to the marriage when Ghulam received a call from the groom's father asking him to come immediately. Ghulam Rasool took Farhan along and went to the groom's residence. The groom's father received them at the door. There was a deathly silence in the room. Farhan could hear a wailing somewhere in the back of the house. They sat in silence for some time.

"What is the matter?" asked Ghulam to the groom's father.

"They killed him," he replied. "They killed my son, my only son..."

And he started sobbing.

Ghulam was shocked. He did not know how to react.

The groom's father continued.

"He was surrounded by a mob. They killed him because he was a Muslim. My son, he always said that it would be his honour to lay down his life fighting against the enemy for the honour of the country. But, he was not killed by the enemy, Ghulam *Saab*; he was killed by his own countrymen for being a Muslim..."

The house had become silent. Farhan's elder sisters had gone. They had stayed back for a few days, but then they had to leave, they had their families, husbands to take care.Ghulam Rasool had barely spoken since that day; it was Farhan who had conveyed the news to the family after they returned back. The joy seemed to have gone from Mumtaz, who was a cheerful and bubbly girl. She walked like a ghost.Farhan had passed out with flying colours in his exams, but the joy was muted. Farhan's grandmother tried her best to bring back normalcy in the house with her cheerful banter. But even that was forced. When she broached the topic of looking out for another groom for Mumtaz, she was reprimanded strongly by Ghulam and Mumtaz.It pained Farhan to see his father and sister in this pitiable condition.

While at home, the situation was tense and uncomfortable, Farhan's days in his college were enjoyable. All the kids were on a high, due to the new found freedom in the college—wearing no uniforms, bunking classes, chatting away in the canteen. Although Farhan had enjoyed his school, he found the college more to his liking as it gave him more space and was not restrictive. He had taken up the science stream and was performing well in college also. He had also tried to overcome his inhibitions by joining the debating club in college and discovered a hidden talent there. He realised that when he spoke, he was able to attract attention by his precise and logical reasoning. He was soon a member of the college team and enjoyed himself during the intercollegiate competitions.

The 1990s had begun. The young Congress Prime Minister had been out of power for nearly a year and a half but it seemed like he would be back soon to lead the country into the 20th century, as elections had been announced. Fate willed otherwise. On a hot summer evening, during the height of the election campaign, a suicide attack in a small sleepy town, known till then as the birth place of the 11th century philosopher Raamanuja, turned things topsy turvy. It put an ageing war-horse of the Congress party into the hot seat.

Farhan had turned seventeen. He was a slightly built lad. Thin wisps of hair had just started appearing on his chin and his voice had just broken. He had neatly cropped hair and the spectacles sitting on his nose gave him the look of a boy, who did not venture beyond his books. True to his looks, Farhan remained a studious boy who would rather escape into the library during off periods than be seen in the canteen or the playground. His only vice, if it maybe called, was debating and sometimes it was noticed, that the quiet boy could become quite aggressive and emotional during debates. It was during one of the debates that Farhan let go...

It was the final round of the individual debating competition in Farhan's college. The two finalists were Farhan and a boy called Mukul. Both had somehow developed an animosity for each other during their first debate and the rancour persisted.The topic for the debate was 'Muslims in independent India: victimised or pampered?'

Farhan had spoken in favour of the debate quite eloquently, giving statistics to prove his point. As Mukul came up to the podium to speak, Farhan did not like the smirk on his face.

Mukul began "My erudite friend here believes Muslims are victimised. Had they been victimised, my friend would not be standing in this podium quoting statistics. Let them, my friend, go elsewhere if they feel victimised.Who broke up this country? You cannot have the cake and eat it too. They have Pakistan; let them go there..."

Farhan's blood was boiling as he heard these words. The judges interrupted Mukul and conveyed in strong words that the debate would be brought to an end if Mukul persisted with such remarks.

Mukul nodded his head, apologised and began, "We have pampered them so much that even in a debate I am censured. They have been pampered so much that inspite of being traitors..."

The speech was interrupted by the judges again, but before they could intervene, Farhan was up in a flash at the throat of Mukul. Mukul was well built but taken by surprise, he could do nothing. Farhan knocked him down and hit him like he had never done before. Everybody was too stunned to react. By the time they separated the two boys, Mukul was bleeding badly from his face and had to be rushed to the emergency medical services available in the college. The students were shocked to see the timid Farhan reacting in this manner. The principal gave him a dressing down and told him that he should not have behaved in this fashion, even though he was provoked.

The rest of the time spent in pre-graduation college was quite uneventful. Mukul apologised later for the nasty remarks and so did Farhan for his impulsive action. Nobody mentioned the incident again, but the entire episode rankled in Farhan's mind.

The situation had improved at home. Due to constant badgering by Farhan's mother and grandmother, Ghulam and Mumtaz agreed to look for another groom and finally a groom was chosen. The smile was back on Mumtaz's face and Ghulam seemed to have suddenly become younger. The groom to be was working in the United States and a date was agreed for the wedding, early next year. Although there were more than six months for the wedding, preparations at home began with full gusto.

Farhan had topped the college in his higher secondary exams and joined for his Physics Honours course at the same college.

Ghulam was a happy man.Farhan had promised that he would start involving himself in the business after graduation, which was three years away. Ghulam felt that the wait was worth it. He could at last retire and relax after handing over the reins to his son. He had spent forty-five years running the business; but age was catching up; he would be seventy soon and he longed for the day when he could sit at home and enjoy his sunset years.

Ameena was overjoyed at the turn of events. She was proud of her son and the manner he had built up his business and reared his children. She was happy as the family grew and her great grandchildren played with her. If only her husband had been able to see the family! How happy he would have been. She had still one more wish in her life; to see her beloved Farhan get married and to hold his child in her hands. She wondered whether she would see that day.

Nausheen smiled in contentment as she watched her happy family together at the dining table. It was Eid and all her daughters and their husbands and their children had come home. There was not enough space at the dining table so there was much jostling and shoving going on amidst laughter. She saw her contented husband sitting at the head of the table and feeding one of his grandchildren. Their glances met and she smiled shyly. She had come into the family as a child, leaving her parents behind.Ghulam Rasool had taken good care of her and the family. She had shared with him their moments of joy and sorrow. All those thoughts came rushing back to her today—her first sight of Ghulam after marriage; his joyous face as he held Nargis in his hands for the first time; his sorrow when he heard about Ehtesham's death; his laughter when he grabbed Farhan from the nurse's hand; his tears when he held the broken Mumtaz to his heart; his anguished face during those trying times...Ghulam had been her life and soul.

Farhan sat near his father and watched the scene. It was good to see the family happy again. It all seemed too good to be true. They had not been so happy for such a long time and he had a feeling somewhere deep down that this was going to be their last time together. He tried to shake off those thoughts but they remained.

On December 6th, 1992, two months from that day, a mosque was razed down at the temple town of Ayodhya, culminating into that eventful evening at Bombay, which would change Farhan's life forever.

❀❀❀

Madhav

Madhav Karve was born in the same year as Farhan in a small nursing home near the Dadar railway station. He was a noisy child; his screams could be heard even above the noise of the suburban trains which kept passing at regular intervals. He kept the nurses on their toes on all three days that he spent in the hospital.

Madhav was the first born child of Narendra Karve and Malti Karve. They belonged to the Chitpavan Brahmin community which had its origins in the coastal belt of Maharashtra.

Like his father and uncles, Narendra was very active even at a young stage in the freedom movement of India and after independence in politics. He was so involved in the affairs of his country that he refused to get married until very late and Madhav was born when he was old enough to be a grandfather, at fifty eight.

Narendra's father Dattatraya was so enamoured by the charm of a man called Gandhi who had recently arrived on the Indian political scene like a messiah that he plunged into the movement along with his young wife, Veena and son. Dattatraya was at the forefront of the "Swadeshi" movement which called for the boycott of foreign goods. He, along with his family, travelled across the country rallying the people against usage of all things British. What attracted Dattatraya to this man was his concept of "*ahimsa*" or non-violence. He refused to be provoked even by repeated acts of aggression by the ruler, and this seemed to be slowly frustrating the British. Dattatraya firmly believed that nothing could be achieved by violence and strongly disapproved of the groups which advocated violence to terrorise the British government. In Gandhi*ji,* he found a leader whose thought process was very similar to his. He was particularly impressed by one of Gandhi*ji's* sayings 'There are many causes that I am prepared to die for but no causes that I am prepared to kill for'.

The Swadeshi movement had evolved into a non cooperation movement against the British and had snowballed into a mass movement. However, the movement ran aground in a sudden halt as a result of a vandalism in a police station in the state of Uttar Pradesh, which resulted in the death of twenty two policemen. Gandhi*ji* called for the end of the non cooperation movement, fearing further violence and thus the mass movement died down. Gandhi*ji* was arrested and sent to jail, so were many of his followers among whom was Dattatraya. Dattatraya spent the next five years of his life in jail. Narendra was now six years old and the constant travel since his birth was affecting his health.Veena decided to settle down at Poona till Dattatraya came out of prison. She admitted Narendra to a local school and also began to teach there. Narendra's health slowly improved. He was a bright child and was doing well in school, though he missed his father very much.

Dattatraya was released finally during the winter of 1927. He came back home to his wife and son. After a brief period of hesitation, Narendra was all over Dattatraya wanting to know all about those years, his father had spent in prison. Those were happy days, as the family tried to catch up on lost time. Six months passed by, and Veena was pregnant again. For the past few days, Veena had sensed a growing restlessness in Dattatraya. She could feel him caught in the conflict between staying at home and taking care of the family and going back into the freedom movement. One night after dinner, they were sitting on the verandah. Narendra had gone to sleep. The night was dark and silent and all they could hear was the sound of the crickets in the background intermittently.

"You want to go, don't you?" asked Veena.Without waiting for a reply, Veena continued, "Don't worry about us; I can take care of Narendra and our unborn child. You have work to do, go and may freedom come soon."

Yadavendra was born eight months later, on a day of unseasonal rains. The city was flooded and she gave birth in the house.Dattatraya was away in Bengal. Over the next few months, as the child started growing, she was in touch with her husband through intermittent letters. He was travelling the country along with the Mahatma. During those trying months, Narendra was her source of strength. He was a strapping young lad of thirteen, very much in the mould of his father. Yadavendra was nearing his first birthday and Veena wanted Dattatraya home for the child's' birthday. He had been away now for nearly two years.

Dattatraya spoke to her from Ahmedabad.

"You have to bear with me Veena, he said. I cannot come now. *Bapu* has launched a '*Satyagraha*' and we are going on a long march. But, I promise I shall be back soon." Veena was disappointed. But she replied, "Don't worry, the country needs you more."

Dandi is a small village on the coast of the Arabian Sea, near Surat in Gujarat, about 250 km north of Bombay. Gandhiji's march from the Sabarmati Ashram in Ahmedabad to Dandi signalled the beginning of the end of the empire. The march was against the imposition of tax on salt by the British Government. Everyone needed salt and the civil disobedience movement launched against the salt tax, caught everybody's attention and imagination. The frail old man, Gandhiji was sixty one years old then and he walked nearly four hundred kilometres in those twenty four days. Thousands of people joined him. On the morning of April 6th, 1930 at Dandi, he picked up a lump of mud and salt, boiled it in sea water and defied the mighty British Raj. Thousands of people, in the coming days and weeks, made salt and were arrested and put in jail. Thus was born a mass movement.

But India had to wait—wait another seventeen years till the British were ready to let go...

Dattatraya was among those thousands who were arrested in Dandi and elsewhere. He was imprisoned and sent to jail in Poona. News of his arrest and imprisonment in Poona reached Veena and she desperately tried to meet him, but the authorities refused to give permission. One afternoon, nearly three months after his imprisonment, she received a call from the jail asking her to come there immediately. Taking her child in her arm, she rushed to the jail. She was taken to a cell where lay a body covered with a piece of cloth.

"Remove the cloth and have a look," said the policeman softly.

And there he lay; her husband of sixteen years. The punishing schedule had taken its toll and Veena could barely recognise the once tall and strapping young man. She broke down and cried; seeing her cry, the child Yadavendra cried for a father, he never knew.Narendra lit the funeral pyre of his father, a man whom he admired but whom he regretted had never got to know well.

A year went by Narendra had passed out from school.Veena's parents had been urging her to come and stay in Bombay, but she had been resisting so far. Finally, she relented, packed her bags and left Poona, which had been their home for the last ten years. Ten years, in which she had barely spent a year with her husband.

She took up a small place near her parents' house; the house where she had been born and had grown up. Life had turned full cycle. Both the houses were located at a stone's throw from Shivaji Park. She was able to get a job as a school teacher and Narendra joined college while Yadavendra entered school. The children spent lot of their time at their grandparents' house, who were delighted to see them.Veena had been their only child and they had been very lonely these years after her marriage.Veena's father was a retired school teacher and the children soon had a father they never had. Those were happy days, after a long time, for all of them. They would go for long evening walks in the Shivaji Park and the nearby beach. And then, one day it was all over.Veena's father had a fall; it broke his back, reducing him to an invalid lying on his bed. He lost his will to live and passed away soon in his sleep.Veena's mother was heartbroken. Her entire world had revolved around her husband and within a month, she was also gone.Veena's world had crumbled a gain. She moved in with her children into her parental house, nineteen years after she had left as a shy bride.Narendra was seventeen and Yadavendra was five.

Narendra had grown up to be a fine, young man. He was profoundly influenced by Gandhi and felt that he had to finish his father's incomplete task. But he did not want to hurt his mother. As he had grown up, he understood the sacrifices she had made in her small way and felt she had suffered enough. But he could not ignore the call of his motherland and he now understood better the conflicts that must have waged in his father's mind. He had to take a call someday and he knew he was just postponing the decision.

Narendra had passed out of college and like his grandfather and mother, he became a teacher. He joined the same school where his mother continued to teach. He was the youngest there, being twenty one years old and became quite a hit there with the children and teachers alike with his impeccable manners and teaching style.Veena was proud of him and often wished her husband had been alive to see this day.

Yadavendra was nine now and the complete antithesis of his elder brother; both in looks and behaviour.Veena could not believe, at times, that she had given birth to both of them. So different they were. Narendra stood six feet and with his light brown eyes and fair skin, was a handsome sight.Yadavendra,on the other hand was the shortest and frailest student in his class and the only resemblance was in his pale skin. While Narendra had been an obedient and studious child from the beginning, Yadavendra was the opposite. He hardly lifted his books to study and the moment he was back from school, used to rush into the expanse of the Shivaji Park. He was full of energy and kept the entire household on its toes. He was mostly at the bottom of the class and both his mother's and brother's attempts at pleading, coaxing and finally threatening, did not seem to have any effect.Veena used to sometimes get worried but Narendra used to shoo her worries away saying he was a child.

World War had broken out and the political temperature of the country was rising.Narendra was becoming increasingly agitated and restive. He felt it was now or never. On August 8th, 1942, the Quit India resolution was passed at the Bombay session of the Indian National Congress. As he heard Gandhi speak on that day urging his countrymen to start a non-violent protest, Narendra made up his mind. The next day morning, as the nation slowly started stirring up into what was growing to be the beginning of large scale demonstrations, Narendra conveyed his decision to his mother.Veena listened as Narendra forcefully explained his need to complete his father's unfinished mission. Listening to her son sitting and talking to her, she was reminded of her husband. She could see the same zeal and fire in him. It was as if history was repeating in front of her. She longed to hold him closely and ask him to forget everything and just be her son and nothing more. But she knew; she could not. She could not break his heart and say no. She continued to listen and was amazed at his clarity of thought. He finished and looked expectantly at her.

"Go, my son!" she said.

Narendra took leave from the school and plunged headlong into the Quit India movement. All the major leaders including Gandhi had been arrested and put in jail. New leaders emerged; large scale demonstrations were being held in all parts of the country. The non-violent movement turned violent; with bombs being exploded and government buildings being set on fire. The British responded with a vengeance; hundreds of protestors were killed and thousands arrested. Narendra escaped from being arrested and went underground and aided in the struggle by distributing pamphlets and help setting up clandestine radio stations.

It was a trying time for Veena.There was no news of Narendra. Yadavendra had managed to pass out from school, but he seemed totally disinclined to study further. He remained absent from the house for long hours and refused to answer her questions.Inspite of repeated coaxing, he refused to spend his time in a constructive manner. And then one day he vanished. He came back after three months, as suddenly as he had left and refused to answer any of his mother's queries. He said that he had managed to get a job in the Middle East and he was leaving.Inspite of his mother's repeated pleas, he left one day. Veena was to never see him again. Time passed slowly for Veena, who now got fully immersed in the school. She was now fifty one, but could feel herself ageing faster.

One January evening, almost a year and half since Narendra left the house,Veena was sitting on the verandah and reading a book; when the main gate of the house opened, and Narendra walked in.They held each other and cried.Narendra was shocked to see his mother's condition. Her hair had turned completely white and the once blemish free face was full of wrinkles. She looked old. He wept like a child. Over the next few days, they shared their experiences.Narendra vowed never to let her alone and go. The Quit India movement had petered down.Narendra went back to work, but still kept attending party sessions. He had been a little disillusioned by the increased use of violence in the movement but firmly believed that the path of non-violence would eventually triumph. In the meantime, he also got fully involved in the activities of the school along with his mother.

Subsequent to the Quit India movement, the tribulations of the Indian National Army in Burma and Singapore raised the national fervour of the people. The armed forces joined in, resulting in the Naval Mutiny. By early 1946, the British had begun a political dialogue with the Indian National Congress and on 15th August 1947, India became a free nation, nearly two hundred years after the British East India Company had been established.

How many men and women sacrificed themselves at the altar of freedom! How many lives were lost like that of Dattatraya! How many widows like Veena were created, who lived unsung and unwept! How many families were badly torn apart like that of the Karve family!

Much water has flowed down the river since then. Newer generations have grown up and British rule remains a lesson in history for most of us and Independence Day; a day of rituals for a few teachers, school children and leaders and a day of rest or recreation for most others. The deeds of Gandhi and Nehru and Bose and Patel and...others are enshrined to the archives of Indian history. A country; caught in the buzz of economics, stock markets and foreign investments, seems to be forgetting the lessons of history.

Like so many others, Veena and Narendra wept tears of joy as they heard Nehru's speech declaring India an independent country. Their sacrifices had finally born fruit. At last, it seemed there would be some stability in their life. Their life fell into a routine; mornings and afternoon in the school; evenings at home or Shivaji Park or at some cultural programme.Both of them liked theatre and dance and were, at last, able to indulge in them.Narendra still kept in touch with his colleagues who had been with him during the Quit India movement. Some of them had become legislators, some others ministers and they urged him to join the party and the Government. But Narendra refrained. He told them that he had completed his father's unfinished mission and would now like to spend the rest of his life with children, the citizens of tomorrow.

Life went on.Veena had turned sixty and she finally decided she should call it a day. She felt at peace now, with Narendra by her side. But two things rankled her.

One was Yadavendra. It was ten years now since he had left, and still there was still no news from him.Narendra made lot of enquiries but there was no trace of Yadavendra.It was as if he had vanished from the face of the earth.

And the other, Narendra's decision not to get married.Narendra was thirty seven now and inspite of his mother's repeated requests for a daughter- in- law and grandchild; he did not relent. He said he was happy with his home and work, and did not feel it necessary to get married.

Narendra had quickly become the Vice-Principal of the school in which his grandfather had been once principal.Veena was now more or less confined to the house and their walks to the nearby Shivaji Park slowly stopped.Veena's eyesight was also fading and she was not able to read properly. Evenings were spent with Narendra reading her the newspaper or some Marathi novel inspite of her protesting loudly that he should not spend time with her and should go out and meet people his age and get married. The end came peacefully one evening as he was reading aloud from her favourite author, Hari Narayan Apte.

The small two roomed house appeared too large now for Narendra as he sat one morning in the verandah where he last read to his mother fifteen days back. His mother had been his constant companion through his life all these forty years, except for the brief period during the Quit India movement. He realised how empty his life had suddenly become without her. Even the time spent in the school did not cheer him up. One day the Principal called him up to the office.

"Sit down, Narendra," he said. "You need a break. Why don't you take some leave and go away for some time."

Narendra had not taken any leave since a long time.

"But where do I go?" he asked.

"Travel the country, my son," replied the old principal, "and rediscover it. This job will be waiting for you when you return."

Locking the house, he put all his worldly possessions in a box and set out. He had not seen anything beyond Poona and Bombay. He embarked on a pilgrimage. His first port of halt was the Sabarmati Ashram. He had planned to stay there for a couple of days; he remained there for a year. It was one place where it seemed Bapu's message was still alive. From there, he travelled to Dandi and then to Porbandar; where the *Mahatma* had been born. His pilgrimage was not yet over. That night he took a train to Delhi. He went straight from the station to Birla House; the abode where Gandhi spent the last days of his life. He walked silently retracing the path of the *Mahatma* from his room to the park.

As he sat in the park, he remembered the day Gandhi was shot. He had been working late in school and was returning home, when he found shopkeepers downing their shutters and people standing in groups and talking. He instantly sensed something was wrong and hurried to his house. There he found his mother, sitting and weeping in the darkness before a radio, from which came some mournful music.

"What is the matter?" cried out Narendra.

"The *Mahatma* is no more," replied his mother.

He remembered both of them sitting in the darkness and talking; talking of Gandhi*ji,* his father and all those bygone days. It was all over now.

Now, as he sat in the twilight at the spot where the Mahatma had fallen, he realised that his mission was still unfinished. India had woken to freedom nearly a decade back but the lights were still not burning bright in every household. He had to make some difference somewhere. He pondered on this issue for two days and then light dawned. He took the night train and got down at Nagpur, the next day afternoon. It was the height of summer as he caught a bus and landed at Sewagram, the ashram started by Gandhi*ji* nearly twenty years back.

Narendra quickly settled down to the life at Ashram. He discovered that lack of proper schools was a major problem in that area as was also the reluctance of the locals to send their children to school. His persistence paid off. His first class, under the tree had five children. Narendra had converted an abandoned house, by taking over it, into the school and named it after his mother. Within a year, the school had expanded. He held classes in two batches; one for children below eight years old and the other for older children. There were now thirty children in the school. He charged them a nominal fee, but provided them with books, which he managed to buy with funds from his savings and contributions from the Ashram.

The years passed; the school had grown. The original building had been expanded to make way for more students, there were nearly two hundred of them as also five teachers and Balram,the peon-cum-clerk cum-administrator, all rolled into one. Narendra was now fifty and sometimes he felt his age. His life completely revolved around the school and he went home-which was a one room tenement near the school building, only for sleeping. He had not been outside Sewagram, since he set his foot there nearly nine years back. But he felt a sense of contentment, as he looked back upon those years.

Nine years; a new Prime Minister, a woman, was in power now. The baton had changed from the old to the new guard. India had fought two more wars, lost some territories, gained some. The second and third five year plan had run their way. Three steel mills at Bhilai, Durgapur and Jamshedpur had started production; the Bhakra Nangal, Hirakud and Mettur dams were completed. The Green revolution had commenced. India's GDP was increasing, albeit slowly; the population was increasing; a bit too fast for comfort and poverty and illiteracy was decreasing; though ever so slowly. The country was slowly trying to find its feet in a new world.

He had debated it for a long time with himself before taking the decision to go. He had avoided going to any functions after arriving at Sewagram but the persistence of Balram, had paid off. It was Balram's second daughter's marriage and she was one of the first students to have joined the school. Taking time off from school, Narendra went to the marriage ceremony. The arrangements were quite elaborate and the marriage went off quite well.Narendra enjoyed the break from his routine and was glad he had accepted Balram's invitation. But, something, he had observed in the marriage had troubled him. He noticed a young girl of no more than thirty, who seemed to be a close member of the family, was running around actively coordinating all the marriage activities. But, when it came to the marriage rituals, she receded into the background; albeit reluctantly.Narendra was puzzled and could not find any logical answer to the dichotomy. He wanted to ask Balram about her, but could not find the courage to do so.

Ten days passed by, but the girl's face seemed to haunt him everywhere. He could not take it any longer and decided he had to find the answer. It was evening, the school was closing for the day.Balram came to him to ask him whether he was needed or could go home.

"I need to talk to you," said Narendra to Balram. "Can you stay for some time?"

"Of course, *Saab*," replied Balram and he stood beside Narendra.

"I had a nice time at your daughter's marriage" said Narendra, "and I am glad I came."

"Thank you, *Saab*," replied Balram. "It was kind of you to come."

There was a brief moment of silence as Narendra struggled with himself to ask the question.

"The arrangements were all perfect," said Narendra. "You must have had to do a lot of running around."

"No *Saab*, it was all done by Malti,"replied Balram. "She is my elder daughter and she has been my biggest strength. You must have seen her, Saab; she was the one who was running around."

"Yes, yes..." replied Narendra. "But one thing puzzled me, Balram; she seemed to get pushed to the background when the marriage functions were happening."

Balram sighed.

"She is a widow, *Saab* and you know how it is about widows..."

"But she is so young,"remarked Narendra. "What happened?"

"We married her off about fifteen years ago, she was only fifteen then," said Balram. "Her husband was a shopkeeper in Nagpur. He used to drink heavily and beat her. One night he came home, very drunk and started beating her with a rod. Malti tried to defend herself and remove the rod from his hand. In the melee, the rod hit him on the head and he dropped down dead. She was arrested for murder. His family and the lawyers tried hard to implicate her. The case dragged for two years; she was refused bail and spent those years in jail. Those days were hard. We prayed and hoped for a miracle. God listened to our prayers. She was released. She returned home; five years after she had been married off. It had been traumatic for her. She often had nightmares and it took a long time for her to become normal. But the stigma remains..."

"Then you came, *Saab* and I decided my younger daughter should not face the same problem. That is why I sent her to your school and then to college, so that she could be married to an educated person."

There was a long silence, as both Narendra and Balram were lost in their thoughts.

"Shall I go now?" asked Balram.

"But you cannot spoil her life like this," replied Narendra, "she is still young."

"What can be done?" replied Balram. "She helps my wife and myself around the house and is always doing all sorts of chores for the neighbours."

"But, she needs a life of her own," replied Narendra.

His voice had become raised.

"Why don't you marry her off to somebody who can give her a new life?"

Balram looked at him in shock.

"But who will marry her," said Balram, almost in tears now. "She is a widow, has gone to jail and is illiterate. Who will marry her, *Saab*?"

"I will," replied Narendra.

Balram was too shocked to react.

"But *Saab*, you are an educated person and she is a ...and besides you are a Brahmin," he finished lamely.

"Those things do not matter to me," replied Narendra. "If you think my age is an issue, let me know and I will not talk of this any further."

"No, no, *Saab* ..."replied Balram.

They were married ten days later in a small ceremony at the Sewagram Ashram.Narendra discovered that for all the ordeals that Malti had undergone, she still retained an air of innocence, which fascinated him. She was eager to learn and she became his newest and oldest student. He discovered that unknown to her father; she had managed to pick up a few things from her sister and could read reasonably well. Every evening after returning from school, the lessons would start; Marathi, Hindi, English, History and so on.Narendra would tell her in bits and pieces his entire life and how he had landed up at Sewagram. Malti opened up after a lot of persuasion and then the dam burst. She told him about those years in hell and after the end of it, felt much better.

The years rolled by quickly; Narendra could not imagine a life without Malti.Their age difference hardly seemed to matter.Narendra felt happy and contented. He was fifty five years now and beginning to bald, but still retained his lean physique.

It was a Sunday. Narendra's practice of going to the school even on Sundays had stopped slowly after marriage. Winter had set in and the sun was mellow. Malti was cooking and Narendra was going through the newspaper, when he heard a knock on the door.Narendra went up and opened the door. There were two strangers at the door; a couple.

“Yes...,”said Narenda, questioningly.

“You are Narendra aren’t you,”asked the gentleman.

Something about the man rang a bell in Narendra’s memory; but he could not figure out what?

“Yes,” he replied mechanically.

The other person suddenly grasped him and hugged him with all his might. And then it dawned on Narendra and he also held on to the stranger, his only link to his past. It was strange seeing the two old men holding each other. One tall and balding in a *dhoti kurta*, with a shawl wrapped around him and the other, short and stout and nattily dressed in a suit. They appeared to be from two different worlds, but for Malti who saw this sight as she abruptly came out of the kitchen, it was all very clear.

Yadavendra had returned; Narendra’s brother was back. He had left home as a child and was back now; middle aged and married.

For a few minutes, everybody was too stunned to react and then the words started flowing.

Over the period of the next few days, Yadavendra’s life started to unfold before Narendra’s eyes. He had managed to get a job in Kuwait as an assistant in a trading company. The hours were long and the pay was poor. It was an ordeal initially for him, since he had never been used to a disciplined life earlier. He thought of running away frequently, but with his passport in the employer’s hand, he was trapped. But what motivated him and kept him going was the desire to become rich. He had seen his mother struggling to make ends meet and was determined that he would go back only as a rich man. So he worked and worked, harder by the day. Soon, his diligence caught the eye of the owner of the agency. He brought Yadavendra into his office and made him his personal assistant. Before long, Yadavendra knew all the nuts and bolts of the business. The Sheikh was happy with him and rewarded him well and Yadavendra was on his way to achieving his ambition. The years passed by, the Sheikh was becoming older and had no son.Yadavendra was now literally running the business. He had also become immensely wealthy. But he was also getting older and feeling lonely. So, twenty years after he had left the country, he took a flight back to Bombay. He went to the place where he lived and found it locked. Inquiries revealed that his mother had died and his brother had left for an unknown destination. He had taken a month's leave; he had time and money on his hands and he decided that he would enjoy the good life of Bombay; as he had never done before. He checked into a five star hotel and started enjoying the sights of Bombay. He became a frequent visitor to the Mahalakshmi Race Course and discovered the thrills of gambling. During these visits, he became friendly with one Sunil Ghorpade; a small time politician who had made his money through real estate. Ghorpade invited him to his house; a luxurious flat near the race course. Ghorpade had a daughter of marriageable age. One thing led to another and Yadavendra and Anita were married within ten days. Yadavendra went back to Kuwait after completing his leave and Anita followed within two months. Years went by; the Sheikh had practically become senile and Yadavendra ran the business. They did not have any children and Anita was getting restless cooped up in her mansion in a strange country. She wanted to go back to Bombay. After a lot of fights with her, Yadavendra finally decided to quit the country which had made him a wealthy man and returned back to Bombay. They bought a penthouse beside the sea in Worli. Anita was happy now but Yadavendra was restless. His father-in-law suggested to him to join the new political party, which he was now part of. The party firmly believed that the locals-the Marathis had been given a raw deal and all the jobs were being wrested away by strangers from the South of the country. They had launched an agitation and Yadavendra liked the idea of joining an agitation; like his brother and father had done before. He was soon into the thick of things and became a prominent leader. Anita did not like the happenings, but she had no other option and kept quiet. In all this time, he had never once gone to his old house. Anita kept suggesting that he should do something about the old house and also find out about his brother. Due to her repeated cajoling; he finally agreed to look at the place. They went there one morning; the locks gave away easily. The house was dark, dank and full of dust. On a corner table in the sitting room, he saw the photos––his family photos; he sat by the table and broke down. He sat on the dirty floor and wept; for a father whom he barely remembered, for a mother whom he had reviled while she had lived and for a brother, whom he hardly knew. He wept for a family that never was...

He had the house cleaned up. He started making enquiries about his brother's whearabouts. He met the principal of the school where his brother had taught. The principal was very glad to meet him and was able to provide him with some information. He said he had received a letter from Narendra about six years back wherein he had mentioned that he was living in Sewagram.That was the last he had heard from him; although he had written to Narendra a couple of times asking him to come back and take charge as the principal as he was getting too old to continue.

They, Yadavendra and his wife had taken a car to Sewagram and had finally landed up here.

They spent the next day or two catching up and discussing Sewagram, Bombay, Kuwait and their past.Narendra showed them the school he had built from scratch. Although Malti was initially reticent; Anita's easy going nature and her ability to adapt to the new environment impressed her and very soon they got along famously. A week passed and it was time now for Yadavendra and his wife to go back. For the last couple of days, they had been urging both Narendra and Malti to return back to Bombay, to their home. Narendra had been initially hesitant; he was so used to his life and the school at Sewagram that he did not want to go away. But after repeated persuasion, he said he would think over it seriously.

Narendra returned back home; to Bombay, with Malti nearly seventeen years after he had left. They had left Sewagram with a heavy heart. Narendra had handed over the administration of the school to Balram, who agreed after a lot of reluctance and repeated persuasion by his daughter and son- in- law and the other teachers. One of the senior teachers was appointed the principal. Narendra's mission in Sewagram was over.

For several days after they came to Bombay, both Narendra and Malti were lost. At Sewagram, their days had been extremely busy, but suddenly they had time on their hands.Yadavendra and Anita visited them often and tried to make the transition smooth.

One day, the Principal of the school where Narendra had been teaching earlier visited them. He urged Narendra to join back; he said the school was having financial problems and needed a strong administrator and a Principal to set things right and begged Narendra to join.

Narendra's second stint in the school thus began; this time as Principal. His hands soon became full as he tried to straighten out things. After years in seclusion; Narendra slowly started going to the theatre and started renewing ties with his old friends. Malti was his constant companion and source of strength. The hustle and bustle of Bombay soon enveloped their activities and Sewagram now remained a pleasant memory. And then, after nearly seven years of marriage, Malti announced that she was on her way to become a mother.Balram and his wife came visiting; they wanted to take Malti with them and insisted that their first born grand child should be born in Sewagram; but Narendra was adamant. He refused to let Malti leave him.

Madhav was born nine months later, a few weeks ahead of time on a sweltering day just before the onset of the monsoon. He screamed his heart out as he was passed from hand to hand; his parents, grandparents, uncle, aunt and a host of well-wishers. Malti's parents moved in with them to help manage the child, in the initial months. Yadavendra and Anita often passed by and spent a lot of time with the child. They did not have a child of their own and embraced him as their own child.

Madhav was a noisy child. He was always shouting and screaming for everything. Malti and Narendra found it difficult to quieten him. But his uncle,Yadavendra had a way with him and the child would become quiet the moment he lifted him.Yadavendra would carry him even when he was just six months old to Shivaji Park and Chowpatty beach and the child would jump with joy. Thus, began the bond between uncle and nephew.

As Madhav grew older, Yadavendra used to spend more time in the house; from which he had run away as a child. Often, he and Narendra would spend time sitting on the verandah and discuss about the affairs of the world. The topic would often veer around to politics; and the discussions would often turn heated and Malti or Anita would have to intervene to quieten things up.Yadavendra would leave in a huff, but would be back the next day, everything forgotten.Yadavendra was now a prominent politician; but the brand of politics that he practiced made Narendra very unhappy. He did not like the politics of hate, and was deeply troubled by it.

Madhav was growing up into a very naughty and unmanageable child. He could barely sit in one place and was turning the house upside down. He would raise a tantrum for everything that was not done, the way he wanted and Malti would more often than not succumb to his whims. Narendra did not like the way Madhav was behaving and tried hard to reason with him, but this was not yielding much of a result. Often, his behaviour reminded Narendra of his brother and this worried him. Madhav joined the same school where Narendra was teaching.

Madhav disliked school; he did not like to sit in classrooms and study. He got bored and irritated and started troubling the other children. He became a bully. The complaints against him started coming from all quarters; the children, their parents and the teachers, and became a source of great embarrassment to Narendra. He tried hard to explain to his young son, but this was not getting anywhere; as Madhav would go into a sulk and Malti would then intervene and chide with him for being too harsh on the child.

The years went by; Narendra was into his mid sixties and wanted to call it a day. He had spent the last ten years in bringing up the school to its old standards. He had appointed a capable vice-principal who could take over and was slowly trying to disassociate himself from the affairs of the school. But the school management refused; they wanted him to be there for at least two more years and help plan and organise the golden jubilee of the school. So, Narendra continued. The school at Sewagram was also running well, Balram would send him updates very often and also ask for his advice. Both the schools flourished, and Narendra felt a great sense of satisfaction. He felt and often remarked to Malti that he had reared children of two generations successfully. The school at Sewagram was like a child whom he had reared with his own hands; nursing it through the formative years and holding hands till it was strong enough to walk and now run on its own. The school at Mumbai was like a middle aged man, who had stopped learning and was stagnating and who needed patient coaxing and affirmation on his abilities so that he could bring the spark back into his life.

In the same breath, he would often remark that he had failed his third child; Madhav. His long years of experience as a teacher had come to a naught with his son. Malti would console him and tell him not to take things to his heart. She would remark that he was but still a child and would grow up to be a fine man. Narendra would nod hopefully.

Madhav was now eight years old and in the second standard. His performance at school continued to be poor; it was not that he could not grasp the subjects; he was totally disinclined to pay any attention or study. He continued to irritate the children and the teachers who tolerated him, because they had no option.Madhav wanted a way out of school; his restless soul could not tolerate the regimen in the school. He urged his parents to withdraw him from school and let him be. Both Narendra and Malti were unable to understand him. Madhav also refused to join any sports or cultural activities and just lay around the house doing nothing. The gap between the child and the parents was growing. The only time Narendra and Malti could see happiness on Madhav's face was when Yadavendra came to meet him. Often, he would go away and stay at Yadavendra's place for two or three days and return much more cheerful.Yadavendra would often discuss about Madhav with Narendra and Malti.The conversation would often go in this fashion.

"He feels suffocated here, he is unhappy here," Yadavendra would say. "Let me take him; he likes being with us. I will put him in some other school and let's see whether things improve."

Narendra and Malti would refuse to listen to his line of argument and Malti would start crying.

One day, after such a bout of argument and crying, they agreed to look at options. After a lot of discussions, it was finally agreed that Madhav would be admitted to a convent school near Yadavendra's house and stay there for the course of the week and come back home during the weekends. When the idea was mooted to Madhav, he yelled in joy.Yadavendra managed to pull the right strings and Madhav was admitted to his new school. The time came for Madhav to leave; his bags were packed and he left happily on a Sunday night. Although, Madhav was going only a few kilometres away but for Narendra and Malti, it seemed as if they were losing him forever.

Madhav enjoyed his new environment. He found the new school, with its more relaxed atmosphere, more to his liking. He also started enjoying the atmosphere of the apartment where he was staying. In a few months time the transformation was complete; from a loner he had become the monitor in his class and a leader of sorts in the apartment complex. Madhav also developed a good rapport with Yadavendra's in- laws who used to drop in often. The tantrums that were the norm earlier completely stopped. However, he used to turn sullen during weekends when he had to go back home. Soon, he started inventing new reasons to stay away from home and the weekend visits gradually reduced to monthly visits. Narendra and Malti became resigned to the fact that they could do nothing about it. The Shivaji Park residence became a desolate place and Narendra and Malti suddenly felt very old. Both of them wanted to get away from the place and go back to Sewagram, but they did not bring up the subject. They felt trapped as in a prison and helpless.

In the Yadavendra household, there was more happiness. After nine years of marriage, Anita was pregnant. There were lot of celebrations and Madhav was in the forefront. His meeting with his parents had now become very infrequent and even at these meetings, he exchanged a few words with his mother but hardly anything with his father. The break was nearly complete.

Madhuri was born in the same nursing home where Madhav had been born twelve years back. She was named after the actress who had suddenly caught the imagination of the country. The Yadavendra household held a grand party to celebrate and gave pride of place to his elder brother and sister-in- law, but they felt totally out of place. Yadavendra was now a member of the state legislature and several leading politicians attended the celebrations. Narendra and Malti sat through the function with difficulty and were glad when it was all over.

That night, they sat in the verandah of their home and talked about old times and the present. The golden jubilee celebrations of the school had gone on well but the school authorities had persisted with him to stay a bit longer. Now it was time to quit. Balram had been calling them time and again to come and stay in Sewagram for some time. They had been postponing the decision for quite some time now. But it seemed the time had come.

"I think we should go to Sewagram and stay for some time," said Narendra, broaching the subject for the first time.

"What about your school here?" replied Malti.

"I have decided to quit; I have told the school authorities informally but I shall inform them formally tomorrow," answered Narendra.

There was a long silence.

"What about Madhav?" asked Malti.

"What about him?" replied Narendra, his voice quivering.

"I mean, we cannot just leave him and go, he is our son," answered Malti.

"Yes, our son..." replied Narendra. "We gave birth to him but..."

"But what?" asked Malti.

"You know Malti," replied Narendra. "I think we have lost him for ever. I know it is hard but let's face it, it's true."

"It's strange isn't it; I was a teacher to so many children, so many of them still come back to meet me, thank me. But...I failed; failed with my son. Where did I go wrong Malti?"

The Lebanese-American poet Khalil Gibran in his famous book 'The Prophet' has this to say about children. I quote:
'Your children are not your children.
They are the sons and daughters of Life's longing for itself.
They come through you but not from you,
And though they are with you, yet they belong not to you.
You may give them your love but not your thoughts.
For they have their own thoughts.
You may house their bodies but not their souls,
For their souls dwell in the house of tomorrow, which you cannot visit, not even in your dreams.
You may strive to be like them, but seek not to make them like you.'
Generations of parents have not understood or wanted to understand this and maybe never will...

Once the decision was made, it was a matter of days before Narendra and Malti set off for Sewagram. Fifteen years after they had come home, they were off again...

Yadavendra had taken Madhav to party meetings, a couple of times. Madhav found these meetings interesting and was attracted by the firebrand speeches given by the leaders. Ayodhya had become the clarion call and Yadavendra was in the forefront. Several marches had been organised to gather support for the movement to liberate the birthplace of Lord Ram and Yadavendra was a key organiser. Although, he was initially reluctant to take Madhav along; he slowly started involving him in the various activities. Anita was not happy and was apprehensive, but Madhav's youthful enthusiasm persuaded Yadavendra.

Narendra and Malti were back at their home in Bombay after a prolonged stay for a year in Sewagram.

The Ayodhya agitation was reaching a crescendo. Bricks were being collected from various places throughout the country to be sent to Ayodhya to lay the foundation of a temple of Lord Rama. Processions and *pujas* were being held across the country and tempo was building up for the foundation ceremony.

Yadavendra was getting ready to leave for the event. Madhav insisted that he would accompany his uncle and created a ruckus. Inspite of opposition from Narendra, Malti and Anita; Yadavendra decided to take him along.

Malti wept and Narendra fumed in anger.

In his moment of grief, Narendra confronted Yadavendra and asked, "Why did you ever come back? Why did you come back to our lives and mess it up?"

Malti had never seen Narendra raising his voice and was shocked.

"Why don't you leave us alone," continued Narendra. "Give me back my son and go away from our lives."

Yadavendra listened to his brother's cries and said, "I did not take your son away from you. You drove him to me. You and your antiquated ideas made him suffocate. He was choking; dying...I gave him life. Ask your son if he wants to come with you, I am sure he will not, you know the answer. Go away Narendra, let us live in peace."

A fuming Narendra stormed out of the house.

The break was complete. A bond which had hung tenuously all the years snapped.

They were back in Bombay. Those ten days at Ayodhya had been overwhelming for Madhav.The town had been swamped with hundreds and thousands of people from all over the country and was a sea of saffron. He had listened to hundreds of speeches. He was back home but a thousand questions rose in his mind. He needed to find answers to them and he hoped his uncle could provide those answers. But Yadavendra was extremely busy and repeated attempts by Madhav to get some time for him failed.

One night, after dinner as he was getting ready to go to sleep, Yadavendra came to his room and sat down on his bed.

"Yes, Madhav," he said, "you wanted to talk to me. Tell me what is troubling you? Do you want to meet your mother, your father?"

"No, no...that was the last thing on my mind. The way he behaved with you, the less I see them the better," he replied.

"Then what is the matter?" asked Yadavendra.

"It is about our visit and the agitation and those speeches and what I have been studying at school," replied Madhav. "The books, teachers––they keep saying that we are a great nation because of our mix of cultures and religions."

"I understand..." replied Yadavendra. "Madhav, those books are doctored and your teachers; after all they need to make a living."

"Don't look shocked my son! We are paying the price for the follies of our forefathers. They allowed Islam to enter our country; those barbarians plundered and looted us and as if that was not enough they preached their religion, destroyed our temples and forcibly converted people. And they kept on growing and then one day they wanted a country of their own. We, our so called leaders gave them their country, but unfortunately we messed it up. We called ourselves a secular country and instead of driving all of them away into their promised land; we allowed them to stay here, sheltered them and spoilt them. And today, we are third class citizens in our motherland. In return, those people they keep on growing and very soon they will swamp us and drive us out. They care two hoots for the country; you know most of them are agents for Pakistan and are conspiring with them. Yet, they want all the privileges of this country and much more and our government sitting in Delhi keeps pampering them. But our party and our leaders will not allow this to happen; we will put them in place. If they want to live in this country, they will do at our terms; if not ...We need to teach them a lesson they will never forget and I need you to be in the forefront. Don't be misled by all the nonsense that they teach you at school and get confused. Follow me and I shall lead you up the right path. Now, go to sleep and wake up a changed boy; sorry man, you are quite grown up now."

The seeds had been sown. As the days passed, the seeds would sprout and get nurtured in the impressionable Madhav's fertile mind and from there they would slowly grow and become entrenched strongly.

Madhav had passed out from school and was now in college to complete the two years required to take up a graduation course. He had not done too well in school in his studies but had been a popular guy thanks to his leadership skills. At college also, he quickly formed a group of likeminded boys and was soon their leader. He and his group liked to loiter around in the canteen and attended classes when they got bored. Most of the guys were rich and they often spent the weekends boozing and chasing skirts. Often, he used to return home early in the morning after those late night binges and would then profusely apologise to his uncle and aunt. He would then wake up late and rush to college to drown himself in endless cups of tea in the canteen. Yadavendra indulged him and although he reprimanded him due to the nagging from his wife, he secretly envied him. Madhav reminded him of his younger days and the opportunities he had missed out.

It was the summer of 1991. Madhav had completed his annual exams and was hopeful that the college would take mercy on him and promote him. Madhuri had completed her first year in school. Elections to Parliament had been declared and campaigning had begun.Yadavendra was now past sixty and due to his irregular habits was not very fit. Anita wanted him to call it a day, but Yadavendra was too involved with the party and its politics, and refused to quit. And then the party nominated Yadavendra to contest a seat from Bombay and there was now no looking back.

The election campaign had begun and the atmosphere was charged up because of the Ayodhya issue. Yadavendra wanted to kick off his campaign by first visiting the holy shrine of *Vaishno Devi.* It was a long time since he had taken his family out and so, it was decided that Anita, Madhuri and Madhav would accompany him.

The shrine of *Vaishno Devi* is located on a three peaked mountain called Trikuta which is located twelve kms uphill of Katra which serves as the base camp for the journey to the shrine. Pilgrims travel the distance by foot, on ponies or palanquins. The Yadavendra family had decided to make the journey by foot. They began their walk uphill in the evening. The road was well lit and there were hundreds of people like them. Soon the little child Madhuri and Anita were tired, and could walk no further. They proceeded on ponies while Yadavendra and Madhav followed on foot. The shrine was an exhilarating experience for the family and after dinner and some amount of rest, they began the journey back. They reached back late in the morning tired but satisfied. The original plan was to return back to Jammu the next day and from there to Bombay by the evening flight. Fate willed otherwise.

It was Anita's wish from her childhood to visit Kashmir and have a ride on the Dal Lake in Srinagar. They were only about 250 km away from Srinagar and the opportunity was too good to miss.Yadavendra was initially reluctant; he needed to get back to Bombay and kick off his campaign. Also, there had been sporadic terrorist attacks in and around Srinagar and he did not feel too comfortable. But the coaxing by Anita finally turned him around.

After breakfast, they caught a luxury bus which would take them to Srinagar by evening. It was a pleasant morning and although summer had set in, the journey was pleasant. They had passed by the heavily fortified town of Udhampur; wherein the Indian Army's Northern Command HQ is located. They had gone about thirty kilometres from Udhampur when the vehicle slowly came to a halt. Madhav was dozing but was woken up when he heard loud voices coming from outside. He peeped out from the window and saw a jeep and about four to five persons dressed in army fatigues talking and gesticulating to the driver. The driver seemed to be having an argument but finally he agreed to whatever they wanted. He got into the bus and followed the jeep which started driving away from the highway through a small road. Some of the passengers started getting fidgety and began shout. The driver calmed them down saying that the army wanted to check the bus completely because they had received some tip about the bus and they wanted to do so away from the main road so as to not stop the traffic. The passengers looked at each other with discomfort and distrust.

After about half a kilometre, the jeep stopped and so did the bus. The bus door was opened and in marched three of the persons dressed in army fatigue and carrying automatic rifles.Madhav had a feeling that something was terribly wrong about the whole situation.

The tallest among them suddenly spoke, "Are there any Muslims here?"

A few hands were raised fearfully.

"Come out all of you," he said.

They got up fearfully and a couple started pleading that they had done no wrong.

"Kindly go out, it's an order," said the man, his voice raised.

They went out followed by the other two armymen. The tall man simply stood there, impassively looking up and down. The other two returned back soon after. And then it began and was all over in a flash.

"*Allah O Akbar*!" shouted the three in unison.

"Die you bloody Hindus!" shouted the tall man and then began the firing.

The hail of bullets rained on the hapless passengers and stopped suddenly as it began. The three men got down and off went the jeep.

Madhav had been sitting near the window. On hearing the bullet sounds, he had instinctively ducked and remained in that position. In that instant, he realised that they were caught in a terrorist attack and he was about to die. He did not want to...The sounds stopped. He remained in the crouched position. He could hear in the distance the sound of the jeep starting and going away. He still remain crouched, he could not believe he was still alive. Slowly, he got up and turned and shrieked. His shriek pierced the silence in the bus. Madhuri's life less and blood splattered body lay beside him, her hands seemed to be imploring him to save her. He shrieked again and again and wept. And then he passed out.

He suddenly woke up; he was lying on the grass outside the bus and an elderly lady was sprinkling water on his face. He looked in puzzlement and then remembered and ran to the bus. The sight made him wince in horror. There was blood everywhere, bodies lay at all angles and there was no sound. He somehow managed to gather enough strength to go up to his uncle's seat.Yadavendra was dead and so was his aunt. He closed his eyes and screamed and screamed; he could feel unseen arms holding him and pulling him away from the bus.

The next few days were like a dream to Madhav and the images from those days would continue to haunt and torment him forever. Images of his uncle, aunt and Madhuri bundled up, incessant sirens of the vehicles, unknown faces screaming and sobbing, men in uniform asking him a hundred questions, fleeting images of his father and mother holding him and three pyres burning-his father lighting them one after the other.

As the days went by, details of the incident became clear.Madhav was the only person inside the bus who had miraculously survived. Sixteen passengers including the Yadavendra family had died on the spot, while seven others died later in the hospital. The eight passengers who had been offloaded were questioned but it appeared they knew nothing and had escaped only because of their religion. The bus driver who had been missing had been traced. He had run away when the firing had started. It appeared he was innocent and had been deceived by the dress worn by the terrorists. The attackers were still at large. There was a large uproar all over the country, the incident had happened very near the Army HQ and also involved an upcoming politician. The blame game started.

The days went by; Madhav walked as if in a daze. He was back in his house at Shivaji Park and spent most of the time in his room. His parents hovered in the background. They seemed to have aged all of a sudden to Madhav. Narendra's tall, stately figure seemed to have shrunk. He suddenly felt a surge of pity for them; they appeared to him like two lost children. The moment of grief had somehow suddenly brought them together. It appeared as if Yadavendra in his death had at last united the family together.

Madhav felt a great sense of despair and hopelessness, at his inability to do nothing. Soon this feeling transformed into a feeling of anger; anger at the system, the government, the army and the Muslims. His uncle's words to him echoed back, "We need to teach them a lesson..."

"Yes!" He said to himself, "I need to teach them a lesson."

Narendra and Malti noticed a great change in Madhav. He seemed to be coming out of the depression and was much more cheerful now. His college had reopened. Narendra did not want to press him to go back to college immediately. But one day when Madhav told him he wanted to resume his studies, he was happy. Narendra and Malti felt that they had got back their long lost child, but at a heavy price. Madhav was still not very communicative with them but his hostility towards them had vanished.

His college mates found him much more serious; he stopped going to parties and started attending classes more regularly. But often he would disappear from college; he would go to his old residence and relive his memories.

The ruling party was back in power. Sympathy for the slain ex- Prime Minister was able to counter the call of Ram.

Madhav had to pass by the party office while returning home every day from college. He was tempted to go inside but could not muster the courage to walk in. One day, he finally managed to gather enough courage to walk up to the gate; the gatekeeper refused entry but one of his uncle's colleagues recognised him and took him inside. He joined the party the same day. He was very vocal and soon came into the spotlight and was hailed by the party as a worthy successor. His attendance in college started dropping as Madhav became more and more involved in the affairs of the party. His parents started getting uneasy since he started returning home late and at times, did not return for two to three days in a row. However, they were too afraid to ask him; as they did not want to lose him again.

Madhav also became active in college politics and was soon a prominent member of the students union.

The academic year went by quickly. Madhav himself was pleasantly surprised when the results came out and he discovered that he had managed to pass and was now eligible to join for a graduation course. He did not want to pursue any studies further and wanted to devote all his time to the party; and his parents had all but given up and were therefore, extremely surprised when he came one day and declared that he had joined the Law college. His friends had convinced him that with his leadership and oratory skills, he could become a good lawyer. But what tipped him to take a final decision was a telephone call from a senior party leader and a close confidante of his uncle who told him that a stint in the law college would help his progression in politics.

The atmosphere was getting tense. Hoardings had appeared at many places in Bombay calling for volunteers and asking them to proceed to Ayodhya. Trains carrying volunteers started moving to Ayodhya. Madhav joined the bandwagon.

He arrived at Ayodhya on a cold December morning. It was a homecoming of sorts. Three years had passed by since his last arrival. But there had been a sea change in his thought process; he was a bystander then and confused; he was a leader today and very clear on what he wanted.

On December 6th, as the nation watched in horror; the Babri Masjid was razed to the ground. Madhav was in the forefront. As the dust settled down on the rubble of the imposing structure, he felt a deep sense of satisfaction. Little did he know at that time, of the orgy that would be unleashed very soon, and his unsavoury role in it.

❀❀❀

Sanjay

Karachi was abuzz as was the rest of the country as Gandhiji's Quit India movement caught the imagination of the people. Large scale demonstrations were being held, thousands of people were on the road and the city was in turmoil. Most of the shops were closed and only a few essential services were functioning.

Mayank Dave paced up and down the corridor of the hospital. His wife was in labour. She had two miscarriages earlier and her health was frail. Mayank was worried. He was also worried because his factory was closed down for the past one week as most of the workers were striking. Mayank was patriotic and supported the Independence movement by donating generously and also by printing books and pamphlets but he did not like the chaos and confusion associated with it. He wished people would act in a civilised manner.

Mayank had taken over the factory from his father Chandrakant Dave, at an early age. His father had moved from his native village in the outskirts of Bhuj to Karachi at the turn of the century and had established a printing press by sheer hard work and determination. About five years back, he had a stroke which had rendered him partially paralysed. His mental faculties were still intact but he felt that the time had come to hand over the business to his only son who was just out of college. Mayank had taken over the business at the age of twenty six and he ran it efficiently.

"Congratulations! Mayank, it's a boy."

Mayank turned around; it was the doctor; Dr.Ahmed, a contemporary and close friend of his father.

"And, yes, your wife is also doing well. You may go in and meet them."

Mayank rushed inside. His wife lay on the bed; she looked tired but happy. Their son lay beside her, fast asleep.

They named him Suresh after the only brother Mayank had, and to whom he had been deeply attached. His brother had been two years younger to him. It was January and the kite season had begun. Like other boys, Mayank and his brother were flying kites from the terrace of the house. A broken kite was flying towards their terrace; it seemed to be landing straight onto Suresh's hand. A gust of wind suddenly blew the kite a bit further; Suresh ran after it, tripped and fell head first over the terrace wall. Mayank watched in horror as Suresh vanished from his sight. He ran over to the side and leaned. Suresh lay there on the ground quite still. He quickly ran down; Suresh was still alive and gasping. Mayank rolled him over and Suresh opened his eyes and tried to grasp his hand. And then it was all over. Suresh had been twelve.Mayank had been inconsolable and had taken more than a year to recover. But he could never forget those last moments...

The entire family fussed over Suresh. Celebrations were muted, but the arrival of the child brought a sense of peace to the family in those troubled days. The ladies of the house were busy with the newborn; feeding, dressing and playing with the child. Chandrakant seemed to have a new found meaning in life and spent all his time sitting beside the child and smiling happily. Only, Mayank was troubled. He was happy to see his family contented but the situation outside had him worried. His printing press was working on and off; there had been raids by the British and now he had completely stopped printing any propaganda material. Some of the workers had quit and he was finding it very hard to manage. But what worried him more and more, as time went by was the talk of Pakistan. What started as a wishful thinking seemed to be growing by leaps and bounds. If it were to come true, Karachi would be in Pakistan and he and his family would have no place in this new country. He spent sleepless nights thinking over it.

Where would he go; taking his aged parents and child? He had been born in this place and this was home to him; why should he go and who were they to decide? They never had any problems in the city and he had never been conscious of his religion. Why should his religion now become an issue?

He searched; groped for answers but could find none.

Religion!
All religions, they say, lead to God.
Religion, they say is personal; but hey, why in the name of God have so many people been killed. My history maybe poor, but I think more people have been killed in the history of mankind in the name of religion than anything else, perhaps with the exception of starvation, disease and patriotism.

What is that quality in religion which turns a human being into a barbarian? Or, is religion a nice pretext, an excuse to settle scores?

No religion, they say, preaches violence. But, then why this unending violence...
Why this mistrust, this hatred...
All in the name of God...

Suresh had turned one. The celebrations were again muted. The country was in turmoil and so was Mayank. His wife was able to sense his uneasiness, but could not do much to allay his fears. Rajni had been born and brought up in Bombay. She had come to Karachi seven years back after her marriage and had quite started liking the place; it had the same atmosphere like Bombay and people were all friendly. Before Suresh was born she had been busy managing their huge house and now, her hands were full with the growing child.

"What do you think will happen?" she asked Mayank, one day.

The last few days, the papers had been full of news of violence in Calcutta; riots had broken out between Hindus and Muslims and the situation was extremely tense.

"I am afraid," replied Mayank. "People who have lived peacefully for ages, are suddenly killing each other. Maybe, it would be safer to go away to Bombay."

"But, what would happen to our business, our home here," asked Rajni.

"We could sell them and start all over again in Bombay," answered Mayank.

"Maybe you should talk about this to your father," replied Rajni.

As he thought about the idea, Mayank became more and more convinced that they should leave Karachi and go away, but he could not summon up the courage to talk to his father.

Finally he raised the issue with him, one day

"You can do that over my dead body," screamed Chandrakant.

Mayank had never seen his father in so much rage.

"I have built the business from scratch and Karachi is my home; I have nothing to fear from anybody. If you are so afraid, go away and leave us here," shouted Chandrakant.

Mayank did not bring up the subject again until much later and plunged himself back fully into the business. He did not have time to think now as he started to spend most of his time at the press. He was able to get new workers and very soon the press was working to capacity. Things seemed to be improving.

The New Year dawned. A year momentous in the history of the country; as it would split it into two halves and the wounds would continue to fester...

It was late evening; most of the workmen had gone and Mayank was sitting in his office, planning for the next day. Suddenly, the front door burst open and three men barged in.

"Yes," asked Mayank, "what do you want?"

None of them answered. They came slowly and stood in front of his desk. One of them sat down, while the other two stood beside him. Mayank had never seen them before.

"I am Nuruddin," said the person who was sitting. "I used to own a shop in Ranchi; they drove me away. These two guys, he said pointing to the others, they used to work with me. Today, they call us refugees. Your people; they have made us into refugees."

His voice was now rising.

"But," replied Mayank "Why are you telling me this? Right now, I have enough people here, if I need anymore people, I shall call you. Please leave your address here."

Nuruddin bristled with anger and got up.

"We have not come here to ask for jobs from you. We have come here to warn you that if you do not pack up and leave, we will be forced to take action..."

"Where do you want me to go?" shot back Mayank. "My father established this place more than forty years ago; why should I go?"

"This country is no longer yours," shouted Nuruddin; "go away to your India..."

And then they were gone.

Mayank was aware of the influx of people from the eastern part of the country for the past two months. He used to wish them away, but here he was being threatened by them.

The old misgivings rushed back to his mind and he sat there not knowing what to do.

He went home and repeated the incident to his father. His father laughed it away and told him not to get paranoid.

"I know all the policemen and judges here," he said, "don't worry, the next time they come, we will have them put behind bars. Of all the gall, asking us to go away to India!"

The next few months went off as in a daze to Mayank. Riots had spread in many parts of the country; Punjab was aflame and the influx of refugees continued. Karachi remained peaceful but along with the influx of refugees; there was a steady outflow of people from Karachi. Partition was announced and the outflow soon became an exodus and on 14th August, 1947; Karachi became the capital of the new country of Pakistan.

Yet, Chandrakant refused to budge.

"I do not care," he shouted. "You may call this country, whatever you want, but this is the place which gave me my bread and butter and this is where I will continue to live and die, when the time comes."

Even Rajni was getting anxious now, her parents kept calling each day from Bombay, asking them to leave immediately. As the days went by, Chandrakant became more and more irritated and one day he called his wife, son and daughter- in- law and told them that they were all free to go; but he would not go with them. Faced with a piquant situation, they kept quiet and resigned themselves to fate.

Mayank continued to run the press and hoped for the best. Many of the houses and businesses vacated by the people leaving were being allotted by the Government to the refugees. Many others were simply being occupied by the locals.

Another New Year dawned; Suresh was nearly two and a half years, but in those years, the child had hardly ever ventured out; not even to the beach, which lay hardly fifteen minutes away.

And, then it started all of a sudden. Karachi, which had been simmering slowly, erupted. There was mayhem everywhere; people were being dragged out of their houses and being killed. Houses and shops were aflame. Chandrakant's friends urged him to leave the house and take shelter in their homes. Chandrakant refused. The family panicked.

Several of Chandrakant's friends personally came to their house to take them to safety. They went away sadly, nodding their heads in despair. Only Nasir Ahmed remained. Nasir lived only a few blocks away and was a retired government servant. He had been Chandrakant's closest friend.

"Listen," he told Chandrakant, "you are old and anyway don't have many years to live; but you cannot endanger your sons and grandson's lives. They are still young and have a life in front of them. If not for you; come for them. You can come back after the madness is over."

Chandrakant pondered over it and then said, "Mayank, take your wife and child and go with Nasir *Chacha*. Your mother and I will wait here..."

With a heavy heart, Nasir left the old couple and took Mayank and his family home.

Mayank and Rajni hardly slept that night as gunfires echoed and flames leapt in the background. As morning dawned, Mayank said that he would go home and have a look. Nasir refused to let him go saying the streets were unsafe. The mayhem continued through the day and night with no sign of the police. The early next morning, they heard police sirens on the streets and an eerie silence. Curfew had been clamped. Mayank was getting worried about his parents; the phone lines had gone dead. Finally by afternoon, curfew was relaxed for a couple of hours. Nasir and Mayank along with a posse of policemen ventured to their house. As he neared his house, Mayank had a feeling of dread. The front door was open. They ventured inside. It was dark and all the belongings were strewn all over. Mayank quickly ran up the stairs into his parents' bedroom. They lay on the bed and blood was all over the place. Mayank sat on the ground and cried aloud. Nasir held him and together they wept.

Nearly fifty years after Chandrakant had made his journey to Karachi and made his fortune; his son's family left the city as paupers. Their house had been completely looted; the printing press had been razed to the ground. All they had was the clothes on their backs. They arrived in Bombay ten days later.

I sometimes wonder how the country would look today if Radcliffe had not drawn those lines, which uprooted and changed millions of lives forever!

The honourable men in power in their collective wisdom took a decision to redraw the country's borders and Pakistan was born.

As if in response, the teeming, voiceless masses went on a killing spree. What drove these voiceless, ordinary mortals to indulge in killing of such mammoth proportions? Killing of; not the enemy, but one's own. None of the killers; there must have been thousands of them, were ever arrested or tried for their crimes. Most of them must have become old today or would have died.

I wonder what drives a man to kill; to kill in the name of religion. Did the God in whose name they had killed reward them with 'Jannat' or 'Swarag'?

Friends and neighbours turned into foes and Pakistan became independent India's enemy number one and vice versa. The countries fought three wars on the field and numerous battles off it and invested millions of dollars in acquiring sophisticated weapons. The masses loved it and as if the killings of 1947 were not enough, indulged in periodic bloodletting, all in the name of "Allah" and "Ram".

The killings keep recurring-Mumbai, Kolhapur, Meerut, Hyderabad, Ahmedabad...

It was a difficult time. Rajni's parents gave them shelter. But after having lived all his life in a sprawling house with servants at beck and call, the two room house was becoming claustrophobic to Mayank.He desperately needed to find a job and a home for himself.

After some frenetic searches, he managed to get a job in a small printing press as an assistant. After toiling there for a few months, they were able to take a one room house in a chawl on rent. Those years were one of struggle for the entire family. Mayank went in the morning and came late in the evening. The money they got was barely enough to make ends meet.

And then one day the press closed down. Things became bad to worse. Mayank became moody and irritated; he attributed his misfortune to the politicians, the Muslims and God; in that order and spent most of his time cursing them.

They were now surviving on money from Rajni's parents. Suresh was six years old, but had still not seen the inside of a school. Rajni's father finally got Mayank a job as a worker in a textile mill. Mayank refused to take it up saying it was beneath his dignity.

In defiance, Rajni threatened to take up a job as a house maid. This enraged Mayank and he joined the new job, forcing Rajni to relent. At last, they were able to eat and live properly. The money was not great, but Rajni managed the meagre resources well and finally got Suresh admitted to a nearby municipal school. Mayank was accustomed to long working hours but not to the physical effort that he had to put in now. That and the dusty environment were taking toll on his health. He now took to drinking. He used to come home late and drunk and fall asleep, cursing and shouting. Rajni was pained to see her husband's decline but did not know what to do. Suresh was also finding it difficult in school; he was quite timid and not doing very well in his studies also. The once prosperous and happy family was progressively going on the long road to oblivion.

Rajni decided that unless she intervened and took things in her hand, they would reach a point of no return. In spite of heavy resistance from Mayank, she managed to get a loan from the textile workers union and set up a small tailoring shop. She employed a couple of wives of the mill workers. Soon, her business started picking up and within a year, she was doing well.

Suresh was now twelve years old; Rajni shifted him from the local school and admitted him into a convent school. The new school environment did a world of a good to him and slowly but surely, he picked up the threads. After ten long years in Bombay; life was picking up for Rajni and Suresh.

For Mayank, however, it was all the way downhill. He lost interest in work; the mill provided him work out of compassion. He started drinking heavily. Often, he never came home. Rajni told him to quit and stay at home. She said that she was earning enough to run the family. This upset Mayank further and he went into a rage and started beating Suresh. Rajni drove him out of the house.

It was monsoon; Mayank got drunk and lay on the road; completely soaked and lost to the world. A neighbour noticed him and brought him back home. Mayank was sober for two days; he wept and apologised for his behaviour and said he would quit his job and help Rajni in her tailoring shop. Rajni was overjoyed; but it was shortlived.He stopped going to work, but started pestering her for money, initially at home and progressively at her shop. One day, he came drunk to her shop and abused her and the customers. That was the last straw. That night when Mayank came back home; she handed him hundred rupees and told him not to come back again. Mayank cried, whimpered, shouted and then threatened her. But, Rajni closed the door on his face. That was the last she saw of him alive.

They found his body ten days later; he had been run over by a train. Some bystanders claimed he had slipped and fallen from the platform; others said, he had jumped in front of a running train. Rajni would never know; though she suspected the latter.

Suresh took the absence of his father in a matter of fact manner. Since his birth, his life had been full of trauma and Rajni hoped that at least now things would become normal for her son. But inspite of her repeated attempts, she was not able to bring him out from his shell. He continued to improve in his studies but continued to be a loner.

Rajni's business was now really doing well; she had appointed a supervisor who managed all the routine activities and she went to her shop for a couple of hours only. She had also managed to take a two room flat on rent.

Suresh had by now passed out from school and was studying accountancy. He had seen his mother struggle from his childhood and wanted to take up a job at the earliest so that she could at last get some rest. Rajni on the other hand wanted Suresh to continue his studies. Things were coming to a head. And then Rajni fell ill. The doctor said she was exhausted and needed a long rest. That settled the matter. Suresh completed his graduation and joined a bank as a clerk. He was twenty.

The tailoring shop now had become big and there were several offers from prospective buyers. Rajni did not have the mind to sell off the business started by her, but Suresh did not show any inclination to join the shop. She knew left to itself, without supervision, things could go wrong. Eight years after she had founded her business; she sold it off with a heavy heart.

Suresh worked hard. He did not gossip nor waste his time. He was able to grasp things fast and complete tasks on time. Very soon, he caught the eye of his superiors and his career was on an upswing. He rose up the ladder very fast and within five years he had become an officer.

Rajni wanted Suresh to get married. Suresh was reluctant; he felt marriage would be a distraction to his performance at work and asked her for some more time. The years went by and Rajni got worried. Without consulting Suresh, she started hunting for a daughter- in- law. One day at office, Suresh got a call saying that he should immediately rush home. Fearing the worst, Suresh dropped everything at work and rushed home. He found his mother sitting on the drawing room sofa.

"Get ready son," she said. "We have to go out."

"What is the matter *Ba*?" asked Suresh. "Why did you ask me to come home immediately? Are you not feeling well?"

"I am quite well," replied Rajni. "Change your clothes, put on something nice and let us go. They will be expecting us."

"Who are they?" asked Suresh. "You are not making any sense to me. I had to leave some important work in the office and you don't even tell me what is this all about."

"Ok, you want to know," answered Rajni. "We are going to the Bhatt house. They have a lovely daughter Pooja; your horoscopes match, you are going to meet her."

"How dare you do this to me?" shouted Suresh.

"I am doing this for your own good," replied Rajni.

"I am going back to office," replied Suresh.

This was the first time Rajni had seen Suresh getting angry at her and shouting.

"I have informed them we will be coming," replied Rajni. "You cannot let me down. They must be expecting us. Please, Suresh, I beg of you..."

And she started crying.

The blood was rushing to his head. Suresh had never felt so angry in his life. How could his mother do this to him? He had always been an obedient son but this was just too much. But he could not bear to see his mother crying.

"Ok," he said. "Stop crying. I will come since you have given your word. But do not expect anything more from me."

They arrived at the Bhatt household in the evening. Nilendu Bhatt was an editor with a leading newspaper and he lived with his daughter in their flat in Matunga. Pooja was the youngest daughter and had just completed her graduation in English. She had an elder sister and brother who were both married and well settled. Their mother had died when she was young and Nilendu had brought up all the three children.

"Welcome!" said Nilendu to Rajni and Suresh. "Please come in and make yourself comfortable."

"Where have I got myself into?" thought Suresh.

He had half a mind to turn back and run away. He smiled back at Nilendu and took his seat. All around he could see new faces and the urge to run became stronger in him.

Rajni could feel him fidgeting and getting uncomfortable; she could only hope for the best.

Well, since I have got myself into this. I might as well endure it, thought Suresh. He again smiled at the faces looking at him expectantly; there were so many of them. Some of them were sitting, others standing. Suddenly, he was aware of a small kid standing next to him, who was pulling at him and trying to catch his attention. Suresh was always uneasy with children and he squirmed in his seat. But the kid was persistent and Suresh had to finally turn his attention to the child.

"Are you going to marry Pooja *Maasi*?" asked the child.

Suresh blinked not knowing what to answer and everybody burst out laughing.

"Oh, I am sorry," said Nilendu to Suresh and Rajni. "I have not introduced you to anybody here. You must be wondering who they all are. Where do I start? Maybe, I will start with Aditi, who has been troubling you Suresh. She is my elder daughter Archana's child. And Archana is the one who is standing there," he said, pointing to a young lady who had a baby in her arms.

"That is her second child and he is called Kiran. Standing next to her is my daughter- in- law, Anjali.This is my son-in-law Ritesh," he said pointing to a bespectacled young man who was seated. "He also works in a bank like you. My son Pradeep, here, is an engineer and works in Bangalore. They are here on a holiday."

Suresh was overwhelmed. He had never known a family. He could barely remember his grandparents and he did not know of any other relative.

"It was kind of you to come at such a short notice, *Behnji*," Nilendu told Rajni. "My son and daughter- in- law are leaving in a couple of days and hence the urgency."

Meanwhile, a servant had kept plates full of sweets and savouries in front of Suresh and Rajni.

"Please have them," said Pradeep.

"You must be wondering about Pooja,"said Nilendu. "She will be here in a moment. Archana, why don't you get her here."

In ancient India, there was the Swayamwara. All the suitors used to be lined up before the girl and she used to indicate the person she liked by garlanding him. Things changed, I guess, somewhere along the way. The suitors are lined up today also in front of the girl, but they come alone (if you disregard the large family that usually tags along); the girl is also represented by her near and dear ones. This tamasha is repeated with various suitors until the boy and the families (and the girl-if she has a say) like each other and then the marriage is arranged. Arranged marriage (as these are called), they say are on the decline. Although no records are available, the great majority of all marriages in India are arranged. Of course, there have been changes to the old format; the family/girl/boy meetings continue but at various places like hotels, movie theatres, chat rooms...India's liberalisation policy seems to be catching up. The days of the liberalised arranged marriages have arrived.

They (except Suresh) were all talking nineteen to a dozen and nobody (except Suresh) noticed when Pooja came slowly into the room led by her sister. Her head was bowed, as was the custom and Suresh gaped at her as she slowly came nearer. Somebody,suddenly realised that Pooja had walked in and called everybody's attention to the fact.Pooja came slowly and touched Rajni's feet as a mark of respect and sat down beside her. The conversation resumed. Suresh still sat tongue tied.

"*Behnji*,"said Nilendu to Rajni, after some time, "if you allow, can we let the children, Pooja and Suresh have a separate chat, they maybe feeling shy here."

"But, of course," replied Rajni.

"Pooja *beti*, take him to your room," said Nilendu, "and, Suresh, be at home..."

They entered Pooja's room. It was sparsely but tastefully furnished. Pooja pointed a finger at a chair and Suresh sat down. She sat down on the bed facing him.

He wanted to say something witty, something smart; but nothing came out of his mouth. He just sat there fidgeting. The seconds ticked, it seemed an eternity to Suresh. He had never heard his wrist watch ticking so loudly.

"Well," said Pooja, "you must be aware of my background."

Suresh could only nod his head.

"I heard you are working in a bank," she said and not waiting for an answer continued, "Must be boring?"

Suresh smiled and nodded his head in return.

"I want to teach," continued Pooja, "on second thoughts, maybe not. I am quite lazy, you know," and she giggled.

Suresh did not know what to answer; he had not spoken to any girl in his life. He had kept clear of them in school and college.

"But," replied Pooja, "I can cook well. I do cook sometimes, when the cook does not turn up, which is not really often..."

"I am talking too much, isn't it? All my friends say so. You do not talk much, do you? You seem to be like my sister..."

And very soon she was painting a picture of her family, her friends, teachers and Suresh just sat and listened and nodded and smiled.

The monologue was interrupted by a call from Nilendu.

"Pooja *beti*," he said, "if you have finished, why don't you come out. You can do all the talking after the marriage."

Suresh could hear the laughter in the background. He looked at his watch; forty-five minutes had passed. They came out.

"Well," said Nilendu to Rajni, "maybe you would like to discuss with Suresh. Pooja take them to your room and come out, will you."

There was more laughter.

"What do you think?" said Nilendu to Pooja after she came out.

"Well," she said, "he seems to be ok, he did not say much..."

"Hey!" shouted her brother, "Did you allow him to say anything?"

Pooja went after him.

"Behave yourself," shouted her sister.

"Come and sit here," said Nilendu to Pooja. "Have you made up your mind?"

"I don't know Papa" said Pooja.

"You have to make up your mind child," said Nilendu. "Or do you want more time to think; we shall tell them so."

"No, no..." replied Pooja. "I am ok with it," she replied shyly.

Her brother let out a whooping cry and everybody cheered.

"Sshh..." said Archana, "Behave all of you. What will they think of us?"

Mother and son heard the shouts coming from outside. Rajni smiled as Suresh frowned.

"They are a happy family and I think you will like it," she told Suresh.

For the past ten minutes, she had been trying to get an answer from Suresh but was getting irritated by his lack of response.

"I think Pooja seems to be a good girl and her influence will do you a world of good," she continued. "So, is it yes? Shall we go out?"

Suresh felt himself cornered. But this was not the place and time to argue with his mother. He just nodded his head. They went out.

Suresh and Pooja were married two months later, on an auspicious day.

It was 1969. Richard Nixon had taken over the American presidency, Yasser Arafat had taken command of the PLO, US had begun their withdrawal of troops from Vietnam, Wal-Mart had been incorporated, Beatles legend John Lennon had got married and Man had landed on the moon.

Closer home to India; the life expectancy of an average Indian had reached about 49 years, the Congress party had split into two factions, the commercial banks had all been nationalised, a new superstar: Rajesh Khanna had emerged in Bollywood and cricket fans had set fire to the stands in Bombay's Brabourne stadium after India lost the Test match to Australia.

Closer to our story; Suresh and Pooja had set up home. They had taken a larger flat in Dadar overlooking the Shivaji Park and moved in there along with Rajni.

Marriage brought some degree of stability to Suresh's life. Pooja was happy to be a homemaker and did a good job of it. The coaxing and cajoling by Pooja forced Suresh to come out of his shell slowly. His frequent interactions with his boisterous in- laws also helped. He slowly found in Nilendu a father figure whom he could rely on to provide sound advice. Beneath the bluster, Nilendu had a razor sharp intellect. His long association with journalism had exposed him to various facets of human life and he was able to quickly make a judgment on people and more often than not, he was right.

Rajni felt at peace. She was glad to see Suresh happy and contented. Her years of perseverance had finally paid off.

A child was born to Suresh and Pooja five years later. Holding her grandson in her hand, Rajni thanked God and prayed that he should not undergo any of the horrors that his father had undergone at a young age. She named him "Sanjay"-the victorious.

Unlike his father, Sanjay was born in a country which was slowly shedding the baggage of its past and trying to make its presence felt. Suresh was now heading the branch where he had first joined as a clerk and the family was now living comfortably.

There was a lot of celebration and joy in the Dave and Bhatt households. Pooja's siblings and their families had come down and the atmosphere was one of grand merriment for a week.

Sanjay was an inquisitive and mischievous child. He kept the entire family on their toes.

Nilendu had now retired but still continued to provide advice to his old newspaper. After years of running around, he had time on his hands. He often paid a visit to his daughter's house and very soon a close bond developed between the child and his grandfather.

Nilendu would take the child to the adjoining Shivaji Park and play and talk to him for hours. As Sanjay grew up, he would tell him many stories: from the mythologies, freedom struggle, his experiences as a journalist and the laws of nature. The more he heard these stories, more were his questions and as the days went by more were the complexities of the questions. Nilendu introduced him to the world of books and by the time he was admitted to school, he became a voracious reader. At school, he amazed his teachers with the breadth of his knowledge and had many of them foxed with his innumerable questions.

Sanjay was popular at school. He had a pleasing personality and inquisitiveness which endeared him to everybody. He made friends aplenty in school and in his neighbourhood.

The house was always bustling with children in the evening and during weekends.

Nilendu was a cricket buff and very soon Sanjay was also obsessed with the game. He spent many hours along with his grandfather watching the game at Shivaji Park. Soon, he was playing the game whenever he got the opportunity with his friends in the neighbourhood.

He was fascinated by various cricketers, but one cricketer had caught his imagination.

Kapil Dev had taken the country by storm when as a teenager he had made a dent in the Pakistani batting line up in the winter of 1978, in their own soil. His rustic air and dashing approach to the game was like a gust of fresh air and had caught the imagination of the nation and the followers of the game. Sanjay was also caught in this euphoria. Very soon, he had all the cricketing statistics of Kapil Dev's career on his fingertips and every time there was a match, he would update the data.

It was the summer of 1983. West Indies were playing India in the finals of the World Cup in England. It was a sultry evening in Bombay. Suresh and Pooja had gone out for a wedding. Sanjay was at home with his grandmother, grandfather and a friend Vivek, who lived next door. They were listening to the cricket commentary on the radio and were quite crestfallen. India had been dismissed for a paltry score and the mighty Vivian Richards was hammering the Indian bowling all around the park.

Nilendu was blasting the Indian batsmen for their spineless response but Rajni asked him to be patient and have faith in Kapil. Sanjay had taught his grandmother the rules of the game and now she was hooked to it and like her grandson adored Kapil.

The commentator was droning on, Madan Lal was bowling to Richards and Richards had hit the ball. It was a lofted shot and the ball seemed to be running away to the boundary again, but wait, Kapil Dev was running towards the ball, backwards, will he,won't he? And,the catch was taken. Richards was out. India was back in the game. The commentator's voice rose to a crescendo. The boys shouted in glee; joined by the grandparents. After that, wickets fell in quick succession and the atmosphere was one of festivity in the Dave household and millions of other Indian households. Suresh and Pooja returned home to find the house in a riotous mood and soon joined the fun. And when the last man, Andy Roberts, got out to an innocuous looking ball from Mohinder Amarnath, everyone in the house jumped up in joy. Cricket and Kapil Dev had given the nation, besieged by innumerable problems, a reason to celebrate. And celebrate they did. People rushed onto the street, strangers greeted each other and the whole of India went wild. It was a proud moment for Indians...

What binds nations together? Language? Race? Religion? Maybe, maybe not. A common aspiration? Convenience? Maybe, yes.

What binds India together? Many pundits had predicted after India's independence that the country would split and go the Europe way...The British, they said, had held the country together, and in their absence there would be riots, anarchy and chaos. Yes, there were riots, there were separatist's movements; they still continue to be there. But India has survived and thrived.

So what binds this diverse country together? Maybe, it is the way the country bounces back after each adversity. And, adversities have been aplenty; each time the country seemed to be moving fast forward; there have been obstacles; which has pegged back things. So, perhaps it is the resilience of its people which has kept the country moving, albeit ever so slowly. And, perhaps it is their resilience which would probably keep this country together!

The evening when India won the World Cup would forever remain in Sanjay's memory and so would another evening more than a year afterwards. That would also mark the beginning of the end of Sanjay's days of innocence.

Sanjay was ten years old and was now in class five. He was doing well in studies. His favourite subjects were English Literature and History. He was also active in the sports field and was a member of the sub-junior cricket team in his school. He was slightly built and had started wearing spectacles. His closest friend was Vivek Raman; who lived next door. He was a year older than him and went to a different school, but they had known each other from the time they could remember and at their age, each could not imagine a life without the other. Sanjay was also quite close with his cousins Aditi and Kiran.Often, they would all get together and have a roaring time.

Suresh had now got transferred to the head office of the bank and was doing well. Pooja kept herself busy, looking after the house and taking care of the family members. She had also started writing articles for a couple of magazines since the last year and that gave her lot of satisfaction. Rajni kept herself busy visting the nearby temples and attending various cultural programmes. Nilendu had slowed down on his activities in the office and was leading a retired life.

There had been no school that day. India's third prime minister had been killed by her bodyguards inside her house; the day before. Sanjay had come straight to his grandfather's house as he sometimes did. He had not returned back home as he usually did, since the city was tense. He had spent the day reading and talking to his grandfather, who seemed to be unusually pensive. He kept receiving phone calls and was on the phone for long periods. It was now evening. Sanjay was sitting on the balcony of the house along with his grandfather. They were on the first floor of the building and their building was on a side street leading up to the main road. From their verandah, they had a good view of the main road also. It was deserted.

Suddenly, Sanjay noticed somebody running from the main road and into the side street and following him were a group of people. Sanjay saw his grandfather stiffening.

"You sit here," he told Sanjay, "I will be back in a moment." And he was out of the flat in a jiffy.

Sanjay had never seen his grandfather move so fast. As he watched rooted in the balcony, he saw his grandfather rushing to the main gate of the building and at the same time, the desperate man who was running, reached the gate. Nilendu opened the gate and pulled him in a flash.

"Run inside," he shouted to the man, and closed the gate.

The group of people arrived in a moment and started banging at the gate. They were so near, Sanjay could see their features clearly. They were shouting and screaming but Nilendu stood still before them. Sanjay was suddenly afraid; afraid for his grandfather. He did not know what to do, but he knew he had to do something. The security guard had backed away; the mob had prised open the door and now there was nothing between them and the old man. And Sanjay ran like he had never run before. He ran down the stairs two at a time and out of the door straight to the lonely old man, who was trying to reason with the angry crowd. Nilendu was shocked to see his grandson and did not know what to do. The mob surged on.

"Stay there!" shouted Nilendu, "you go inside over our bodies," he said, pointing to himself and Sanjay.

Sanjay was now shaking with fear and holding onto his grandfather. There were four persons in the group. All of them were in their twenties. They started advancing and then they stopped; as if undecided on what to do. Nilendu sensed their hesitation.

"Why are you stopping?" he said. "You can kill us first before you can kill that man; how does it matter?"

"We do not want to kill innocents," replied the guy who was in the front and seemed to be leading the group.

"What crime has that man done?" Nilendu asked. "If he has committed a crime, I shall hand him over to you.

"They killed our Prime Minister," shouted the leader.

"They?" "Did that man kill our Prime Minister?" asked Nilendu.

"His people," shouted the mob.

"You mean he was the leader of the group which killed the Prime Minister. What is your name son?" asked Nilendu.

"Rajan," blurted the leader.

"Rajan, the people who killed the Prime Minister, they did not have any religion. Religion does not teach anybody to kill; to hate. Do not tarnish the entire community because of a few people. And assume you do kill him; what do you achieve? You must be having a wife, parents at home, maybe a child like him," he said pointing to Sanjay.

"Look," he said and turned back to the building.

The balconies were filled with people; who had been watching in silence.

"So many people are watching you. What if they report to the police? Maybe somebody has already reported to the police? Where does that leave you? Do you want to spend the rest of your life in prison, while your family waits...?"

Nilendu was now talking directly to Rajan and ignoring the others.

One of them shouted, "You cannot fool us by all this talking. Enough is enough; move away."

Nilendu ignored him.

"Go home Rajan," he said. "Go home to your family. They need you."

Nilendu could now sense Rajan weakening.

"I am like your father; you would not kill me or will you?" he said looking intensely at Rajan.

Rajan turned back and started talking to his group. There was a long argument. It seemed to be going on and on.

"Yes," interrupted Nilendu. "It's getting dark; we cannot be standing here and talking all night."

Rajan turned back to him.

"We are leaving," he said. "You seem to be a respected person; we do not want to harm you and the child also."

"Thank you," said Nilendu "and may God be with you."

And then, they were gone. Sanjay held on and started crying.

"You were brave, my son," said Nilendu. "Do not cry. You were really brave..."

"You gave me the courage," replied Sanjay. "You were wonderful."

Sanjay had always admired his grandfather. But this incident reinforced his belief.

The year rolled by fast. Sanjay was now captain of his school team. His days were full. Early morning was cricket coaching at Shivaji Park; there was just enough time afterwards to have a quick bath and rush to school. Breakfast was mostly eaten on the way to school. School kept him busy for the better part of the day. Other than his studies,

Sanjay was an active member of the Literary Society. He continued to read voraciously, especially works on history, biographies and was now a virtual encyclopedia of facts and historical events of India and the world. Evenings were spent in "gully cricket" or catching up with his neighbourhood friends, especially Vivek. Although Sanjay was thirteen now, his bond with Vivek had endured the passage of time.

Vivek was the youngest son of his parents; both his siblings were much older than him. His eldest sister had just been married off and his brother was in engineering college in Bangalore. His father had come to Bombay nearly thirty years back after passing out from school from a small village in the Palakkad district of Kerala. He had enrolled in a night college while working as a typist. He worked hard and slowly but surely worked up the ladder and was currently a General Manager at the same company where he had joined. Vivek's mother passed away when he was just five years old and the children were reared by their father. Pooja developed empathy towards them, especially for Vivek, who spent most of his time with the Dave family. Very soon, he was fully conversant in Gujarati and usually conversed with Rajni in that tongue. Thanks to Vivek, the entire family also picked up a smattering of Tamil.

And then, Sanjay's world came tumbling down.

Nilendu was now seventy years old; for the past couple of months, he had started forgetting small things. It reached such a stage that sometimes he forgot who he was and where he lived and lost his way. One day, an acquaintance found him wandering aimlessly on the roads far away from his house and brought him back home. Pooja and her sister became concerned. They took him to a doctor, much against his wishes. After a series of tests, the doctors concluded that it was the onset of Alzheimer's disease. He needed care. It was decided that Nilendu would move in to the Dave household. Nilendu protested, but finally gave in. Sanjay was happy that he could spend more time with his grandfather but was pained to see his condition. Nilendu was slowly deteriorating. His movements started getting affected and his lucid moments were gradually reducing. Often, he failed to recognise his family members. Sanjay used to sit with him and Nilendu would forget the present and talk to him about his childhood. He would often ignore Sanjay completely and talk to an imaginary companion. Sanjay was pained but could not do much about it. He kept asking his parents whether they should consult other doctors and have another opinion. They did consult many other doctors but the prognosis was same and there was no cure. Their advice was to handle him with care and hope for the best and pray that he did not have to suffer much. They had never been very religious; but in adversity, man clings to God for hope. So did the family. They went to temples, conducted *pujas*, kept vows; they hoped for a miracle...

It is often said that faith moves mountains. Religion and mythology are full of such occurrences: the river Yamuna parting the way for Nanda as he took the young Krishna to safety; the parting of the Sea of Reeds as Moses led the Hebrews to their Promised Land. Even today, one hears of miracles: the blind being able to see, the dumb being able to speak and terminally ill patients becoming alright when all modern medicine had failed.

Maybe these and other miracles have happened; maybe not, but one thing is quite clear, when science fails to provide answers, mankind turns to the unknown, to God.

Six months after the symptoms were first noticed Nilendu passed away. Sanjay could barely recognise the man in his last days; his descent from an energetic and knowledgeable person to an incoherent old man had been fast. Sanjay was devastated. This was the first time he was seeing death at such close quarters and he was overwhelmed. He cried like he had never cried before. He felt a deep sense of sadness; as if he was adrift. His grandfather had been a man full of life and Sanjay had never imagined a life without him. He had prayed and prayed fervently during those last days, but those prayers went unanswered. He felt a deep sense of anger, of helplessness and a feeling of betrayal. His grandfather had not harmed anybody; in fact, he had helped so many people; why had he been subjected to this sorry end. Was there really a God; who cared, who helped? Or was he a myth, for people clutching at straws? In his moment of despair, he read; about God, religion, life and death. There were no answers.

Time is a great healer and time did heal most of Sanjay's wounds. He discovered that life could go on without his grandfather and life would go on irrespective of who lived or died. He was in his last year at school and the board exams were round the corner. His days were full again and he barely had time to think. But sometimes when he lay on his bed and tried to go to sleep, he would remember those happy days he had spent with his grandfather and cry silently.

Vivek had joined the science stream and was hopeful of getting into an engineering college like his brother and sister. His cousins had also joined engineering colleges. His parents also wished he would take up a professional course like engineering or medicine. But, Sanjay was not quite sure-he did not want to get into engineering like his friend or cousins. So, when Sanjay took up Humanities instead of Science stream for his two years in junior college; there was a lot of opposition at home. Sanjay had been an obedient child and had never gone against his parents. But he had been defiant this time. He said he wanted to become a journalist like his grandfather and no amount of persuasion could change his decision. Suresh was very upset. He had struggled on his way up and did not want his son to do so. He tried his best to convince his son that journalism would not pay and the life would be hard.

"You are a good student," he told him, "and can easily get into the best engineering colleges and thereby the best jobs. Why do you want to let go off an opportunity like that and get into something which would be demanding and less paying."

"Papa, please let me do what I want," pleaded Sanjay. "I want to follow in my grandfather's path. That is where I will be happy and maybe successful."

"Your grandfather was a noble man and led a simple life, Sanjay;"replied Suresh. "But times have changed..."

Suresh did not speak to Sanjay for nearly a month after that. But slowly he became reconciled to the idea, that his son was different and would not go the way he wanted.

Sanjay enjoyed those years in junior college. He became very active in many of the societies in college. The college had a magazine. Very soon, he became the editor. He put in an entirely new editorial team and gave the magazine a whole new shape and meaning. He showed his parents his new creation; they were happy for him. A year passed. Vivek had got admission at IIT-Khargpur in his favourite branch. He was to leave in a couple of day's time.

They sat one day afternoon on Marine Drive. The monsoon had just hit Bombay; it had poured for the past week and there had been a let up only since the morning. The sea was roaring behind them and often, the waves would come and crash very close to them. The sky was dark and grey. People were hurriedly passing by, though there were some children and couples, who seemed to be enjoying the weather.

They sat in silence for a long time; a companiable silence. They did not need to talk; they understood each other and how the other felt.

"We shall meet during holidays," said Vivek. "Come on cheer up."

"I heard your father is thinking of going back to the South, now that he has retired," enquired Sanjay.

"Yes, he is," replied Vivek. "Both my brother and sister are in Bangalore and with me going to hostel, he will be all alone."

"So you will be going to Bangalore for the holidays, won't you?" asked Sanjay.

"Hey come on, I will not forget you, Sanjay," replied Vivek. "Holidays or no holidays, we shall meet. You are more than a friend to me, Sanjay," he said. "You are family."

Both of them fought back tears and looked the other way.

Vivek and Sanjay kept in touch; through letters, phone, whenever they could.

Vivek's father shifted to Bangalore. Six months later, he passed away suddenly.

"I guess he missed Bombay very much, as much as I do," wrote Vivek in a letter soon after that to Sanjay. "One starts to realise and miss those small things that were part of one's life, only when you go away from it. My father swore at Bombay's crowds, filth, rain and so much of it but realised later, that the city and he lived and thrived because of it and not in spite of it. It is said that when a person visits a place, he leaves behind a part of him there; forever. My father lived more than thirty years in Bombay, perhaps he left his soul there!"

Sanjay's magazine was thriving. Besides reporting on the college affairs and events; they soon started reporting on happenings in Bombay. Often, Sanjay would attend political rallies and report interesting tidbits. He reported on an old man whom he had seen cheering, vociferously, at three different rallies of different political hues. After an initial reluctance, the man told him that it was his job. He went to any political rally which paid him and his job was to go there and shout and raise slogans. He made a decent living out of it. During these rallies, Sanjay also noticed a disturbing phenomenon-the attempts to rake up caste, linguistic and religious issues not to raise awareness but to divide; to deride.

Sanjay was astonished to see how ordinary, seemingly well behaved, law abiding citizens behaved quite irrationally on the issue of religion and caste. And this was being used to stir up a deadly cauldron. He could not understand why the people were getting so passionate about a place called Ayodhya and the need for building a temple there. Could two wrongs correct a right? He watched with amazement and growing concern the movement to build a temple, gaining momentum and the passions being raised in the name of the Lord. He was further surprised by the reaction from some of his friends in college; some of them were even ready to join the movement. He watched with growing concern the divide between those who were supporting the cause and those who were not and the ranks of the former seemed to be increasing. He could only hope for sanity...

Sanjay passed out at the top of the class and took up admission for his graduation in Political Science. There were still some days for college to begin. Sanjay was now eighteen years of age and he felt on top of the world. Aditi had just passed out from Engineering college and was now planning to do her post graduation in US; she already had got admission in some university there. Her brother was also in IIT-Kharagpur and both he and Vivek had come down to Bombay for the holidays.Pooja was happy to see them together after a long time. It was a balmy evening, the monsoon had yet to set in, dark clouds were threatening in the horizon and people were sweating and swearing. They, all four of them had gone out for lunch, then for a movie, and were casually walking on "Fashion Street" adjoining the Churchgate station. Suddenly, they saw a procession making its way with huge banners. There was a person standing on a jeep and he was speaking, or rather shouting onto his microphone.

"The time has come," he was saying, "to liberate this country from the invaders. They invaded our beloved country, tore down our temples and imposed their religion. Ayodhya will be the first; Mathura, Varanasi and the others will follow. Nothing can stop us now. Come join us and fulfill your duty..."

The procession wound its way. Some people cheered others looked away. Sanjay looked at his cousins and Vivek, and saw their troubled faces.

"Don't worry," he said, "that is only a show of bravado; the barking dog does not bite, they say."

The vacations went off fast. Sanjay joined his graduation course and was busy with his assignments and lectures. Since joining college, his cricket playing days had come to a halt. He had resumed the same a month back and started playing club cricket at Shivaji Park in the evenings. It was a December evening; the 6th of December, they had just finished the match and Sanjay was packing up when he heard a huge shout. It seemed like people were cheering. The sounds seemed to be coming from the gymnasium area. He took his cricketing kit and went up to the gymnasium. The T.V. was on and was blaring. The pictures there told him the story, several hundred people attacking the mosque at Ayodhya until it crumbled and fell.

The barking dog had bitten and now the resulting venom would spread and unleash an orgy two months later, wherein Sanjay would get inexorably sucked.

❀❀❀

CHAPTER-II

The day

Farhan, Madhav, Sanjay

64 BC, Rome; according to legend, the great fire began and burnt itself out after seven days. It is still uncertain what caused the fire but about a tenth of the city was supposed to have been completely burnt.

Associated with the fire is also the story of Emperor Nero; who was supposedly playing his fiddle and singing while the fire raged. Whether there is any truth to this story or whether it is the creation of somebody's imagination going haywire, will remain a source of conjecture.

However, history is witness to circumstances-much of them manmade; wherein the leaders and administration chose to play the fiddle while mayhem reigned and anarchy prevailed.

The demolition of the Babri Masjid led to one such situation-wherein a wave of hate and violence engulfed Bombay.

India's financial hub and city of a million dreams was ravaged. The image of the city lay shattered; its underbelly viciously exposed. The country, the leaders(or rather the politicians) watched in a collective state of inaction as men turned into beasts and enacted the dance of death. Children,women,men were killed ruthlessly; the lucky ones turned into destitutes; their houses burnt, shops ransacked and looted. The madness began in December of 1992, raged for a few days and subsided and reached its crescendo again for a fortnight in January 1993.

At the end of this orgy; at least nine hundred people lost their lives and property was destroyed in many areas- from the slums in Dharavi to apartments in Bandra. Around two hundred thousand people fled from their homes for safer havens and the demographics of the city changed forever.

The city lay divided on religious lines.

Farhan, Madhav and Sanjay were sucked into this bloody whirlpool...

□□□

Ghulam Rasool was getting worried. The year had ended on a troubled note. Riots had broken out, people had been killed. The situation had returned to normal in the New Year but the city was on the boil. Preparations for the wedding of his daughter had got affected and time was running out. He hoped things would come back to normal soon...

□□□

Madhav had returned home triumphant; he and the others who had brought down the mosque were felicitated. This was just the beginning; he was told. Much more needed to be done. They had to be taught a lesson to last...

□□□

The scene on television and the newspaper reports brought back memories of Karachi. Rajni was afraid; afraid for her son's family. She pleaded with Suresh and Sanjay to stay at home and not venture out.

"But, *Ba*" said Suresh, "we cannot sit at home forever. We will take care, don't worry."

However, Karachi continued to haunt her and sometimes she would get up suddenly in the middle of the night, sweating. Sleep would return slowly. As the New Year dawned, Rajni remembered another New Year nearly half a century back when they were forced to flee from their homes...

□□□

The situation had turned from bad to worse. The air was thick with rumours. Bombay was under siege. The police were either absent or going berserk. The politicians blamed each other. Hooligans had taken over the streets and the common man was at their mercy. Societies and apartments tried to barricade themselves against outsiders. Some succeeded; others failed. Families were targeted and pulled out of apartments and killed. Vehicles, shops and people on the road became easy targets. Might was right. Those who could fight, stayed; others fled...They were a few brave souls, who tried to make a difference; helping, saving people from the mobs. However, the majority of the people watched in horror from the safety of their homes; helpless. The mobs had taken control of the city.

Madhav was in the forefront. He had taken a backseat initially when the violence had started, preferring to control and direct the actions from behind. His strategy had been simple; target the areas where the Muslims were in a minority. Destroy their property, drive them away into their ghettoes, and kill them if they did not comply. He and his group of trusted lieutants had planned carefully. They had, over a period, obtained information on shops, houses owned by Muslims in Hindu majority areas and targeted them.Outnumbered, the people there were an easy target. Emboldened by their success and coupled with inaction from the police force; Madhav entered into the fray. He had experienced the thrill earlier when the mosque came down in Ayodhya and felt a similar thrill running through him. The sight of the people cowering and crying for mercy gave him a high. He grew bolder and reckless.

□□□

Ghulam was resolute. He was unwilling to listen to his daughters' pleas to shift to their house temporarily. His older daughters lived in Thane on the outskirts, which had comparatively been unaffected by the violence. But Ghulam felt he was safe in his house in Dadar; though there had been reports of Muslims being targeted in apartment blocks nearby and being killed. As a precaution, the society in which they lived, had removed Muslim name plates from the reception area and replaced them with fictitious Hindu names. For the past week, they had locked themselves in their house and had barely ventured out.It appeared to be safe. But their delusions were rudely shattered one night. It was about nine pm; they had spent another restless day and were ready to retire for the night. Ghulam was standing in the verandah when he heard a loud shout. A large crowd armed with swords and sticks had barged inside the two storey house, a couple of blocks down the street. He watched in horror as they pulled out people from inside. In the glow of the streetlights, he could see them pleading. He knew those people. They were a family of five; decent and god fearing. He watched in horror as they were mauled and assaulted. He wanted to do something, but all he could was rush inside. He had to do something; he could not let them die.

"Maybe we should call the police," said Farhan.

"Yes, yes," replied Ghulam.

He dialled the emergency number for the police; it kept ringing. He tried again and again. Finally, he heard a voice at the other end.

"Yes, what do you want?"

"Please help," shouted Ghulam. "A mob has attacked a family next door and they are in grave danger. Please come quickly..."

"Don't shout," replied the voice at the other end. "You know we are hard pressed, we cannot be sending people everywhere."

"Please..." begged Ghulam.

"Tell me the address," answered the drawling voice at the other end.

Ghulam spelt out the address in a hurry.

"Ok," said the voice at the other end and then it went silent.

The family sat in silence. They could hear shouts coming from outside; there was no sign of the police. They barely slept that night. The shouts died down, but the police never turned up.

"I think we should go," said Ghulam to his family members.

They were sitting silently and having breakfast.

"I spoke to our security guard; none of them were spared, even the child."

"When will the madness end?" he cried out aloud. "I called up Nargis and told her we are coming. Pack up your essentials and we will leave as soon as possible."

The family packed their belongings quickly and loaded them into their car.

"Should we tell somebody, our neighbours, that we are leaving," asked Ameena.

"No, no..." replied Ghulam. "Let us leave."

They got into their Ambassador; Ghulam behind the wheel and Farhan beside them; the ladies behind.

The security guard opened the door and off they went. The car wound its way through the deserted streets. It wound its way past the Sidhivinayak temple, past the Catering Institute on Veer Savarkar Marg and towards Shivaji Park.

The departure of the car from the building did not go unnoticed. Madhav had deployed his cronies to watch and report on the activities of the few Muslim families in that area. Unknown to Ghulam and his family, they had been under observation for the few weeks.

"Stop the car," ordered Madhav to his men, when he got the information. "I will be there soon."

As the car approached Shivaji Park, Farhan noticed a group on the road near the Park. They seemed to be armed and were looking at them.

"*Abba,*" he said, "maybe we should turn back. That group looks menacing."

Before Ghulam could react, the windshield was shattered by a huge stone. Ghulam swerved; he could barely see anything ahead and came to a stop. For a moment, they sat in stunned silence.Ghulam opened the door and stepped out. Five young men stood there, looking at him. They were armed with swords and sticks.

"Where are you off to?" asked one of them.

"I am going away," replied Ghulam.

"To Pakistan?" asked another man.

Ghulam did not answer.

"You cannot drive all the way to Pakistan, can you?" he persisted.

"I am just going to my daughter's house," replied Ghulam.

"We don't want you to go there," replied another man. "We want you to leave—go away to Pakistan.That's where you all belong don't you? You sit here and work for them. We can't have this anymore."

"I am an Indian first and last," replied Ghulam. "As good as anyone of you," he added.

The group started laughing. Farhan and the ladies inside were getting restive. Farhan stepped out.

"Another Indian," they said pointing to Farhan and started laughing again.

Ghulam looked around; there were hardly any people around. The few people walking at the distance scurried away, as if nothing had happened. He then noticed a man on a motorcycle coming towards them. Hope flickered. The motorcycle came towards them. The man got down and looked at them.

"What is the joke?" he asked the others, "Why are you all laughing?"

"They are Indians, they claim," one of them said and again burst into laughter.

"That is no laughing matter," replied the man.

Farhan noticed that the man was barely older than him but had a swagger and haughtiness which belied his age.

The last six months had been a defining time for Madhav.It was as if the diffident and troubled boy had suddenly grown up into a leader.

"All of them claim so, don't they, but we know better," Madhav said.

It now dawned on Ghulam and Farhan that he was part of their group.

"You think by living amongst us, you can become one of us," he said in a measured tone. "That will never happen. You have been pampered and spoilt; but now all that is over. Today, Bombay is burning; tomorrow the rest of the country will follow. We will pick each one of you and destroy your lives. We will make your life so miserable that you will run away and if you don't..."

He left the sentence unfinished.

He suddenly advanced towards Ghulam, pulled the car keys from his hands and flung it at one of his men.

"Who is inside?" he asked with a sly smile.

"Don't!" shouted Ghulam and Farhan in unison.

"Let them go," pleaded Ghulam. "Do whatever you want to with me. Take my house, my business, let them go," he pleaded.

"We will do all that," replied Madhav. "But first we have to dispose all of you."

"We will go away," pleaded Ghulam.

"To Pakistan?" asked Madhav.

"Yes," replied Ghulam, "if that is what you want."

"No!" shouted Farhan. "We are not going anywhere. This country is ours also, who are you to drive us away?"

"You think this country is yours," shouted back Madhav. "You live in a fool's paradise. You have no place here..."

"Get in the car!" he ordered Ghulam.

"Lock them," he ordered his men.

"What are you doing?" shouted Farhan.

He could see his family banging at the doors. They had now lowered the windows.

"There are ladies in the car," sneered Madhav. "They are your family aren't they," asked Madhav to Farhan. "And you don't want to go away to Pakistan."

"Hold him!" he shouted at two of his men.

Two men pinned Farhan down.

"Easy," said Madhav.

"I will go away wherever you want," shouted Farhan. "Let them be..."

"I will deal with you later; let me first send them—your family packing..." replied Madhav.

"Hey guys!" he shouted to the other men, "let's get started."

As Farhan watched in horror, one of the men opened the fuel tank cap and started siphoning the petrol into a broken down can. Ghulam and the others in the car were trying to force themselves out through the window, but were being forcibly pushed by the group, whose numbers had now increased. The petrol was forcibly thrown inside the car. Ghulam and his family cried in terror realising the gravity of the situation.

Farhan struggled to escape but the men holding him were too strong. He could only watch in shock as they kept soaking his family and car with petrol.

"Stop!" shouted Madhav.

The men withdrew.

As everybody watched, Madhav soaked a piece of cloth in petrol, lit it slowly with a match and threw it inside. The car burst into flames.

□□□

Sanjay had got up late. His college was closed because of the situation in Bombay. He was cooped up in the house for the past one week and decided he would take a stroll outside.

"Why do you want to go?" asked Rajni. "The situation is so unsafe."

"I am just going to the park, shall be back in an hour's time; don't worry, there is nothing to fear," replied Sanjay.

"Let him go " said Suresh.

Sanjay stepped out of his building. The roads were unusually quiet. He walked slowly to Shivaji Park. There were very few people there. He started to jog slowly around the periphery. As he reached the last stretch which abutted the main road, he saw a car in flames with people standing around. His first reaction was that it must have been an accident, but then he realised that the people standing around were not trying to help but were shouting and cheering. Something terrible was happening. He went nearer and through the gaps in the crowd, saw the gruesome sight. A car was burning quite fiercely, there were occupants inside and they were fighting a losing battle with the flames. A lone person, a young boy, ran around the car screaming in anguish and trying to pull out the occupants, while the crowd cheered wildly.

□□□

As the flames started consuming the car and himself, Ghulam cried out in despair. He could hear his family screaming from behind for help. The heat was intense and he knew these were his last moments. A feeling of intense sadness came over him and as he slowly passed out, he could see somebody familiar beckoning him from far away...

Death- the final frontier. An unsolved jig-saw puzzle. A question mark.
What lies beyond? Mankind has struggled to find answers.
Theories abound: Rebirth, immortal soul, karma, heaven, hell, spirits, ghosts...
Treatises, religious texts abound.
However, one of the world's greatest mysteries remains unsolved.

Farhan tried desperately to get near the flaming car. He could see his family dying a slow death but all he could do was to run helter skelter. The heat was so intense, he could do nothing but watch...

Madhav watched the scene being enacted in front of him with no remorse. He had lit the spark which was devouring four lives.

"Let us go," said Madhav to his men. "Our job is done."

"What about the boy?" asked somebody in the group. "He will identify us. Let us finish him."

"No..." said Madhav. "Let him live; his life will be more painful to him than his death."

The mob moved away. Sanjay stood there facing the nearly burnt car and the young boy grovelling beside it. He could see people in the distance watching, walking away; not wanting to do anything with the incident. Sanjay walked slowly up to the boy, he was no more than his age and tried to pull him away from the burning car. The boy resisted for some time and then his body shuddered and went limp. Sanjay did not know what to do. He tried to hail some passing vehicles; nobody stopped. He was getting desperate, the boys breathing was becoming shallow. He needed to do something and fast if the boy had to be saved. He lifted Farhan onto his shoulders and began to walk...

□□□

Farhan opened his eyes slowly. He seemed to be lying somewhere; he then remembered and screamed and passed out. For two days, Farhan hovered between light and darkness, between life and death.

The doctors told Sanjay that Farhan was in complete shock but were hopeful he would recover.

The third day, Farhan woke up from his stupor and gazed at his surroundings. He seemed to be lying on a bed. A lady walked in, she was dressed in white.

"Who are you and where am I?" asked Farhan.

"You are in a hospital and I am a nurse here," replied the lady. "You seem to be much better today. I shall get the doctor; you might want to talk to him."

Farhan watched her going away. The image of his family kept reappearing again and again...He hoped it was a dream; he hoped they had managed to survive. He had to get out from here and find out.

A middle aged gentleman walked in along with the nurse.

"Good morning, young man," he said. "I am Dr. Nag."

"I want to go," said Farhan. "I want to see my family, I need to go."

"Yes, yes," replied Dr. Nag, "you can go, but I think you need a day's rest. Also, the police would like to talk to you before you leave."

"Police!" shouted Farhan, "Where were they when they burnt my family? What do they want now? I don't want to have anything to do with them."

And he burst into tears.

Dr. Nag tried to calm him down but Farhan shouted at him and asked him to go away.

A feeling of intense grief enveloped him. He wept...

□□□

Sanjay had been visting the hospital daily.

As he walked that day carrying Farhan, he had been helped by an auto rickshaw driver who dropped them off at a nearby hospital. He had got Farhan admitted and had narrated the entire story. He was later questioned by the police. They took him back to the scene of the crime. As he watched in horror, they removed the remains of the people, bundled them into gunny bags and took them away. They left him after recording his statements.

Sanjay was badly shaken. He could barely talk or eat.

"What is the matter?" asked his mother as he sat on the dinner table that day. "You seem to be troubled."

"It is nothing Mummy," replied Sanjay. "It's just what's happening in the city. It's terrible."

"There is nothing we can do about it," replied Pooja. "Go to sleep early, you will feel better."

That night as he lay on his bed, the happenings of the morning flashed by. He could see the car burning, with the inmates still alive. He could see the group around the car, watching and shouting. He could see their leader; he was no more than his age, grinning wildly...

What drove these guys to kill?

He had given the description of those guys to the police, but was skeptical. There had been so many killings these days. The police did not seem to be keen to catch the culprits. They would all be walking free on the roads...

He could see the face of the young boy; he still did not know his name, as he lay cowering in the hospital bed, all alone...

□□□

Madhav felt refreshed, alive today. He had buried the ghosts of the past. He had avenged the killing of his uncle and his family. He could not bring his uncle and his family back to life, but at least their souls would rest in peace now. But his job was not over. His mission was just beginning. He had to complete the unfinished job of Partition. He looked back at the events of the morning. He had felt no pity at the family whom he had so horribly killed. He had killed for the first time and he realised, he felt no remorse. He had spared the boy; he had wanted him to suffer...

□□□

Sanjay peeped into the hospital room. The boy was sitting on his bed, staring blankly outside the window.

"May I come in?" he asked.

Farhan turned, looked at him and then looked away. Sanjay came in slowly.

"I am Sanjay," he said. "I brought you here."

Farhan turned and looked at him squarely.

"Why?" he asked. "Why did you save me? Why did you not let me die there? And what do you want from me today? Thanks? Go away; I do not want to see you again."

"But I was only trying to help," replied Sanjay. "I want to help you now..."

"Help me!" screamed Farhan. "How can you help me? Can you bring back my parents? Can you punish those guys who did this to me? Can you turn back the clock? Can you at least take a knife and slit my throat? No, you cannot do any of those things. You can only stand here and talk. Go away and never come back."

Sanjay stood there shocked. Farhan had turned away from him and was again staring outside. He walked out slowly.

□□□

Sanjay tossed and turned. He was trying his best to sleep, but sleep eluded him. He could hear the voice of the boy ringing in his ears again and again. He had only tried to help. He got up and paced the room. He went up to the balcony and stood there. There was a nip in the air and he suddenly felt cold and alone. He wanted to share his feelings, his sense of helplessness. But with whom? His parents, his grandmother would get alarmed. He could not take it anymore. He went in and sat down at his desk. He sat in the darkness for sometime, trying to collect his thoughts. And then he decided. He switched on his table lamp, and took out a piece of paper. He was going to write; a letter to Vivek...

□□□

Madhav entered the house. He switched on the lights. It was quite dusty. He walked up to the balcony. He could hear in the distance the roar of the waves and see the lights twinkling. He was back here after a long time. He took a chair and sat down. This house was his sanctuary. It gave him strength; it strengthened his resolve to go on. He stood up and went to the drawing room. A framed photo on the wall caught his eye.

He removed the photo and sat down on a sofa. He looked at it; they had taken the photo in a studio. His uncle sat with his aunt on a sofa. His niece was in between. He stood behind. All of them were smiling. He touched the photo fondly, tears rolled down his cheeks...

□□□

He had to get out. He could not take it any further. The lights had been switched off in the room and it was silent.

Farhan climbed out of the bed and crept slowly out of the room. He was wearing a hospital gown and that would make people suspicious. But he had no other option. He was fed up living in this sanitised building. He had to get back into the real world. They had killed his family and now were trying to soften him up. He had to go.

The corridor lights were not fully lit up. He moved quickly down the stairs. Nobody had seen him as yet. He had been lucky. He walked faster and faster. He could see the reception in the distance. The nurse sitting there seemed to be dozing. He had to take his chance. He walked slowly but confidently. Luck was on his side. The nurse continued to nod at her seat. He had reached the main door. A security man stood on the road outside the compound wall, smoking, very much awake.

Farhan walked out of the main door, only the wall separated him from freedom. He had to take a chance; he had to scale up the wall and jump out. He went to the farthest corner and began to climb. He slipped and fell. He tried again. This time he was successful. He reached the top; the watchman had to be distracted so he took a stone, that he had carried and aimed it at a window. It hit with a dull sound. The watchman heard it and ran inside.

Farhan jumped. He hit the road and began to walk. He turned back but there was no sign of the watchman. No one had noticed him.

He could hear the sound of a dog howling in the distance. It was followed by more howls. The howls reached a crescendo. He remembered his grandmother telling him that dogs howled at night, because they could see dead spirits. He suddenly felt afraid and ran and ran...

❀❀❀

CHAPTER-III

After

Farhan

The uneasy peace that had descended on Bombay since the latter half of January 1993 was broken. On the afternoon of March 12th 1993, within a span of two hours, a series of bomb explosions rattled across the city, killing more than two hundered and fifty people and injuring thousands. A city, already torn apart by the riots, lay shattered.

Farhan heard the news that evening when he switched on the television. He was not surprised. He had been expecting it...

The last month had been extremely trying; he had refused to listen to his sisters' pleas to vacate the house and move in with them. He had shut himself in his house, refusing to venture out. He had cried, until the tears had dried out. He had felt a great sense of loss and despair. He could not imagine spending the rest of his life without his family. Nothing seemed to make sense.

Why him and his family? What had they done to undergo such a painful end? Was there no justice in the world? Where was God and why was he doing nothing about it? Was being a Muslim a crime? Why was the Government, the police, the people silent?

His sense of loss and despair soon turned into a sense of deep injustice against which he could not keep silent. This is not what he had been taught in school and by his father. He could not become a party to the injustice; he had to act.

What could he do alone? What next?

It was an evening and nearly a month after he had run away from the hospital. It was nearly dusk, but he had not switched on the lights. He was sitting on the sofa staring at the wall clock while hundreds of questions rose through his mind. The door bell rang suddenly; interrupting his thoughts.

Who could it be? He thought. Maybe it was one of his sisters. They used to come often; clean the house, supply him with food and plead with him to come along. He hoped they were not back.

The bell rang again. He walked slowly upto the door and opened it. In the fading light, he could see a young man standing. He was slightly built and clean shaven.

"*Salaam Aleikum*," he said.

Without waiting for a reply, he continued.

"My name is Salim.You do not know me, but I do. We do. We need to talk. Will you not let me in?"

Farhan let the stranger in slowly.

"I do not like the darkness," said Salim. "Why don't you put on the lights?"

Reluctantly, Farhan switched on the lights. He grimaced as the tube light lit up. Most of the past month; he had spent in darkness and had not ventured out.

He stood in silence as he watched the stranger settling down on a sofa.

"Sit down," said the stranger and Farhan sat down.

They sat in silence for some time as the stranger sized him up.

"I know how you feel," he said slowly. "They killed my family too; my parents and my brothers."

There was another period of silence, each of them in their own thoughts.

“I was also feeling helpless, in despair, like you,” said Salim breaking the silence.

“But, now I am clear. We shall not take this lying down. We shall strike back. We have endured enough. They destroyed our mosque; they killed our elders, our children, our women. We will destroy them too. We have a plan. I want you to join us. Be ready, I shall be here tomorrow morning at nine.”

And then he was gone.

That night, Farhan slept fitfully. He woke up several times; everytime by the same nightmare which continued to dog him all these days. He finally got up at five o’ clock. He had made up his mind. He would go with the stranger; maybe he had a solution to his nightmare.

Salim was back at nine as he promised. After a month in seclusion, Farhan ventured out into the streets for the first time. The noise and the light overpowered him and he had to make an effort not to run away. They reached their destination after catching a train and walking for half an hour. It was a crowded market place. Farhan had never been to this part of the city. Salim led him up into a run down building, which however seemed to be fully occupied. They walked up the rickety flight of stairs, onto the third floor. Salim knocked on the door. There was a whisper from the other side and Salim whispered back. The door was opened slightly and Salim quickly pulled Farhan inside. They were inside a corridor which seemed to lead onto a large room, from where he could hear a voice; a very agitated voice. Salim led him slowly into the room and motioned Farhan to sit down. There were nearly twenty people crammed into the room and they were listening to a middle aged person, who was standing at the front and talking. He motioned slightly to Salim and continued. His voice was loud and gravelly.

“The time has come to wage a *Jihad,*” he said. “The infidels have to be taught a lesson. We have tolerated injustice and oppression long enough. We have to wage war against the Government, the Hindus and this country—they massacred our loved ones and want to destroy our religion. We cannot watch in silence as they destroy us. Our faith, our religion is in danger. They want us to become Hindus or run away from here. We shall do neither; we will hit them so hard that they will gasp in pain. All of you, who are here, have suffered. You are all in pain. I want to wipe out the pain from your faces. I want to see the pain on our enemy's faces. But we have to be careful. Our enemy is more powerful. But fear not, they are lazy. They are complacent. We will strike and strike in stealth. But each one of you will have to make more sacrifices. You will have to put your lives at stake; so that we are successful."

The voice went on. Farhan heard and watched, as he saw the entire audience roaring and applauding as if in a trance. Farhan had never felt any particular attraction to Islam; but the last two months had made him acutely aware of his religion. And today sitting here, he felt he belonged. The language, the tone was becoming more and more strident, but something drew Farhan to that voice.

"We have a plan," the voice continued. "We want to create a big impact. You can all help; if you want to. If you want your loved ones to rest in peace. If you want to fight injustice. If you want to save our religion and ourselves from getting destroyed. We have powerful people behind us; they will give us money, arms and their brains; we will—You will execute the plans and bring our lost glory back. We will tell you what to do and when to do; and that will be soon."

He paused for effect.

"Some of you here," he said and he gazed at the people sitting before him, "may feel that they are not upto this. They are cowards."

He paused again.

"*Allah* forgive them. Maybe, some of you here, would like to talk about what I said to others outside. They are traitors. We shall not forgive them."

The voice went on and on. Suddenly, it stopped.

"It's time for our prayers," it said. "And then we shall disperse in ones and twos as we came."

They were on the way back. Salim and Farhan had lunch at a restaurant near the market and now were sitting on a train.

"I shall be getting down in the next station," said Salim. "I shall call you back in a couple of day's time. Think and let me know.But, not a word to anyone, if you value your life."

And then he was gone.

Farhan mulled over it again and again. At the end of two days, he had made up his mind. He was ready for Salim.

"Yes, what have you decided?" asked Salim.

He had reappeared again mysteriously after two days.

"Well," replied Farhan. "The last few weeks, I was trying to run away from reality. The fact stared right at my face, but my upbringing stopped me from accepting harsh facts. I was like the cat which closes its eyes if it does not want to see what it does not like to see. You have prised open my eyes. To be born a Muslim in this country is a curse. I believed, I wanted to believe that all people are equal in this country. But, now I realise that some people are less equal. They talk of fair mindedness and equality from the comforts of their houses and offices, but in reality, it is a jungle out there and they are the hunters. Unless we are prepared and retaliate, we will become extinct."

Farhan stopped, got up from the sofa and went over to a corner table. As Salim watched, he picked up a framed photograph and came over and sat next to him. He stared at it for a long time and handed over to Salim.

"This is what remains of my family; only photographs and memories," he said. "But I am not going to cry anymore. I want justice; an eye for an eye. I want to live amongst them; with them, be friends with them, however painful it maybe, but strike at them slowly and suddenly and create fear in their minds. I want to become the hunter."

He paused and looked at Salim and said, "But I am not ready yet."

"But why?" asked Salim.

"I am still weak, my mind still wavers. I have to become stronger mentally and physically and then, I shall be ready to join your, our war. May you succeed in your mission. *Khuda Hafiz.* "

"*Khuda Hafiz*," replied Salim. "I shall come back ..."

And then he was gone.

Farhan joined his college back. His classmates and teachers expressed their condolences. He thanked them for their concern and said he would like to forget the past and begun afresh. His sisters were glad that he was back to his routine but something about his demeanour had quite changed, which they could not quite grasp. He seemed to have grown up into a man suddenly or rather, he seemed to have grown up into a different person altogether.

Farhan showed no interest in the affairs of his father's business. Since his father's demise, the business was being managed by Iqbal Ahmed, who was a close confidante and distant cousin of Ghulam Rasool. Iqbal had tried to meet Farhan several times during the last few months, but Farhan had turned him away. He finally agreed to meet Iqbal in the presence of his sisters and co-brothers. Despite a lot of persuasion, Farhan refused to associate himself any further with business. Finally, it was agreed that Iqbal would run the business for the family and would only interact with the elder sister Nargis on matters of extreme urgency.Farhan would get a monthly sum depending on the profits generated.

Farhan started to jog everyday morning; it helped him focus his mind and also feel better.

The first few days he could run barely a few hundred metres, but by the end of two weeks, he could run one lap around the park quite easily.

He had also started going to the mosque for Friday prayers. He had never been regular before and had felt uncomfortable earlier. Now he felt at home, at peace.

That Friday; the 12th of March he had not gone for prayers; in fact, he had not gone to college also. He was not feeling well and had decided to stay at home and take rest.

As he saw the images flitting on the television, a smile crossed his face. They had struck and struck well. Panic was writ large on everybody's face; the armchair messiahs were running scared. The tables had turned. Now the hunters were the hunted.

There was a movie, released about twenty years back in which a team of commandos, on a mission in a jungle, find themselves hunted by an extra-terrestrial warrior; an invisible one. They watch in horror as they are killed one by one. They do not know who is killing them and who is going to be next; the uncertainty is worse than the killing itself.

It is the uncertainty which makes terrorism so frightening. The vulnerability to sudden death; the absence of an enemy or rather the enemy within, makes it more frightening.

It is said that terrorism is a 20th century phenomenon. But then, what about those wars and battles which have been part of human history; which have caused unimaginable misery, destruction and loss of lives of millions of innocents. Are these not acts of terror and the instigators, terrorists?

But what separates these acts and terrorism as it is known today, is the identity of the terrorist or rather his lack of identity. The terrorist could be anyone; the guy next door, your driver, your school mate, your brother...This is what makes it frightening. What triggers a guy/gal like you, me, and them to suddenly turn into monsters?

Unless we-the society, the government machinery look for those triggers and try to find answers, we will continue to create more enemies within, more Salims...

Farhan passed the first year of college; he had done well in all the subjects. He was now able to run three laps around the Shivaji Park without stopping. He was going stronger and almost ready. But he needed help; he could not do this alone. He waited for Salim.

Just as he had appeared so many evenings back, Salim reappeared. He smiled as Farhan opened the door.

"You seem to be ready," he said.

"Yes, I am," replied Farhan "and I need your help."

"The police are hard on our heels," answered Salim. "We need to lie low now. You will have to wait."

"No," replied Farhan. "I cannot wait. I have waited long enough."

"Come with me then to our group," replied Salim. "You will have to be away for quite some time and maybe never come back to this life."

"No!" replied Farhan. "I do not want to run away; I want to be within the system and strike them and I do not want to be part of any group, not yet..."

"Then, what do you want?" asked Salim.

"I want your help in locating the guy who led those people and murdered my family," answered Farhan.

"But why?" asked Salim.

"I want to wipe out his family," replied Farhan. "Only then shall I be at peace and ready for bigger things."

"Are you sure that is what you want?" asked Salim.

"Yes!" replied Farhan.

There was a long pause as both of them seemed lost in their thoughts.

"It is not going to be easy," said Salim. "I do not think anyone will come forward and give any clue about that man. Maybe the police have some information, but even if they do, they are not going to do anything about it and neither can we approach the police, can we?"

"There is a way," replied Farhan. "There was this boy who saved me and took me to the hospital. He must have seen this guy and informed the police about him and the others. He will lead us."

"But, how will we locate him?"asked Salim.

"Leave that to me,"answered Farhan. "I shall find out who he is and then, you have to help me further."

"Ok," replied Salim, "I will be back soon."

He got up.

"Wait," said Farhan. "I want your help only to locate this man; the rest I will do myself and myself alone. I do not want anyone getting involved. We shall go ahead only if that is acceptable to you, otherwise let's forget it."

Salim smiled.

"We need people like you with us. I will only give the information that you want and wait...till you join us."

And then he was up and gone.

Farhan waited two days, before he had the courage to enter the hospital from where he had run away. He approached the reception.

"Yes?" said the lady at the reception.

"I am looking for details of a person who was admitted here," said Farhan diffidently.

She stared at him in suspicion.

"Why?" she asked rather brusquely.

"I think you misunderstood me," replied Farhan. "I was admitted to this hospital in an unconscious condition. This man saved my life and brought me here. I was under lot of stress and never got to thank him. I want to find him and thank him."

"Ok," replied the lady, still suspiciously. "Please wait here and I will be back."

She returned back soon and said, "Come with me, our registrar, Mr. Bhide would like to meet you."

The Registrar was an old man, nearing seventy.

"Sit down my boy," he said. "How can we help you?"

Farhan repeated the story.

The man nodded and rang a bell. A peon rushed in.

"Ask Mr. Pande to come with the admissions register for January."

They sat in silence as they waited for Mr. Pande.

There was a knock at the door and Mr. Pande walked in timidly.

"Mr. Pande,"said the registrar. "This boy here, Farhan wants your help. Can you tell Mr. Pande what you want," he said pointing at Farhan.

Farhan repeated his story for the third time.

"That is easy," replied Pande.

He looked through the register and said "Ah, there it is. Farhan: Age -18 years, admitted on 12th January, in a complete state of shock."

He beamed widely at Farhan. Bhide also nodded his head.

Farhan was getting frustrated.

"That is me," he said. "But I wanted to know who brought me here."

"Oh!" replied Pande. "That is also very easy."

He thumbed through the register and said,

"I have found it. One Sanjay Dave brought you in. Do you want his address?" and he repeated it as Farhan quickly wrote it down. It was very near his house.

"Wait!" said Pande and both Farhan and Bhide looked at him.

"The register also says that ten days later you simply vanished. The night nurse came looking for you but you had disappeared."

Mr. Bhide looked at him intently. Farhan wriggled on his seat under those stares.

"I was under a lot of stress and wanted to go home. So I ran away, he said. I am sorry."

Mr. Bhide nodded his head.

"I hope you are ok now, would you like a doctor to examine you?"

"No, no..." replied Farhan in alarm. "I am quite well now and thank you so much for all the help."

He got up from his chair and literally ran away from the hospital.

Salim returned after five days.

"This is the lead," said Farhan, handing over the name and address to Salim.

"I shall be back soon," Salim said.

The days went on. College was interesting and Farhan delved further into the mysteries of the physical world. He sometimes went to his sisters' place when he felt alone, but would return back quickly. They were all busy in their own world and he had never been too close with them or their families. Weeks and months went on and there was no sign of Salim. Farhan was becoming restive. It would be a year now since that ghastly incident. He was feeling the urge to do something soon.

And then, Salim reappeared one evening; as suddenly as ever.

"I am sorry," he said as he walked in.

Farhan noticed that he had lost weight and appeared to be tired.

"I had to go away...outside the country. That is why it took so much time."

"But," he smiled, "your job is done."

He took out a paper from his pocket and gave it to Farhan. It had a name with an address. "A proper character he is; your man. Wants to drive away all the Muslims.Was, I understand, in the forefront at Ayodhya also. He lives there with his parents, they are very old," said Salim. "His father was a freedom fighter and they are well respected."

"My father, my parents too were decent people," replied Farhan. "They did not harm anyone. These people have to pay the price. "

They sat in silence for some time. Salim got up.

"I am going away," he said. "But I will be back one day and then, I think you will be ready to join us."

"I do not know how to thank you," answered Farhan. "You came like an angel into my life and changed it, gave it a direction. I can never forget you. I shall be ready when you are back."

Salim reached Farhan and hugged him closely.

"May *Allah* be with you," he said and then he was gone.

Farhan sat on the sofa for a long time looking at the name; Madhav Karve; this man had devastated his life. It was his turn now to pay it back.

It was the first anniversary of the death of his parents, grandmother and Mumtaz.There had been prayers and a feast at Nargis's house. He returned home in the afternoon. He had chosen this day to make his peace.

It was a pleasant evening and dusk was falling. Narendra and Malti were getting ready for their dinner when there was a knock on the door.

"Wonder who it is?" said Malti aloud.

"It can't be Madhav," replied Narendra, "he will not be back so soon. I shall answer the door."

Narendra slowly went upto the door and opened it; there was a young boy at the door and he seemed to be carrying a bag.

"Yes," asked Narendra, "what can I do for you?"

For an instant Farhan panicked. He wanted to turn back and run away. But he stood his ground.

"Sorry," replied Farhan. "May I come in? I have something to discuss," he paused, " regarding your son Madhav."

"I hope he is alright," said Malti who had rushed in overhearing this conversation.

"He is quite well, it is just that I want to talk to you both regarding him."

"Yes come in," said Narendra.

Farhan walked in. The room was spacious but sparsely furnished.

"Sit down, will you," asked Malti. "Will you have some tea?"

"No, no" replied Farhan. "I don't have much time."

"What is it son?" asked Narendra.

"Your son killed my family—my parents, grandmother and sister, exactly a year back. He burnt them in their car. I was spared, so that I could suffer. This last one year has been a terrible period for me."

As Narendra and Malti listened in horror, Farhan narrated the incident.

He finished his story, Malti was silently weeping and Narendra looked shattered.

"Now the time has come for you to redeem this deed," said Farhan pointing at Narendra and Malti.

"Where is Madhav's room?" he asked.

Narendra pointed.

"Come with me!" said Farhan.

"The room is locked; Madhav does not like us to enter it," replied Narendra.

"Then open it up!" demanded Farhan. "We need to go there."

Malti obediently opened the room and they went inside. The room was in a mess. Lots of pamphlets and posters lay here and there. The windows were all closed.

"Sit down," Farhan said pointing to the bed.

Narendra and Malti sat down tentatively.

Farhan kept the bag on the floor, opened it and took out a long rope.

"What do you want?" asked Narendra.

Farhan smiled.

"You have to pay the price," he said.

Quickly Farhan tied the old couple to the bed. They could hardly offer him any resistance. He went back to the bag and removed a large can. He unscrewed the cap and emptied the contents on the old couple and the bed sheet.

The smell of petrol filled the room.

"You cannot do this to us," said Narendra. "You cannot, should not stoop to his level. Your family is not going to come back; why do this to us."

Farhan smiled again.

"I want Madhav to suffer."

"But, where is this going to lead?" asked Narendra

"I do not know and I do not care," replied Farhan.

And then he lighted a match stick and threw it on the bed. The sheets caught fire instantly and as the old couple writhed in horror, the flames engulfed them. He could hear their shouts as he coolly walked out of the door, bolted and locked it and slipped away into the darkness.

By the time, the neighbours could call a fire engine and douse the flames, the room was an inferno. All they could retrieve later were two charred bodies.

Farhan slept well that night; his nightmares had gone.

The police did an investigation and concluded that it was an accident.

Hate begets hate and hate begets anger. Anger destroys reason and incites people to act irrationally. Anger fuels them and drives them into a world of self pity, injustice and a grudge against society. This deadly cocktail spurs them further away from reality into a world where the line between right and wrong becomes blurred. Farhan had become entrapped in this vicious world. Only time would tell where this vicious circle of hate, would lead him.

Salim returned one night, after almost a year of that fateful evening. Farhan was in his final year in college.

"Come in," replied Farhan. "I was expecting you."

Salim smiled.

"I am ready now," said Farhan.

"I knew you were," replied Salim. "Our group is meeting in a week; I will take you there."

"No!" replied Farhan.

"What is the matter?" asked Salim in surprise.

"I do not want to be part of any group," answered Farhan. "I want to do this myself; with you of course. Will you join me?"

"I do not want to get into the nitty gritty," continued Farhan. "My personal battle is over; now begins the war. I will plan along with you our future course of action and you will execute the plans through your men."

The tables had suddenly turned. The transformation from a timid and afraid young boy to a man—a leader, who had a mind of his own, was complete. Salim smiled again. He was not much older than Farhan but the years in the battlefield made him look much older.

"Well, well, well..." he answered. "But, why do you think I will join you?"

This time Farhan smiled.

"From what I could gather, your leaders are on the run and your organisation is in tatters. So you don't have much of an option."

A flash of anger suddenly swept across Salim's face. And then he was back to his old self.

"I had seen something of your steely resolve even during the first day I had met you, when you were completely broken. That is why I kept coming back to you," answered Salim.

"I will be back again, I need to sort out a few things," he said.

And then he was gone.

The year was 1996. India had made an unceremonious exit from the cricket World Cup in front of a frenzied crowd at Calcutta. The Communists had for the first time joined a rag tag Government at the Centre. And a mid-air collision near Delhi had killed nearly 350 people. It was business as usual...

Farhan had taken up Physics for his post graduation, after topping his class in graduation. His specialisation was Astro physics. He searched for those answers regarding the creation of the universe, which had perturbed him as a child. He got rational, scientific answers but not the answers he was looking for. His passion for history continued and he read avidly, especially the history of Islam in India. What troubled and fascinated him was the era after the Sepoy mutiny. It seemed to mark the beginning of the decline of Islam in India. He wanted it to change and change it by hook or crook.

Salim had returned back, nearly six months after their brief meeting in the night. He again came in the cover of darkness. He said he was ready to join Farhan and he had a small group of people with him, who could be trusted. Thus began their sessions. It was usually late in the evening after Farhan had returned from college. The sessions sometimes lasted till the early hours of the morning. They discussed on many issues but would finally veer down to one- where, when and how they would strike. They discussed many options but nothing seemed right. The days became months and still they had no concrete plan in place.

Farhan was becoming restive day by day and Salim's visits became more and more infrequent. They seemed to be running out of ideas.

It was Diwali and Bombay had turned into a war zone. The noise and the lights were overpowering and Farhan shut himself up in the house. He wondered how he had once enjoyed this occasion and had burst crackers along with his sisters and the neighbourhood children. Memories of his sister Mumtaz came flooding back and he was filled with an uncontrollable rage.

The door bell rang. Farhan got up reluctantly and opened the door. Salim was at the door.

"And what brings you here?" asked Farhan.

"I have a plan," replied Salim.

"You and your plans," shouted Farhan. "That's what we have been discussing all this while and nothing has come out of it. Go away, leave me alone. We are not capable; neither me nor you."

Salim had never seen Farhan in this mood.

"Calm down," he said. "Unless we think calmly, nothing is going to come out."

They sat silently for some time; the silence broken intermittently by the deafening noises coming from outside.

"They are planning a massive rally in Shivaji Park on the anniversary of the demolition of the masjid. We will strike there."

Farhan listened in silence as Salim laid out the plan.

Over the course of the next few days and weeks, they went over the plan again and again until they could not rework it any further. It was not foolproof, but they were desperate to strike and decided they had to take a few risks.

The plan was quite simple; attach plastic explosives with a trigger mechanism underneath some of the chairs to be used for the rally, and trigger it at an opportune moment. The problem was when to stick the explosives on the chair without being observed. They explored several course of actions and finally decided upon one. Two of Salim's operatives would get jobs with the contractor who would be entrusted with the arrangements for fixing up the meeting. But another problem arose. There were hundreds of contractors who did this sort of a job in Bombay; how would they locate the correct contractor in time to get the guys on their rolls. This turned out to be the most difficult part of the job and the time was running out. A stroke of luck helped them. They discovered that tenders had been floated for this work and after that it was not difficult to locate the contractor who was awarded the job. The difficulty now was to get their men jobs in that company. Money had to be paid. Money was also needed for the explosives, and the operatives who would carry out the job. Farhan arranged the money.

Salim informed Farhan one day that their men had landed up temporary jobs in that company and also that the explosives had been procured. The plan was set into motion.

They had a final meeting, a week before the attack. Everything seemed to be in order. They wished each other and decided to meet again only in the New Year if everything went off as per plan.

The morning of the anniversary dawned clear and bright. As usual, the security had been tightened all over Bombay. A massive rally had been organised at the Shivaji Park. The already stretched police force was stretched further. The crowd started swelling and by the time the speeches had begun, was flowing over. The speeches were mild at first but as the sun climbed up the horizon and the temperature went up, the speeches became more strident. The crowd shouted in unison as the speakers urged for an immediate construction of a temple at Ayodhya.

The blasts occurred almost simultaneously and hell broke loose.

"At least 100 people killed and scores injured." screamed the headline of the evening paper, which Farhan had picked up from a stall on his way back from college. Farhan smiled. The days that had been spent in planning had yielded results.

There was a big outcry and the police went on an overdrive. Over the next couple of days they arrested, questioned and let off many young men. Nobody had yet claimed responsibility for the blasts and rumours were flying around. Suddenly, one day, the police claimed they had arrested the guys who had planted the explosives.

Farhan heard this news with apprehension. There was no news from Salim and every time that the door bell rang, he would pray that it was not the policemen.

Bombay was tense for a few days but the city recovered quickly. The news of the blast slowly moved away from the first page.

The New Year dawned.

Salim appeared again one night suddenly, as usual. They held each other for a long time.

"Who were the guys that were arrested?" asked Farhan, the moment they sat down.

Salim roared in laughter.

"A couple of guys who were at the wrong place at the wrong time," he said.

"And what about our men?"

"Well," replied Salim with a broad smile on his face. "They obviously left their job and are currently away on a holiday."

A hint of a smile crossed Farhan's face.

"Let's get out and celebrate," said Salim.

"No..." said Farhan. "There is nothing to celebrate. We have just lit a spark, we need to build a fire; a fire that will rage through this nation and raze it upto its foundation. From the embers will emerge a new nation; where we can stand upright with our heads held high and not slink and look behind our shoulders every day, every moment. We— you, me and others like us, will run this country and restore our past glory...We shall celebrate then."

They parted, deciding to lie low for some time.

Salim returned back after nearly six months. He had gained more weight and had a broad smile on his face.

"You look happy," said Farhan.

"I am getting married," replied Salim. "The wedding is not in Bombay. I will be away for some time. I need some money, for those people who work with me."

"Money for what?" asked Farhan.

"To retain them; otherwise they will go away," replied Salim.

Farhan looked at him incredulously.

"You don't expect them to do it for free, do you?" asked Salim. "They are in it for the money; they don't have any ideologies, like you and me. They are good at their job but they need money."

He handed over a chit. It had a name of a bank and an account number.

"Deposit some money and don't forget to deposit once in two months at least. I don't want to keep coming and asking you for money. And yes, I will be back soon..."

Farhan progressed in his studies. He completed his post graduation and joined for his doctorate programme. The research work meant long hours in the library and a gruelling schedule throughout the week. But, this had not stopped his early morning jogging around the Shivaji Park which had begun nearly five years back. The regulars there noticed and nodded at the small slightly built harmless man, who ran five to six laps around the park everyday as if he had no tomorrow. They also noticed that he pretty much kept to himself and except for the brief nod or smile, rarely ever spoke to anyone.

Farhan's sisters noticed his increased aloofness in the few occasions that they met him and became worried. They decided to get him married and started scouting for girls. Farhan heard about this one day and went into a rage.

"I don't have any time for this nonsense," he shouted. "I have things to do, much more important than getting married and raising a family."

And he stomped out.

Farhan had other important things in his mind and marriage did not figure in his scheme of things. His association with Salim was proving to be fruitful. They were able to strike at will, wherever and whenever they wanted. They had among themselves engineered four strikes in the heart of the city and each had been more daring than the other. They were far away from their goal, but they were moving in the right direction.

Rahman Ahmed was a hard working young man. His wife had recently given birth to their son. He worked hard and liked nothing better than to spend the evenings with his family and new born child.Rahman was Iqbal Ahmed's only son and as his father's health was failing, he had got more and more involved in the business inherited by Farhan. In spite of Farhan's reluctance to meet him, he periodically came and appraised him on the business. Farhan used to listen without interest and ask a few questions just to keep Rahman happy.

It was a rainy August evening, one of those days in Bombay when it rains all day long in a steady monotonous fashion. The roads were in a mess, the trains were running late, the clothes refused to dry and people's tempers were on a short fuse. Rahman had been particularly persistent that day and was going on and on. Farhan was becoming restive and wished he would stop and go away. The door bell rang. Farhan quickly got up and went to the door, thanking for this divine intervention. Salim was at the door. He barged in; he was quite wet.

"I need to talk to you for ten minutes, I am in a hurry," he said.

He stopped himself when he saw the guy sitting on the sofa.

"Don't worry," said Farhan. "He is Rahman. He runs my business, I mean my father's business."

Rahman got up, "I will go away. I will come back later."

"No, no" said Salim. "I just need a little time with Farhan and I will be off. You sit here. Farhan will be back soon."

He took Farhan by the hand and led him to the balcony. It was quite grey and dark outside.

"There has been some problem," he said. "One of our guys is being tailed. I need money to pay off some of the cops so that he can slip away."

"But I have been depositing money, sizeable amounts nearly every month," replied Farhan.

"I need more," replied Salim.

"But this can't go on and on," shouted Farhan.

"Nothing can be done without money," shouted back Salim. "Do you want the cops to catch you? And do you know what will happen if they catch you. They will hang you. You have the blood of hundreds in your hands."

"So do you," shouted back Farhan.

They turned and noticed Rahman standing just beyond the balcony and staring at them. In the heat of the moment, they had forgotten about him.

Rahman had heard Farhan shout at Salim and rushed in to intervene, if needed. What he heard next from Salim had him rooted to the ground. He could not believe his ears. Farhan, the quiet and learned man, what had he done to be hanged?

"Why did you come here?" asked Farhan to Rahman. "And what did you hear?"

"I ...heard nothing," whimpered Rahman. "I heard you both shouting and came to protect you."

"He is lying," said Salim.

Rahman looked at both of them and started backing away to the door.

"So you heard everything?" asked Farhan.

"You, you...killed people," cried Rahman backing further away. "I will tell everybody, everybody."

And he turned and ran to the door.

Farhan and Salim ran after him and were on him, in an instant.

"Yes, we have blood in our hands," said Salim, "but don't you dare utter a word or you won't leave this place alive."

"Let me go," cried Rahman. "Don't do anything to me. I have a wife, a child, my parents are old."

He wriggled out of their hands and wrenched the door open. Farhan ran like a mad man, caught Rahman and banged him against the door. Rahman's head hit the door with a thud and he started falling on top of Farhan. Salim quickly banged the door shut and dragged them both in. Farhan got up quickly. Rahman lay still. Salim bent down and felt his pulse. He looked up at Farhan.

"He is dead. You have killed him," he said.

"Oh, my God!" said Farhan. "What have I done!" and he crumpled on the floor.

"Get up!" said Salim. "He is not the first one you have killed nor is he going to be the last one. We need to dispose the body."

"But they were different. He is one of us," answered Farhan.

"It does not matter. Anyway let's wait until dark," replied Salim.

The next few hours were one of the most stressful periods for Farhan.

Salim bundled the body in some bed sheets and shoved it inside an old metal trunk. They waited till it was dark. It was raining hard now. They lifted the trunk and moved it to Farhan's car, parked down in the basement. Farhan drove the car; Salim gave him the directions. They drove a long way off and finally arrived at a deserted spot near the railway track. By the time Farhan returned home after dumping the body on the railway track, it was well past midnight. He slept fitfully that night.

He was in college the next day; when a call came for him in the front office. It was his sister.

"They found Rahman's body on the tracks today morning. He had not come home yesterday night. It looks like an accident. Iqbal *chacha* is in a sorry state. We are all at his home. Please come immediately," she said.

Farhan had been dreading this moment. He could not face Iqbal, he wanted to run away.

"Oh!" replied Farhan. "I shall be there immediately."

Rahman's body lay in a coffin covered by a shroud. His young wife sat next to it; her eyes red with crying. The child lay on her lap fast asleep, oblivious to the surroundings. Rahman's parents sat in a corner, in a stupor. Seeing Farhan, they burst into tears. Farhan held Iqbal's hands as the old man cried his heart out. A thousand emotions were running through Farhan's mind. He tried not to show any of them as he muttered his condolences.

It was still raining and the burial ground was full of slush. The body was removed from the coffin and slowly lowered into the freshly dug grave wrapped in the cloth. The cloth was removed from Rahman's face. His face was calm, he appeared to be fast asleep; the train had mutilated only his body badly. One by one, they poured three handfuls of soil into the grave while reciting from the Quran. It was all over soon. The prayers had been said and it was time to leave; leave Rahman to rest in peace for eternity.

Farhan returned home late in the evening. He shut the door. He could not control himself any longer. He screamed and wept uncontrollably. His pent up emotions gave way. He cursed himself again and again. He had become a monster. Where was all this leading to?

He could not do this any more. He had to stop. He had to confess. If they sent him to jail, hanged him—so be it, he deserved it. He calmed down. Tomorrow morning he would go and surrender at the next police station.

The door bell rang. Who could it be now, thought Farhan as he went upto the door.

It was Salim.

"What do you want?" asked Farhan. "Go away!"

Salim barged in.

"You seem to be upset," he said.

"I regret the day you came into my life," shouted Farhan. "You have made me insane. I have had enough .I want to surrender. I want to live, die in peace."

And he broke down.

Salim watched, in silence, Farhan fight his demons.

"Listen to me," said Salim softly.

"No, go away," replied Farhan. "I should never have listened to you in the first place."

"Shut up!" said Salim and before Farhan could react; he lunged forward and gave him a slap.

Farhan was too shocked to react.

"Now, listen!" said Salim. "They killed your family; they destroyed entire families and treated us as vermins. They wanted us to cower in our holes and wallow in misery."

He paused.

"Do you remember the evening I met you for the first time. You were wallowing in self pity. They had succeeded in their plans. You were finished. Everybody falls, at least once in their lifetime. But it is those who rise from that fall, who make a difference. I found in you a man who could make a difference. I was right. You rose from that pit. You hit them; hit them hard and left them bewildered. You have them on the run now, confused and groping. And now you want to leave and go. Because of one man? It is upto you, Farhan. You can either act righteous and let our entire community go to the gallows or, you could fight it out like a man and teach them a lesson they can never afford to forget."

And Salim got up and started walking to the door. Farhan sat there like a statue unmoving; his thoughts in disarray.

"Wait," he said. "I need you Salim. Dont leave me and go."

The human mind (or thought or whatever you wish to call it) behaves in a mysterious fashion. It sometimes seems to have a mind of its own. I know I am sounding crazy here. But it is as if we have no control on it. We become slaves to this mind and are led wherever it wants us to go. Sometimes, it takes us on a roller coaster ride and by the time the ride is over, we turn into emotional wrecks. Farhan was close to being one. He survived...

Farhan, like the rest of the country and the world had entered into a new millennium. His doctoral thesis was progressing well. After a brief slump, the family business was looking up enabling him to satisfy Salim's constant craving for money. Their forays were becoming more and more audacious but Farhan was enjoying walking on the tightrope.

Sometimes, he pondered where it was all leading to. Whether the methodology he had chosen was the correct one. Whether, he alone could bring about any change. Whether, he should join hands with others; more influential, more powerful to really make a big impact. Whether he should join politics which would help him come in contact with the masses and bring about unrest.

But eventually, he would reason out that this was the best option open to him and he would need to continue in this manner...

Farhan was now twenty seven and was called Doctor *Saab* by his colleagues and relatives. His years of perseverance had paid off and he could affix the prefix Dr. before his name like his sisters and co-brothers. Farhan was now Dr. Farhan Rasool-a doctor who hoped to heal the wounds inflicted on himself and his community by inflicting wounds on others. A doctor, who was caught in a time warp and who wanted to right the wrongs of history. A doctor, a brilliant mind gone terribly wrong ...

It was time for celebration in the family as Aalia, Farhan's eldest niece was getting married. A reluctant Farhan was forced into the festivities. Farhan was attending a marriage after ages and the noise and the din made him feel sick and he wanted to run away and get back to his home, but his nephews and nieces kept him on a leash. His sister and brother –in- law were influential members of society and had a huge circle of friends and well wishers. The groom and his family were also from a well known political family and so the festivities were on a lavish scale attended by hundreds of people and spread across the bride and the groom's residences and finally, culminating in a five star hotel.

Farhan was tired and bored. All the small talk and laughter filled him with disgust. He looked at his sisters; they were chatting away gaily, welcoming the guests and busily running round. Their faces were radiating. He saw Aalia smiling demurely, contendently sitting beside her groom. He wondered how they could have forgotten.

His mind went back. He could see his sister's happy face. There was a spring in Mumtaz's step. He had caught her once gazing at a photograph of the handsome young man, who would come riding on a horse and take her far away to US. She had blushed and run away when he caught her. He would miss her when she would go away...His eyes misted.

He felt an arm resting on his shoulder. He turned, it was Salim.

"Surprised aren't you?" he said. "But I guessed you might want some help. Memories..."

They sat silently for a long time. Farhan broke the silence.

"My sisters; they are all so happy, they have all forgotten."

He sounded harsh.

"Don't...you are being cruel," replied Salim. "They have their family, their children. What more do you expect them to do. You cannot expect them to sit and mourn for ever. Time is a great healer and it heals many wounds. But, you and I cannot let it heal our scars. We need to continuously battle against it. We need to keep our wounds festering and— that is our challenge!"

As he lay alone that night in his home, away from the festivities at last; those words of Salim kept echoing in his head. He could not; would not let his wounds heal...

Farhan was now a professor in the same college where he had obtained his doctorate. He discovered that he had a flair for teaching and very soon, settled comfortably into his new role. He was animated and quite at ease in the classroom, but was a different man outside it. Many of the students went to him after classes with their queries and found him quite uncommunicative. Soon they stopped going to him. His behaviour with his colleagues was similar. In between classes, he used to retire to the staff room and would immerse himself into his own world; making notes and studying. He would never take part in the conversations and gossip that went around and would answer in monosyllables to queries from his colleagues. Soon those attempts at conversation from his colleagues' stopped. Farhan was content to live in his own world and was happy when they left him alone. He did not want to get close to anybody and enter into relationships; these would weaken his resolve, heal his wounds.

The year 2002 dawned like any other. But it was not going to be like any other year for Farhan. It would rekindle the memories of an afternoon in January, nearly a decade back and strengthen his resolve. His resolve—to continue to wage war against the country of his birth.

Ahmedabad, in the state of Gujarat, traces its origins to the 11th century but acquired its current name in the early fifteenth century from its ruler Sultan Ahmed Shah. Like many of the cities in India, it changed hands over the centuries- from the Bhils to the Solankis to the Delhi Sultanate to the Mughals to the Marathas and finally, to the East India Company. The early 20th century saw Ahmedabad becoming an important centre in India's war of independence. And with independence came partition and intense riots between Hindus and Muslims. The year 1960 saw the creation of Gujarat state, and Ahmedabad emerging as the capital of the state.Ahmedabad grew and became a centre for educational and research institutions and industry. As the city grew, it also became more volatile as religion and caste divided the city and fanned agitations and riots.

And then, the world came crashing down literally a powerful earthquake flattened buildings and killed hundreds of people. The city was devastated. But aid came pouring and the citizens came together irrespective of their religion, caste and creed. It seemed that the darkest hour had united the city like never before. Ahmedabad showed its brightest side and displayed its never say die attitude and rose like a phoenix from the ashes and thus made the country proud.

But Ahmedabad's darkest hour was yet to come. In a replay of the Mumbai riots, nearly a decade back, the city lay torn apart by unimaginable violence and savagery. As the city and the rest of Gujarat burned, the country watched in shocked stupor.

Farhan had been nominated by his college for a week's seminar being organised at a leading management college in Ahmedabad. He had been reluctant to go but finally agreed. His niece Aalia had shifted to Ahmedabad after her marriage, where her husband, Rafiq worked in a petrochemical company. She was yet to get adjusted to her new home and was delighted to have her uncle stay with her for a few days.

The days had gone by quickly; Farhan used to be back from the seminar by five pm and the evenings were spent enjoying the sights, sounds and smells of the new city with his niece and her husband. After the initial reluctance; Farhan could not but be drawn into the infectious joy of the young couple. He remembered those days; it seemed a million years ago, when the entire family used to go around for those joy rides, how innocent he had been and how cruel the world had been to him and his family. He felt an unease creeping up seeing their joyous faces; a sense of foreboding...He wished it away, he must be getting old, he thought.

A couple of days remained for the seminar to wrap up. As he trudged back home that evening from college, he found groups of people around shops and that sense of unease came back rushing. At home; the television was on. His niece looked pensive, a train carrying pilgrims had been burnt and all sorts of rumours were flying around. They spent that evening at home.

The next day, a *bandh* call had been given and the city was tense. Aalia was scared and asked her husband and uncle to stay back. Both assured her that the city was quite safe and there was nothing to worry. It was Farhan's last day in Ahmedabad and he was supposed to catch the morning train to Bombay, the next day. He waved to his niece who stood in her balcony and was off to his college. He would rue his decision for ever...That was the last he saw of his niece. The seminar concluded early and abruptly. There were reports of violence coming in from various parts of the city.

Aalia's house was about four km from the college and Farhan used to walk the distance in thirty minutes..Today, as he walked, he saw smoke billowing from the distance. The roads were sparsely populated. The people on the roads and the vehicles seemed to be moving with an unnatural urgency. A sense of fear and dread came over Farhan. He walked faster. He could hear shouts in the distance and saw a mob breaking and setting a shop on fire. People were running here and there. He ran and did not stop till he reached the building where his niece lived. He ran up the stairs and reached the flat. The door was wide open or rather what remained of the door. He rushed in; the whole place was in a mess and Rafiq sat there in the centre of the room; his eyes blood shot.

"What happened?" shouted Farhan.

"She is gone, my Aalia is gone."

He cried out aloud.

"They took her away."

"Calm down," said Farhan. "What is the matter?"

"I received a phone call from Aalia, saying a mob had entered the building and was searching for Muslims. I rushed back. But it was too late. They have taken her."

The next few hours and days went as if in a blur for Farhan.They spent the night sleeping in mosques, makeshift refugee camps, in houses of strangers and during the day; they slunk around the city, the police stations, hospitals, morgues, looking for Aalia. However, there was no sign of her. It was as if somebody had plucked her away. The city burned and the people fought and killed on the streets, on the roofs and inside the houses. And, then one day, he spotted him. There was no mistake. It was the same boy; he was a man now, but he had the same swagger and smile. He was leading a pack of men ransacking and looting the shops. The shopkeepers were being pulled out and being brutally beaten. Farhan had an urge to run and stop the madness. But all he could do was stand and stare before Rafiq pulled him away.

Farhan could not remember how they finally managed to get out of the city into a train and landed in Bombay.

His holiday with his niece had turned macabre. He shut himself in his house and did not venture out. His nightmares had returned and returned with a vengeance...

He walked around the house, completely lost. He needed help; he cried out aloud for the only soul who could help him-Salim.

But Salim did not come. Alone and helpless, Farhan wept until the tears dried up. He lay on the bed staring blankly at the roof. It must be his imagination he thought, but the roof seemed to be closing down upon him and any moment he would be squeezed against the bed. He needed to get out, he ran for the door and out like a man possessed. He turned back; saw people running after him, people staring at him, cars honking at him, a policeman blowing his whistle.

I need to run faster, he thought, they want to catch me and kill me. I shall not let them catch me; he whispered to himself, he would out run them and survive.

He ran and ran and ran...

He opened his eyes. He was again staring at the roof. But the roof looked different; whiter. He tried to get up, but was unable to. Somebody or something seemed to be holding him back. He looked around and saw his arms and legs bound to the bed. He screamed.

He opened his eyes and blinked. A faint smile came to his lips as he saw Salim sitting beside him. He went back to sleep.

He had been in the hospital for a month.

A student of his had found him running aimlessly, in a state of near exhaustion, in Shivaji Park and had him forcibly admitted to a hospital. There he lay, screaming and ranting, until they were forced to drug him and tie him up. And, then,one day Salim had arrived. His arrival had calmed him down...

They were sitting in the house having tea. It was now nearly six months after he had been discharged from the hospital. It had been a protracted and painful return to normalcy. Salim had yet again brought Farhan back from the edge. He had not yet returned to college, but had commenced his morning jogging schedule. Salim had told him to brush away the incident as a bad dream and he had successfully managed to do it.

"We need to start again Farhan *bhai*," said Salim.

Farhan nodded his head.

"And, this time I want him first," he replied. "I should not have spared him; should have finished him off along with his parents. I wanted him to suffer...I saw his smile that day on the road; it seemed to have no effect on him."

Salim listened quietly to his friend.

"His time will come," he said. "But that will have to wait. Your personal battle has to wait. We need to strike when it's hot. And this time, he added, we will have plenty of fireworks. We will shake them and shake them hard, he went on. We will watch their children and their mothers and wives weeping. We will watch and laugh to our hearts content. C'mon Farhan; can you not see them before your eyes? Those pitiable old women and the wailing wives."

"Yes, I see them," replied Farhan. "I see them falling at my feet begging for mercy, for pity. I can see their husbands', sons' bodies lying torn apart...Yes, I can see everything, Salim. I can see everything. And, I can see myself laughing. I have never seen myself laughing so much."

"Let us laugh, Farhan," whispered Salim slowly. "Laugh at those wretched creatures. Laugh at the lesson that we shall teach them. Laugh, Farhan, laugh."

And slowly Farhan began to laugh. He laughed like he had never laughed and Salim joined the laughter. They laughed and laughed until the tears ran down their cheeks and the echo of their demonic laughter filled the house...

Farhan was back at college. It was as if nothing had happened.

The blast in the two storey office building at Marine Drive, three months later was so powerful, that it brought the entire building down.

Over the course of the next six months; Farhan and Salim planned and executed some daring strikes throughout the city- explosions in buses, car parkings, cinema theatres, on the sea front...These were less devastating; killing and injuring only a few but random enough to create panic and outcry among the citizens. The police searched and sifted for clues trying to find a thread somewhere, without much success.

Farhan was happy at the turn of events. But he wanted to carry out something big and fiery which would bring down the city to its knees. He was surprised when Salim was not keen on the idea, but knew that he would come around when he had a plan in place. He started planning...

Life at college gave him a respite from the planning and to keep in touch with his first love—Physics.

He was sitting in the staff room one day going through his notes, when the office boy came upto him and said somebody had come to meet him and it was urgent. Who it can be, thought Farhan as he walked upto the reception.

"*Salaam aleikum*, Farhan *bhai*," said a familiar voice.

He turned and saw himself face to face with Salim.

"What are you doing here," asked Farhan in a raised voice. "Why have you come here?"

"Don't worry," replied Salim. "I will go away. I was just passing by and I thought I should just come in and have a look at Prof. Farhan. Phd. and, I am impressed, I may say. Your college, your colleagues, your students and you, all are very impressive. But what if they come to know who you are; Oh! Don't worry, I shall not tell them."

"What do you want?" asked Farhan brusquely.

"Money," answered Salim.

"You come here and blackmail me and you think I will give you money!" Farhan's voice was now raised. "Go, tell them..."

"Shut up!" replied Salim.

The tone was menacing and caught Farhan by surprise.

"I could have done that, much earlier, if I had wanted to," he continued.

And then he paused and the smile came back to his face.

"You worry too much, Farhan," he said. "You need to relax, you need to smile sometimes. You cannot carry the burden of society on your shoulders alone. We are doing what we can, but beyond that, there is not much we can do."

There was a pause as Salim surveyed the surroundings.

"How much do you want?" asked Farhan, breaking the silence.

"The usual," replied, Salim. "I shall meet you soon, take care."

A smile crossed his face.

"And yes, I will have a surprise for you soon; a pleasant surprise."

And then he was gone.

Farhan stood there and watched Salim as he quickly walked away out of the building.

He suddenly realised that he really knew nothing of his only friend; Salim. He knew that he had got married but did not even know whether he had a child. He did not even know where he lived and what he did. He was much like a closed book. While he had bared his soul and life to this man, he knew absolutely nothing of him. He had been so immersed in his life that he had not even bothered to find out more. But now he was filled with an immediate urge to find out, to repay his debts. He ran outside and tried to spot Salim in the milling crowd. It seemed like he was lost. He turned back and then he spotted him again across the road. He was talking animatedly to someone; who seemed to be smiling. He wanted to run and catch him. He started walking towards him. But then, something held him back. He stood there and watched. And then it hit him. Salim was talking to the same boy, man...He felt faint. He stumbled back and ran back. The chowkidar looked anxiously at him as he came back panting.

"Are you fine sir?" he asked.

"Not really," he replied. "Can you catch a taxi? I want to go home."

He lay on his bed; his world was going topsy turvy again.

But how could it be? Salim, his trusted friend...What was Salim doing with this man. What were they conspiring? Salim had talked about a surprise, was this it? Salim,,a traitor? Salim, who had nursed him back from the dead, not once; a traitor?

He could not believe it, but the more he thought about it, the more he became certain.

There was only one way out, he thought. He had to get Salim, before they got him. But he did not know where to search for Salim.He had to wait.Salim had said he would come.

He was afraid to go out; he sent word to his college that he was not well and would not be coming for some time.

He sat and waited for the door bell to ring.

It rang one night. It was past dinner. He had finished his frugal meal and was sitting, waiting in the sitting room. It was Salim, he knew, even before the ring was complete. There was something in the ring, that identified it with Salim. Maybe, it was the softness of the ring, the gentleness...He brushed aside his thoughts. He picked up the long dagger, which was his constant companion, these days. He looked at it; it was shining and pointed. It seemed eager to plunge and bloody itself. It had been waiting for a long time...What an irony, thought Farhan.The dagger had been given to him by Salim, in those early days, as a present, to protect himself. And now...

There was another ring. This time a little too long. Salim must be getting impatient, thought Farhan. He did not like to wait. Farhan walked upto the door and peeped through the eye hole. It was Salim and he was alone. He opened the door slowly.

Salim smiled slightly as he entered.

"I heard you have not been keeping well," he said.

And then, something cold and hard and sharp hit him in his stomach. He had never felt so much pain; his insides were searing. He looked down to see blood gushing out and Farhan holding one end of a dagger. He toppled and fell.

Farhan withdrew the dagger and quickly closed the door. Salim lay gasping on the door, his eyes shocked and dazed.

Farhan bent down and said, "I found out before you did, you traitor. How could you do this to me Salim?" he whispered, "You and that boy, that beast who destroyed my family.Why? Why did you want to do this to me? Was it the money? Tell me," he screamed, "tell me, before I plunge this dagger and finish your misery."

Salim was hardly able to breathe. He knew he was dying. He had seen people dying; he had killed them with his own hands and had seen death, at close quarters. His time was up...He always knew this was how it would end one day; but he was shocked at the manner it had come. That it had to come through Farhan...He lay there as the life slowly ebbed out of him, hearing those words from Farhan. He had to clear this with Farhan, before he floated away. But it was becoming difficult, his eyes were misting and he was choking.

"Hold me, raise me," he whispered to Farhan. "I want to tell you something..."

Farhan lifted him, his eyes still bloodshot, in rage

"Out with it fast!" he said.

Salim smiled, "I wanted to give you a surprise, my friend. I ...wanted to lead him to you."

He gasped...The effort was taking its toll.

"Hold me tight, my friend," he said.

Farhan held him and strained to hear the words coming out.

"I wanted to drive out those demons still in your mind. I knew you could do that only by killing him...But," Salim smiled again, "you did not trust me..."

He was fast fading now and Salim knew it.

"Never mind, my friend," he whispered. "Go out and get him...He is there for your taking. And then, maybe you will find your peace..."

He could now barely see Farhan, the light was fading fast. It was getting cold, very cold.

Farhan nodded, tears flowing out of his eyes.

Salim smiled, one last time and closed his eyes.

It took a year this time. A year to get out of his self inflicted misery. Several times in those dark days, he felt like ending it all. He took long leave from his college saying he wanted to see the world. But, he hardly ventured out of his house. He refused to answer calls from his sisters and shut the door on their faces when they came visiting. They were puzzled and shocked and finally, gave up. He sat hours and days sometimes staring at nothing but reliving those last moments of Salim...He had doubted a man who had given him a path and a vision in life, a man who had nursed him back like his own brother. He had doubted and murdered his only friend, only well-wisher in cold blood. Sometimes, he took the same dagger and stared at it, pointing it towards himself and willing himself to strike it through. But, something stopped him. It was the eyes of his dying friend. They had been kind and forgiving even in those moments, and they seemed to be urging him forward to move on.

He survived...He joined his college back. His students and colleagues were surprised at his appearance. He seemed to have become old almost overnight. He was only thirty two, but his hair had turned grey and his skin seemed to be sagging at all the wrong places. He appeared defeated and lost. But, inside the class, he was like a man transformed. He held his students in rapt attention and astounded everybody by his clear and precise explanations. Farhan knew he had to regain his health, if not for himself, for his friend. He had to complete this mission and complete it all by himself.

The first few days, his legs felt like lead. His chest gasped for air. He would collapse, but would get up and drag on. Bystanders at Shivaji Park would stare as he struggled and urged himself on. Others would try to help him as he crumpled in a heap in exhaustion. He ignored all of them and willed himself on. In a month's time, he was running two laps around the ground and by the end of two months; he was doing five laps comfortably. He felt much better now, both in mind and body.

He was ready to begin afresh. But, where could he start. Where could he find the boy; the man? He remembered now, the house where he had tied that old couple and watched them burn alive. He retraced his steps back to that house. He reached the place in the fading sunlight. There was no house. There was a brand new apartment building. He was confused. Maybe, he was wrong about the location. He walked back and forth but always came back to that same house. He slowly walked to the front gate and asked the watchman...

"There was a bungalow here, my friend used to live in it..."

"Yes, there was," replied the old man. "Maybe your friend sold it off. They built an apartment here."

"Oh!" replied Farhan. "I thought I could locate my friend..."

"Why don't you talk to the builders," replied the watchman. "They may, perhaps, help you."

"Thank you," replied Farhan.

He contacted the builders on some pretext and was surprised to discover that Madhav owned the company. He had demolished the house built by his grandfather and built the new complex. After that it was easy. Madhav lived in a flat; in an apartment complex, opposite the beach in Dadar.

He walked upto the beach, he had not been there since he was a child. He was shocked at its condition. The water was there far in the distance and the sand or what remained of it was a mess. That did not seem to dissuade the citizens, since the place was full with the young and the old. Children ran and howled, the hawkers screamed and the sound of the horns blared from the vehicles, amidst music from the latest blockbuster ....

Farhan retreated back quickly. He would come back again.

He came again and again but could not spot his quarry. He had to be patient. And then, one day he turned lucky. It was a Sunday, and after his morning jog, he had strolled upto the apartment. He had walked up and down the street for some time and was about to leave, when he saw him coming out. He was accompanied by a lady who was carrying a child. He was shouting and talking on the phone loudly. The lady was quiet and was silently following him. He cut the phone angrily and motioned the lady to go back inside the house. A man came running from the distance and stopped when he saw Madhav. He folded his hand and ran inside. Madhav stood there fuming angrily. A car came out, slowly.The man was at the wheel and the lady and the child were seated inside. It stopped. Madhav opened the door, got in and banged the door shut. Farhan watched as the car sped away.

As the days passed, Farhan made more enquiries and slowly was able to gather information on Madhav. He now knew where Madhav went for work, when he returned and what he did otherwise. He had gathered whatever he had set to gather. He now had to make a plan and unlike other times, he had to execute it.

The plan slowly came into being, over many nights, sitting in his apartment. It was like old times-looking at all the options, their advantages and disadvantages. Several plans were created; their minute details were worked out and then were thrown away as the flaws were revealed slowly. The plans had to be reworked again and again, until the perfect one was worked out. He had done this so many times and it always gave him a thrill. At these times, he often felt like God, deciding the fates of so many people.They, he and Salim used to fight, laugh, joke and finally arrive at a plan. The difference now, was that he had to do it alone. All that remained now was for him to execute the plan. He smiled...

I wonder, how many Farhans are created every year in this country and how many more will!
You, we, may say we have nothing to do with this, we did not create him, them. It was circumstances, the politicians, the system...
Are you sure?
Did we–you, me, us–upright, law abiding citizens of this country not do anything? Of course, we did not. We did not violate the law (except minor transgressions here and there), we did not kill anybody; we did nothing.
The country burned and thousandhs were slaughtered when it broke away from the bondages of the foreign ruler; we did nothing.
Bombay burned and the ghastly pictures flashed day after day over newspapers; yet we did nothing.
Gujarat burned. The TV, Newspapers, magazines flashed report after report, still continue to do so. We watched, discussed, felt their pain. Yet, we did nothing.
Do you not hear sometimes, the deafening sound, the sound of our collective silence?
Maybe, one day we shall...

✿✿✿

Madhav

Madhav had been spending more and more time now in his uncle's house. He had avenged his uncle's death. His hand was awash with the blood of so many of them. And, it had not been difficult. Actually, he had quite enjoyed it. The thrill it had given him was exhilarating. Bombay had been his playground and those wretched creatures had been his play things. He was disappointed when it had to come to a halt. He had wanted to continue till they were all exterminated or had run away to their Pakistan or whatever; but he had to stop. He was told to stop. He was told that they had been taught a lesson. He did not agree. They were wrong and he had been right. They had struck and struck across the city that afternoon. They had been caught unawares; the precision and audacity of the bomb attacks had shaken them. He rushed to them, ready to march out and start the battle of retribution. Again he was told to wait; the moment was not right. The time would come.

He sulked. He sat on the balcony and brooded.

He had lost a year in college. He had been irregular and had missed many of the exams. And now, he had to repeat the year. He had joined back and was now busy - he had participated in the student elections and had become a member of the student body. He enjoyed the power and liberty that gave him and utilised it fully.

However, at times, when he was alone, he continued to brood. His visits to his home were untimely and sporadic. He hardly communicated to his parents and did not even bother to answer their queries.

Narendra was seventy seven years now and felt his age. His eyesight was failing fast and it was Malti who often read to him.

"How time flies," he remarked to Malti one day, as she read from one of the journals.

"I remember sitting here, not so long ago and reading out to my mother. And, then, she passed away and you came into my life. Do you remember those early days in Sewagram, Malti?"

Malti nodded and smiled.

There was a long period of silence; a companiable silence, as they relived those days.

"I do not think there will be another man like him," said Narendra, breaking the silence.

"Yes," nodded Malti. "You mean, Gandhi*ji* don't you."

"Yes," replied Narendra.

He smiled.

"We have become like open books to each other, haven't we? They say, with time, husbands and wives even start looking alike, like brothers and sisters. Funny thing, marriage is, I never thought I would get married..."

"You were talking of Gandhi*ji,*" reminded Malti, gently.

Narendra smiled again.

"Yes, I was."

"Do you remember the speech by *Pandit* Nehru that midnight? I remember. I sat here with my mother and listened. Do you know what he said...?"

"On this day, our first thoughts go to the architect of this freedom, the Father of our Nation, who, embodying the old spirit of India held aloft the torch of freedom and lighted up the darkness that surrounded us. We have often been unworthy followers of his and have strayed from his message, but not only we but succeeding generations will remember this message and bear the imprint in their hearts of this great son of India, magnificent in his faith and strength and courage and humility."

"We called him "The Father of our Nation" and killed him. We committed patricide and confined his message to the dustbins of history."

He stopped. They sat in silence.

"I am an old man now, Malti and maybe I am getting it all wrong. Maybe, my thoughts do not fit in today. Maybe his message has no meaning today. So many of my countrymen cannot be wrong..."

"You are an old man now," said Malti quietly. "But you have not got anything wrong. We have strayed from his message; maybe some day, it will come back to haunt us and wake us up from our slumber."

She got up. It's getting dark, she said. Let us go inside. She slowly led her husband inside.

"We will have dinner early and retire," she said.

There was a knock on the door.

"Wonder who it is?" said Malti.

"It can't be Madhav,' replied Narendra, "he will not be back so soon. I shall answer the door."

Narendra slowly went upto the door and opened it; there was a young boy at the door and he seemed to be carrying a bag.

"Yes," asked Narendra, "what can I do for you?"

"May I come in?" said the boy. "I have something to discuss," he paused, "regarding your son Madhav."

In the next few minutes, as Farhan narrated the horrendous incident; their world came tumbling down.

They moved as if in a trance to Farhan's instructions and found themselves bound to Madhav's bed. They watched in silence as the boy went back to the bag and removed a large can. As he unscrewed the cap and emptied the contents on them, they realised what was going to happen.

The smell of petrol filled the room.

Narendra tried to reason with the boy, but he lighted a match stick and threw it on the bed. The sheets caught fire instantly and the flames engulfed Narendra and Malti.They shouted, but it was all too feeble and the flames soon consumed them.

By the time the neighbours could call a fire engine and douse the flames, the room was an inferno.

Madhav had decided he would go home that night; he had not been there for a couple of days. As he neared his home on his motorcycle; he saw smoke in the distance- reminding him about those days a year back. He smiled as he recollected those moments. The smile vanished as he came nearer and found the smoke coming from his house .The entire place was surrounded by people, police and fire engines. He had to fight his way to get inside the cordon. A portion of his house had been completely gutted. A police officer recognised him and took him aside.

"Your parents, were they at home?" he asked.

"I don't know, I suppose so," replied Madhav. "Why, where are they? Did you not locate them? Maybe they have gone out."

A wave of panic shot through him.

"What is the matter?" he asked the police officer. "Why are you not answering me?"

The police officer took him by the hand and slowly led him to his burned room.

He pointed his hand at the two charred bodies. Madhav saw and recoiled in horror.

"It can't be," he said. "It must be someone else; they never go to my room."

"I am sorry Mr.Madhav, but you will need to identify those bodies. You can do it later, it's quite dark..." he petered out.

"No, no..." shouted Madhav. "I want to have a look now, it cannot be them..."

Even in the darkness; lit up by lights from the police vehicles, there was no doubt on the identity of the bodies.

Madhav sat there and cried...

The next few days went off in a flurry of activities. The funeral was well attended; the party and the students union ensured that everything went off in clock like precision.

The charred bodies of Narendra and Malti were confined to the flames yet again amidst the chanting of prayers.

Yet another man of peace had fallen prey to the vicious circle of hate.

Madhav slowly recovered from the trauma of his loss. He had never been close to his parents when they were alive; but felt their absence badly now. He shuddered as he imagined the horror, they must have undergone. He was thankful for the support of his party. Thanks to them, the police had launched an immediate investigation. But the investigation revealed nothing and life went on.

The second anniversary of the demolition of the mosque was on its way and Madhav was in the forefront of the organising committee for a rally in Shivaji Park. Many eminent leaders were participating and Madhav strived day and night to make it a success. The police had warned of possible terrorist strikes

The day dawned clear and bright. Lots of money had been spent. The crowds were better than expected. The speeches began slowly and the tempo built up gradually. Urged on by the organisers, the crowd roared in unison for the construction of a Ram temple at Ayodhya.

The explosions were simultaneous and randomly spaced across the ground. Madhav's first reaction was of irritation; why were they bursting crackers now? But the irritation turned to horror and shock as he saw the people running in confusion, and body parts flying in the air. His worst nightmare had come true.

Madhav did not sleep for the next couple of days. He rushed from one hospital to another, to the victims' houses, to the mortuaries and to the crematorium. At the end of the week, he was so exhausted he could barely keep his eyes open. He was forcibly put in a hospital and there he lay for the next couple of days, recovering. The memories of the cries of the dead, dying and their relatives woke him up repeatedly from his drug induced sleep.

He could not forget one face; it came back repeatedly.

She was a small girl, around seven years old- she lay in the park as if she would get up from her sleep anytime. Her hands were clasped around the body of a woman completely disfigured by the explosion.

Madhav had lifted the girl; unclasping her little hand from the dead woman's hand and shook her to wake her up. But she lay still; there was no trace of injury on her body.

It was his cousin all over again...

The monsoon that year was overpowering and the entire city was caught in its onslaught. The sea had become a partner and was roaring as if in acquiescence. Madhav watched the turbulent sea from the safety of his eighth floor flat in Worli. He had moved in to his uncle's house soon after the fire. Waves of anger and resentment rose again and again. Waves, that seemed to egg him on. Waves, that seemed to engulf him and drive him into a dance of fury.

He retreated...Retreated from the party, his college, from the world. He refused to meet his friends, his party men.

And, then, one day as the sun broke away from the clouds and shone, and the city lay aglow in its warmth; a huge procession of merry makers wound its way to Madhav's house. The noise was contagious and brought everybody out. Madhav had no option. They barged into his house, threw coloured powder at him and thrust sweets in his mouth.Madhav could only gasp in astonishment. They had nominated him as secretary for the University elections, campaigned for him in his absence and he had won an astonishing victory.

Madhav was now the General Secretary of the Bombay University Students Council.

He had no time now; no time to sit and mope and brood. Life was looking good again.

Assembly elections were announced. Madhav joined the campaign trail. He was a great organiser; he arranged meeting venues, brought in the right crowd, large crowds. He ensured they were happy, well fed, paid and not kept waiting for too long in the blazing sun. The meetings went off well. The leaders were happy and his demand grew and kept him busy.

The party came to power for the first time. It was celebration time all over again.

Madhav was now twenty one. He had celebrated his foray into adulthood by an orgy of violence. He now celebrated his foray into marriageable age by contributing to the democratic traditions of the country; he had campaigned, he had voted and he had celebrated hard. The world was at his feet now...

Bombay became Mumbai.

Thus began the renaming spree. Both the main railway station and the airport were renamed after Maharashtra's favourite warrior king, Shivaji. Many of the roads were also renamed and the city's leading engineering college was renamed after Shivaji's mother.

'What's in a name?' said Shakespeare.

Bom Bahia, Bombay, Mumbai... whatever name you wish to call her, continues to draw thousands into her arms. They come from different parts of the country, drawn to her like moths towards a flame. Some perish, torn apart by her seemingly cruel indifference. But those that survive and most do, discover that beneath that harsh veneer lies a warm heart.

There is something about her, something almost magical; which inspires a million dreams.

Dreams of becoming rich, famous, powerful, popular...

Dreams,that draw obscure men and women and turn them into celebrities, college dropouts into corporate honchos, and runaways into powerful gang lords.

A city that reassures you it is still okay to dream...

As the New Year dawned; the party got over the euphoria of the win and slowly got sucked into the business of governance.

Madhav had also come back to earth. Once,the elections were over, everybody went back to whatever they had been doing and the party also left him on his own. Although,he was always surrounded by his friends and hangers on; the loneliness of his existence hit him hard. He had never been close to any of his friends and he had no family left. He had never been close to his parents and after the initial shock of their death, he had all but forgotten the incident and had not even ventured near his house. But,today,as he sat alone in the flat, he felt an urge to go back.

It was a Sunday morning. The street on which his house was located was filled with children playing cricket. Several games seemed to be going on simultaneously and there was excitement all around. His house was at the end of the street. He slowly walked upto it. The iron gate, which enclosed the small garden, lay ajar. He walked in. The garden had gone to seed, and weeds were growing everywhere. He noticed some of the uprooted trees that had fallen down and were lying shrivelled. He went upto the main door and opened it. The smell hit him hard- the smell of neglect. He closed the door and the sounds from the street were cut off. The curtains were all pulled back and the light was dim. He switched on the lights. The lights cast an eerie glow. It was as if he was in another time and age. He was in the living room. It was sparsely furnished, but the room was full of books. They lay on the book shelves, on the table, on the chair, everywhere. And the walls, they were filled with photographs; so many. He had never really bothered to look at them, never cared for them. But, now, they drew him closer. He looked around.

He was everywhere; most of the photographs were his and many of the books were about him. It was as if the room was a homage to Mohandas Karamchand Gandhi, who filled the room with his unassuming self. Madhav felt the blood rush to his head- he wanted to destroy everything about this man. Madhav controlled himself.

He stood there surrounded by a philosophy and way of life, alien and spiteful to him. He felt the hate boiling up again...It was claustrophobic and he wanted to run away.

But one photograph seemed to beckon him. It was in a corner. He went closer. It was grainy. There was a big crowd, it was a marriage photograph. A stern looking man was standing next to a shy girl; his parents. An old man stood next to his mother, his arms folded. His grandfather.

He had never thought about the age difference between his parents. But, now he wondered. He suddenly realised how little he knew about them. He had hated them so much that he might as well have lived with strangers. He suddenly felt an urge to know more about them. He went upto the bookshelf and leafed through the contents. Books, books, books...

He went and sat down on the diwan. It was dusty. He noticed a book lying there. It was a note-book. He opened it and began to read. It was afternoon by the time he finished with it.

He had made up his mind. He had to go back to Sewagram where his father had met his mother and married her.

He reached Sewagram the next day evening.

It was just like any other town. Some people directed him to Gandhi*ji's* ashram. He did not want to visit it, but something drew him close. The place was a museum and in a state of disrepair. It had the same smell-that of neglect. He should have been happy to see the museum in that condition; but he did not feel happy.

He went and sat down under a tree. He felt uneasy. Here, he was at the place where a man he hated had launched many of his successful agitations and it was in shambles. It was his moment of victory; Gandhi and Gandhism seemed to have been pushed into obscurity. But, somehow, the victory appeared hollow. He could not explain his feelings. He must be growing soft, sentimental.

He got up and went in search of the school his father had built. Nobody seemed to know of its existence. He checked into a hotel and had a troubled sleep. He had to leave in the afternoon and wanted to look for the school again, the reason why he had come so far.

And, then he turned lucky. A middle aged man, sitting at a tea-shop said he knew the place and said he would take him there. They walked for about fifteen minutes and arrived at an apartment building.

This was where it stood, he said pointing at the building. The school was not able to sustain itself, the government said it could not allot any more funds and it had been razed to the ground.

"I studied here, long time ago, when you were not even born," said the man. "But then, that was a long time ago and things have changed. Things have to change don't they?'

Madhav returned back. He did not know what he had expected to find in Sewagram; but the entire visit left him feeling perturbed. His parents, especially his father was one of the first objects he had learnt to hate, but somehow the feeling seemed misplaced now that they were dead and gone. Even their philosophy and their legacy seemed to have gone with them. All he could feel now was a sense of pity...

The next week, he went back again to his old home. He had enquired and realised that the property prices had gone up considerably and he could earn a small fortune if he sold the house. He was in the house, trying to retrieve all his belongings when he heard a knock at the door. He hesitated and went and opened the door. An old man stood there uncertainly.

"The house has been lying locked for so long, so when I saw you I was surprised. I thought I should come and see you," he said. "You are Narendra's son, aren't you?"

"Yes," replied Madhav.

"You may not remember me," he said. "But, I remember you."

"Can I come in?" he asked.

"Yes," said Madhav, not too pleased with the intrusion.

He looked around.

"I am Milind Hatangadi.I was with your father in college. I live just across the street. What a tragedy it was, the fire, I mean...You know, he missed you a lot. He never said that, but his eyes told me. He was very sad when you left him and started living away. He was heartbroken. He recovered when you came back, but he was never the same again.

But, Malti took great care of him. He was a great man and she a noble lady."

As Madhav sat there, the old man rambled on about the old times.

"I must be boring you," he said suddenly. "Actually, I came here to tell you something about the day, when the house caught fire."

Madhav suddenly sat upright.

"It did not strike me earlier during the police enquiry and I had all but forgotten it. But seeing you today, I suddenly remembered. That is why I came. I wanted to tell you about it."

"Do you have any enemies?" asked the old man, suddenly.

"I don't understand," replied Madhav.

"No, I mean, Narendra did not have any, so why would anybody want to harm him."

"What do you mean?" asked Madhav.

"It was evening that day, the dusk was falling. You know the time of the day, when everything appears slightly unnatural, exaggerated. So, maybe I am all wrong.

Anyway, I was going for my walk, when I noticed a young man, probably your age. He was very diffident. He wanted to walk up to your house, but he seemed to be in two minds. And then, he quickly went upto the house, somebody opened the door and he went inside. I continued my walk. I went to the end of the street and was walking back when I noticed this man, coming towards me in a hurry. He was literally running. He rushed past me; he was looking back all along. I forgot all about it, when I neared the end of the street and found your house on fire."

He paused.

"By the time the fire engine came, it was all over. It must have been terrible, to be burnt alive. I forgot all about the young man, even when the police started investigating and asking questions. But, I suddenly remembered it, about a month back; I do not know why. I did not know to whom I should tell and then I saw you today...I really do not know whether that man had anything to do, but perhaps he did. That is why, I asked you whether you had any enemies; Narendra was too gentle and kind to have any."

"Can you describe the man?" asked Madhav.

"All I can remember is he was a young man, literally a boy" answered Milind.

It was a pensive looking Madhav who returned to his flat in Worli. He had made any number of enemies already. He had destroyed people's homes, their businesses and had taken a few lives. It could be any one of those disgruntled and dispossessed people, who carried out this deed. The old man had said he was a young boy; he wondered how the boy had found out his wherabouts.He had to find out...

The next few days and weeks were spent in trying to uncover a trail which was buried somewhere in the wilderness. He used his contacts in the party, the underworld and the police, but it all led nowhere. Weeks passed into months but the trail had gone cold.

Rakesh was the son of a powerful builder; who had met his end rather suddenly a year back. He had lost his mother at a young age and inherited all the wealth.

Rakesh had been a class mate of Madhav; but they had drawn closer to each other only during their last year. Both of them were floating along aimlessly and perhaps this was what brought them close. Madhav finally found some one whom he could open out and talk.

Both of them eventually graduated, but neither of them had any interest in practicing law. They spent most of their days, or rather nights visting different bars. But soon, they got tired of it and were restless to do something. Rakesh had left the business to survive on its own and it was floundering. They joined hands but they had very few projects on hand. And then lady luck smiled upon them. Madhav had been getting huge offers from various builders for his father's house at Dadar.One day, he decided that he would not sell the house but demolish it and together with Rakesh, they would build their first project.

He watched, without any emotion, as the bulldozer razed the house flat. He had not bothered to clear the house and all that remained of Narendra and Malti were flattened and dumped into a faraway garbage dump.

The project; a gleaming new apartment was completed in twelve months flat and thus began the beginning of a prosperous partnership. They celebrated their success in style with a weekend party in one of the beaches on the fringes of the city.

State elections were held and the party's tryst with power came to an end.

Land was at a premium in Mumbai and their business met with their first road block. There was no land available for building, or so it seemed, and it looked like their fledgling business would flounder. Rakesh started to panic but Madhav asked him to be calm. Very soon, he had managed to identify a huge piece of land very near an expressway under construction. The land was vacant and empty and would be ideal to construct a small township. But it was not available. It was owned by a small time builder, Ramnath Shetty, who had bought the land at a dirt cheap price.

He had got into the building business more by chance than by intent. His friend had dumped the business on him before moving to the Middle East. He had this huge plot of land but neither had the enterprise nor inclination to do anything about it. He was also not willing to sell it. He wanted to wait and watch till the prices skyrocketed and then he would decide what to do...Madhav had approached him number of times, each time with an increased offer but Shetty refused to listen. One day as Shetty sat in his office, Madhav walked in. He closed the door, took out his knife and cut Shetty's throat. He found the papers stuffed in a bag. He took them and walked out.

Very soon, he had a set of papers very similar to the ones he had stolen from the dead man. Only the name of the owner had got changed. The forgery was perfect.

The new project was launched amid much fanfare, with the local MLA inaugurating it.

Madhav's reputation grew fast and the company prospered.

The new century dawned. The world had survived the prophecies of doom- the Y2K virus had come and gone, if at all there was one. An industry thrived and prospered on a possible glitch in the computers of the world. But all's well that end's well. The virus was soon forgotten and the world went on.

India and Pakistan were again at loggerheads and the object of contention was again Kashmir.

There are several theories on the origin of Kashmir. Kalhana in his work"Rajatarangini" which traces the history of Kashmir states that the sage Kashyap formed Kashmir by draining a lake and asking the Brahmins to settle there. Whatever be the origins, the place has had a chequered history. Kashmir soon became a centre for Buddhist learning. Islam came to Kashmir in the 14th century. It soon passed through many hands- the Afghans, Mughals, Sikhs and finally, back to the Hindus under Maharaja Gulab Singh. The Maharaja's great grandson signed the treaty of accession of the princely state with the Indian union post indepence. And Kashmir became the focal point for India-Pakistan animosity. Wars were fought, debates were conducted, talks were held, elections were organised, proposals were floated; but the problem refused to go away. While all this was happening, Kashmir found itself split into three; between India, Pakistan and China. A once peaceful place became a bone of contention and a human tragedy unfolded. The tragedy is still being played out today and a solution eludes.

A solution eludes because Kashmir is only part of the story which began when the East India Company landed in the early 17th century in a small town on the west coast of India and began a policy of divide and rule across the country, ably assisted by a large section of the local populace (knowingly or unknowingly) and culminated in Radcliffe drawing those lines cutting across an entire civilisation.

I do not know the solution nor the end of this story, but hope, that the day will not be far off when those immortal words attributed to the Mughal emperor Shahjahan on Kashmir "If there is paradise in the world, it is here, it is here..." will ring true.

As the new century unfolded, Madhav's grip over the company increased and very soon he was the one taking all the decisions. Rakesh was happy to be the silent partner and supported all his decisions. The trouble started soon after Rakesh got married. His wife, Lavanya did not like the way Madhav bossed over her husband who meekly agreed to everything. Rakesh was easy going and was comfortable with the situation, but the constant nagging and insinuations from his wife were getting onto him. He went and confronted Madhav one day, saying that enough was enough and he did not like Madhav's style of functioning. Madhav was shocked and tried to reason with him but to no avail. The quarrel soon turned into a rift and very soon it affected the operations.

To find a way out, Madhav proposed that they split. Rakesh, or rather Lavanya refused and one day when he reached office, he found his way barred by a security guard who handed him a letter. The letter was signed by Rakesh terminating his service. All these years, Madhav had continued to be an employee and had never bothered to enter into a partnership agreement with Rakesh. Madhav was enraged and vowed to take revenge.

Every morning when Rakesh came to office, he found Madhav standing across the road and staring at him. The scene was repeated in the evening. He started changing his timings, but Madhav seemed to be there always. He now slowly started appearing before his house. Whenever, he looked out or came out, he found Madhav standing outside. He started dreading going outside. The guilt of throwing out Madhav was now compounded by the fact that Lavanya had completely taken over the business. He seemed to have become a prisoner in his own house. Matters came to a head when Lavanya brought a lawyer one day and demanded that the she be made an equal partner in the business. The mildly mannered Rakesh flew into a rage and tore the papers. The situation went from bad to worse and both husband and wife stopped talking. Rakesh felt claustrophobic; he cursed himself for listening to Lavanya and throwing out Madhav. He was at the end of his tether.

Madhav was patient, the stakes were too high. He knew the mind games that he was playing would crack up the easy going Rakesh very soon. It did, sooner than he expected.

One day, as he waited outside the house, Rakesh came out straight to him. He looked haggard.

"You win," he said. "Let's go to your house. I need to talk."

They drove in silence to Madhav's house. Rakesh went to the balcony and sat down. The sea was placid; he could barely see the waves. He felt comforted; at home. He turned to Madhav who was standing next to him. He caught his hands and burst into tears. Madhav felt embarrassed.

"That is enough," he said.

"I am sorry," said Rakesh, wiping his tears. "I am sorry for everything. Please forgive me, if you can."

Madhav smiled.

"I want to get away from her," Rakesh said. "She has made my life miserable."

"Why don't you file for a divorce!" asked Madhav.

"She refused," replied Rakesh.

There was silence for a long time as Rakesh looked at Madhav expectantly for a solution.

"Are you sure that you want to be rid of Lavanya?" asked Madhav.

"Yes, yes..." replied Rakesh. "Do whatever you want, just get rid of her."

"Ok, relax..." said Madhav. "Let's have a drink; your job will be done."

As the sun set slowly over the horizon, Madhav and Rakesh fell into a drunken slumber...

Lavanya was found gagged and very much dead, when Rakesh returned from office, a couple of days later. The guard's throat had been split. The cupboards were all in a state of disarray. Jewellery and cash were found missing.

Police investigation revealed that robbery was most likely the motive.

Madhav joined back after the mourning period was over. It was back to business...

Madhav wanted to expand; he wanted to look beyond Mumbai. He explored several options before narrowing down to Ahmedabad.The big earthquake had brought down several buildings and the city was looking for better quality builders to offer solutions.

There was a beeline for new projects and Madhav used his connections in the government to set up office in Ahmedabad. His business in Ahmedabad started growing and he alternated between Ahmedabad and Mumbai.

It was late in the evening, the brief winter was on its way out and it was pleasant. Madhav was in the office, ready to pack up and leave. He had to catch the morning train to Mumbai. The phone rang. As he listened, his face became grim and he nodded his head several times.

"Do not worry," he finally said, "we shall give them a fitting reply."

He switched on the television; which was filled with images of the burnt train. He could barely restrain himself; they had burnt the Ram *sevaks* alive in cold blood. They had gone too far this time and they needed to be taught a lesson, they would remember for ever. A *bandh* had been called for the morrow. It was time for action, to complete the unfinished business of Mumbai. He started making telephone calls...

Madhav would replay the incidents of the next few days again and again in his life savouring and enjoying those moments. If Mumbai had been gruesome; Ahmedabad was barbaric. Madhav had been one of the band leaders. He had led groups looting houses and shops, slaughtering young and old alike and wiping out entire families. They had gone from shop to shop, house to house, locality to locality and indulged in acts of intense savagery. The police looked the other way and many of the residents joined hands.

Religion's ugly face was on public display.

Madhav had to stop finally...compulsions of governance and the outcry from across the country forced the army to be brought in.

His job over, Madhav left for Bombay.

"Let's go out," he told Rakesh that evening.

They went to a movie and then got drunk.

Life had never been so good for Madhav.He had overcome his personal turmoil and was doing well. The proposal for his marriage came as a bolt from the blue. He had never thought about it; he was quite comfortable with his life and did not want to be reined in by domesticity. He wanted to be alone, to be free, and to do what he felt. But; he could not reject the proposal outright. It had come from a close friend of his uncle and now a prominent politician in the state. This man had enormous clout and could break or make people and businesses. The marriage would be a good business propostion. He agreed.

It was a gala affair as the rich and the powerful attended the marriage.

Madhav's father in law gifted them a penthouse in a new apartment complex across the Dadar beach, just a couple of kilometres away from the house where it had all begun.

Reena was a timid girl. She was just past twenty one and had recently completed her graduation. She had grown up in a household dominated by her overbearing father. He made all the rules in the house and the other members had never dared to disobey. So when her father proposed her marriage, she was very happy; happy that she would get a chance to escape. She knew nothing of Madhav except that he was the nephew of her father's old friend and a successful builder. But she was willing to take a chance, nothing could be worse than her father, she had thought.

Her hopes were dashed very soon. She found her husband remote and uncaring. He refused to go on a honeymoon saying he was far too busy for all that nonsense. He left home early and returned late, and rarely had dinner at home. Her attempts to bridge the gap proved futile; for him, she did not seem to exist. She had left one prison to arrive at another.

Marriage was proving to be lucky for Madhav. Business was booming and he was extremely busy. The only discordant note was his wife; he did not want her but could not do away with her. So, he tolerated her. He was sometimes afraid that she would go and complain to her father, but he soon discovered that she was too afraid of him to do so.

The love less marriage continued, but Reena kept hoping. And one day, when she discovered that she was pregnant, her hopes soared.

He returned home late that evening.

"I have something to tell you," she said.

"I am tired," he said, "can it not wait till the morning."

"No," she said, "you will be happy to hear the news."

He just walked out and went into the bathroom.

She sat expectantly on the bed.

He returned back from the bathroom to find her still sitting.

"Oh," he said, "you have not yet gone to sleep."

"I wanted to tell you something," she persisted.

"OK, out with it," he replied gruffly, "why can't a man live in peace?"

"You are going to be a father," she said shyly.

He looked at her and frowned.

"I think it is a custom for the daughters to go home for the birth of their first child. Talk to your mother and decide. And now go to sleep," he said. "It's far too late. I have a busy day tomorrow."

He switched off the light and Reena could soon hear him snoring. She lay there and wept in the darkness...

Madhav felt very happy as his wife had gone away to her parents' home, and he was all alone now. His father-in-law often dropped in and they discussed business over drinks. He wanted Madhav to contest for the assembly elections. The ruling party at the centre had changed in the recent parliamentary elections. His father-in-law had contested and lost his parliamentary seat. It was now beneath his dignity to contest for the state elections. He wanted his son-in law to step in. Madhav agreed.

There are six parliamentary constituencies and thirty four assembly constituencies in Mumbai. Madhav was provided with a ticket to contest an assembly constituency in the southern part of the city. Preparations began in full swing. Madhav remembered the last time when he had been fully involved, was a decade back. At that time, he was a foot soldier doing all the running around.Today, he had become a leader. He had hundreds of people running around arranging the logistics. But; he still preferred getting into the small details and would often sit with his party men discussing the plans and strategies. The campaign kicked off a month before the election day. Madhav began the campaign by offering prayers at the Siddhi Vinayak temple near his house. The days were full; the campaign would begin early in the morning and continue late in the evening with brief breaks in between. Strategies were worked out and plans were made and changed in between various rallies. Madhav addressed many rallies; he went from house to house. He said he was a son of the soil, he was born and brought up in the city and knew the people's problems. He said terrorism was the biggest threat, even bigger than the housing problem. It was threatening to engulf the country and now their beloved city. He himself had suffered because of terrorism- he narrated the story of his uncle's family. He talked about the traitors who lived within the city and created terrorist attacks. He warned that these traitors wanted to take control, they wanted another Pakistan. But, he, his party would not let it happen. The ruling party had done nothing to catch these terrorists, who were running free all over the city and the country. He hoped that the people would vote him and his party into power or else, they could all become victims of the menace of terrorism.

And so the campaign went on. Threats and counter threats. Allegations and counter allegations...

Reena was feeling irritated and down in the dumps. Her pregnancy was in an advance stage and her mobility was reduced very much. She was getting tired very fast and short of breath. She did not feel like doing anything and would laze around for hours doing nothing. Her mother would sometimes coax her to do some work to get her into shape but she would refuse and snap back at her. Reena realised she was behaving irrationally but could not help it. It was nearly eight months since she had come back and she could count the number of times her husband had come visting. He also rarely called. She had tried calling earlier but had given up now. The last time she had talked to her husband, was nearly a month and a half back and the last time she had seen him, was around three months back. And they both lived in the same city within a radius of less than five kilometres. What a mess she had gotten into.

The pains started one night. It was sudden and unbearable. She shouted for her mother who slept nearby. The pains grew intense. She was bundled into a car by her father and driven to a hospital. Adarsh was born later in the day as dusk fell over the city. Reena was tired and fell into a deep sleep. The child was healthy and glowing and Reena's spirits rose. She clasped the bundle closely to her and wept tears of joy. She was discharged from the hospital two days later. Madhav had still not come to the hospital nor called her up. Her father said he was busy and would drop in soon. Madhav, came four days after Adarsh was born. He smiled sheepishly at Reena and held his son gingerly in his hands. He stayed the whole evening and had dinner with the family. He kept looking at his son in amazement. Before he left, he went upto Reena and hugged her and said he would be back soon victorious. There were tears in her eyes as she bid goodbye and wished him luck. Her mood improved drastically. The baby kept her busy and cheerful the whole day and in between she tried to catch up on her husband's campaign. It seemed that it was going to be a close affair and could go either way.

Election Day dawned, votes were cast. The counting started. Results started pouring in. It seemed that the ruling party was on its way back to power. Results for Madhav's constituency were one of the last. When it was announced, Reena broke into tears. Madhav had lost by fifty six votes. A recount was ordered, it did not change the election results. Reena tried to contact Madhav but he could not be located.

Madhav listened to the election results in disbelief. He was at his friend Rakesh's house- away from the noise and heat. Rakesh tried to console him but he was inconsolable.

Madhav took the election defeat very badly. His father- in- law tried to reason with him saying he was still young and he could come back very soon. But Madhav could not control his disappointment and from the disappointment grew his anger. He felt everybody had conspired against him to make him loose. One day, he went into a locality where he had addressed a rally and began to abuse the residents loudly. A local party man rescued him when the residents started thrashing him. He barged into his in- laws house one day and started shouting at his wife and kid, blaming them for all the misfortunes.

As days went by, the reality of the situation soon started sinking in and Madhav realised that he had to get on with his life. He started attending office and slowly started taking interest in business and soon the memory of his loss became a small niggle, which pained him only when he felt very low. His father- in- law came to his office one day and said that Adarsh was nearly six months now and it was high time, he took his wife and child home. After a lot of reluctance, Madhav agreed. More than a year after she had left, Reena was back with her husband. She hoped and prayed that things would change, at least, for the sake of their son. And things did start changing. Madhav started returning home early and played with the child. He even tried to make conversation with Reena.

And then, one day, as he was getting ready to go to office; he received a telephone call...

"Yes," he said, after lifting the phone.

"I know who killed your parents," said the voice from his past.

"What are you saying?" said Madhav.

"You heard it right the first time, I know who killed your parents," said the voice and the phone went dead.

Madhav shouted back at the phone, but it had gone silent.

"What is the matter?" asked Reena who was standing nearby.

"Nothing, somebody from the office," replied Madhav. "I need to go."

He shut himself up in the office. There were a thousand questions.

Who had called him and why after all these years. So the old man had been right, it was not an accident. But why now.Why, why?

Reena noticed Madhav had again become irritable and had started shouting at the child also. She tried to help but was shouted at. She went into a shell along with her child.

Madhav waited for the phone to ring, and the same voice to call again, but it never did.

His attempt at tracing the call proved futile.

It was nearly two months later, when he received the second call.

"So, how are you?" the voice said.

Madhav immediately recognised the voice; he tried to put a face to it, but failed.

"You must be in a terrible shape," the voice continued and then it stopped.

"Hello!" said Madhav, "go on."

"I thought you were not interested, that is why I stopped," replied the voice.

"No. no..." shouted Madhav. "Tell me and I shall kill that bastard."

"Like so many others, won't you," replied the voice.

"I do not know what you mean," answered Madhav.

"I am sure you know what I mean," answered the voice sharply.

"What do you want?" asked Madhav.

"What else but those pieces of notes which go around and around. You give me what I want and I give you the name," said the voice.

"And how do I believe you," asked Madhav.

"Take it or leave it," replied the voice sharply.

But, the voice continued, "I could also go and tell the police, the press, how an honourable citizen- a renowned builder, an upcoming politician was very active recently in Gujarat and not too long ago in this city."

"Go ahead and tell them," shouted Madhav. "But it's your word against mine and nobody would believe you."

The voice at the other end laughed; "It would not be my word only, I assure you. There are others who saw you..."

"Stop!" said Madhav. "Tell me how much you want and where."

"I will call you again," said the voice, "and till then, no tricks."

The phone went dead.

Madhav sat pensively; this was becoming complicated.

At the other end, Salim kept the phone down quickly and walked away from the public call office from where he had made the call.

Madhav was slowly but surely walking into his trap. He wanted it to be a surprise for Farhan. He wanted to deliver Madhav at his doorstep and knew Farhan's retribution would be quick and cruel.

Adarsh was growing fast. He kept Reena on her toes. He was a playful child and liked to explore the world- which was mostly the house. One day Madhav returned home early, to find his wife and child playing. They were pleasantly surprised to see him and the child urged his father to join in. After the initial hesitation, Madhav joined in and found it great fun. In the evening, he took them out to the beach and later to a restaurant for dinner.

Late that night as Reena lay in her bed, she smiled to herself- this had been her happiest day for a long, long time.

The next day, Madhav surprised her further. He came early and told her to pack. They were off for their first holiday- to Goa.

Reena had the time of her life at Goa. At last, she felt, her marriage was falling in place. Madhav was at his pleasant best and took them around to some wonderful beaches, churches, temples and restaurants. It was all so good to be true and sometimes, Reena wondered whether she would wake up suddenly and discover that she was having a dream. It was the last evening and they were having a quiet dinner on the verandah of their hotel. They could hear the gentle roar of the sea in the background. Adarsh had finished his dinner and was playing all by himself. The phone rang. Madhav lifted it and soon his face had a frown.Reena knew with a sunken feeling that the dream was about to end.Madhav answered in monosyllables.

The phone call ended and their magical holiday came to an abrupt end. Madhav got up.

"Let's go to bed early," he said. "We have to leave tomorrow."

They arrived in Mumbai the next day and Madhav waited the whole day for the phone call, which would indicate where they would meet. The phone call never came.

The phone call came a week later, when he was in the middle of a meeting.

"Come and meet me in two hours time in front of the Jehangir Art Gallery," it said.

"But how will I recognise you?" asked Madhav.

"Don't bother, I shall," replied Salim.

"And the money?' asked Madhav.

"Come empty handed, I will tell you when we meet," replied Salim.

Madhav excused himself from the meeting. At last he was going to meet the voice, which had been troubling him for more than a year. He hailed a passing taxi and reached the place half an hour before the specified time. He stood near the Art Gallery and waited. An hour passed and he grew irritated. Maybe somebody was playing a joke.

And then he heard somebody calling out his name in a voice which was strangely familiar. He turned to find a slightly built man standing near him. He was smartly dressed, but what struck him immediately was the smile. A knowing smile which could only belong to that voice. Inspite of himself, he could not but smile back.

"Can we not meet somewhere else?" asked Madhav. "It is too crowded and noisy here."

"Yes, we will," replied Salim. "I came here only to show you that it is not a joke, that I exist. You will have to wait for a couple of weeks and then we shall meet again, you with the money and me with the name. Till then, *Khuda Hafiz*," said the man and started walking.

Madhav started walking after him. Salim suddenly turned back and said, "Do not try to follow me. There are others watching you."

And he was gone. Madhav was tempted to follow him, but he resisted, he would get his chance. There was now a face to the voice.

That was the last time Madhav saw the man and heard the voice. He waited and waited for the phone call. It never came. He went several times to that place where he had met the man expecting him to materialise. He never did. Days and months passed. It seemed as if the entire thing was like a dream; had he been hallucinating? It could not be possible; he could hear the voice clearly ringing in his ears and also the face and the smile. A smile which suggested a thousand things. He grew worried. Had the man suddenly changed his mind? Had he suddenly decided to squeal, tell the police. He expected the police to come knocking any day. Should he go and pre-empt and tell the police about the phone calls, the man. But then, they would start asking questions and open a Pandora's Box. Let sleeping dogs lie...

Reena was back to reality, her husband was back to his irritable self and the trip to Goa seemed like an eternity ago.

Rakesh found his friend and partner withdrawing more and more into himself. He used to frequent Rakesh's house often but now, the visits became more and more rare. He wondered what the problem was and whether it was something to do with his wife. Reena seemed to be a docile girl, but he thought, one never knew. He had to help his friend. And then one day, he got his chance. They had a late day and all the office staff had gone home. Madhav was sitting alone in his office and Rakesh could see him lost in thought. He walked in.

"Can I sit down?" he asked.

Madhav nodded, still lost in thought.

"Can we talk?" asked Rakesh.

"Yes, but what?" asked Madhav.

"About you," answered Rakesh.

"I don't understand," replied Madhav.

"Madhav, we have known each other for a long time now and I can sense there is some problem that you are trying to hide. What is it, can I help? Is it Reena?"

Madhav smiled.

"Reena? That poor thing! How can she cause me any problem? I am her problem."

"Then what is it?" asked Rakesh.

Madhav sighed. It was a long sigh.

"My father and uncle," he began, "they were brothers, born of the same parents. It is difficult to believe that; they were poles apart; in their looks, their thoughts, in their deeds.

I believed; still believe that my father was naive, his ideas- sacrifice, truth, honesty and all that do not make sense ...

You live only once, so make the best of it; the end justifies the means. My uncle had similar ideas, my father did not. The conflict that arose was inevitable.

But one thing was common to both of them—they both had a violent, painful end.

That makes me wonder...what is right and what is wrong?"

Right and wrong. Black and white. We like to brand people into two neat compartments; Good and Bad.

We have seen two of our characters; Farhan and Madhav at close quarters. We have had a chance to look at their thoughts, their actions, and their lives very closely, perhaps more closely than we do for most people. Perhaps, some of you had paused to ponder at their actions and wonder at their rationale.

Two young men; gone astray--products of our callous society...

"You have not heard me talk like this, have you," asked Madhav. "You must be wondering what I am leading to? Well, the ghosts from my past have come back to haunt me and I wonder whether I can fight them off. But you know me, I am a fighter, I don't give up things easily. And, with luck, I shall win..."

Lady luck finally smiled upon Madhav. He was leaving for his office and his car had started moving away from the apartment gate, when he noticed from the corner of his eye, a man hurriedly getting into an ancient Ambassador. He would have ignored it, but he saw the car again a little behind him at one of the signals. He now started observing its progress from his rear window. The car was still there. His office had arrived and he quickly went behind the door and watched. The car slowed down, hesitating, and then went off. On his way back, he could not see the car and thought his imagination was playing tricks with him. Just as his car turned inside the gate, he noticed the same car, parked a little way down the street. There was something here, he thought. He got down quickly; he had to have a look at the car and the driver without getting observed. A taxi which had just come inside the building was leaving. He quickly jumped into it and asked the driver to go out. The driver started protesting.

"Do as I say," said Madhav. "I will give you money."

He asked the taxi to take a right from the main gate; the car was waiting on the other side. As soon as the taxi had gone about twenty-five metres, he asked him to stop. The driver put up his hands muttering and stopped.Madhav craned his head and looked back. Somebody was sitting at the driver's wheel of the car. That person suddenly got down and started walking, slowly at first and then briskly. He came to the gate and hesitated. It seemed like he wanted to walk in, but then, he changed his mind and walked off quickly. Madhav had caught a brief glimpse of the man, he was slightly built and his head was grey. He seemed to be familiar, but he was not the person who had met him that day. So who was this person and what did he want? He had to find out.

"I want you to follow that car standing there," he said pointing back to the Ambassador.

"I am an honest man, do not involve me on all of this, please let me go," pleaded the driver.

"You do as you're told,"said Madhav, his voice gruff.

They waited. The Ambassador started and then it drove past them.

"Follow him," said Madhav.

The car wound past Shivaji Park and soon came to an old apartment complex and went inside.

Madhav had noted the car number and the apartment complex. It would be easy now to get the identity of the driver.

"Ok, let's go back," he told the driver.

He went home. The driver and the car were definitely after him. There was no question. Should he start making enquiries now or should he wait for a couple of days.

He decided to wait.

The car was not to be seen the next day, or the day after. He must be getting paranoid, he thought. He spotted the Ambassador as soon as his car turned the gate, the next day morning. He smiled, he was still sane. He could see the Ambassador start up suddenly and following him. It followed him right upto the office. There were no questions now, he was being tailed. He had to find out now, he no longer could wait.

The information came to him late in the evening. The car was owned and driven by one Farhan Rasool. He was a professor and unmarried. He pretty much kept to himself. A harmless guy.

Madhav was not happy with the information. He wanted more.

He got what he wanted late in the night when he was going to bed, and suddenly everything fell into place. He smiled grimly to himself. The ghost of his past had come back. He had nicely fallen into trap. The voice, his meeting with the owner of the voice, was a ruse to draw him in. He had fallen for it. He should have finished it all that day, so long ago. He had erred, perhaps had been too confident. The confidence and arrogance of youth. But now the boot was on the other foot. They thought that he did not know, but now he knew who they were and were after him.

The hunted would now become the hunter...

We shall leave Madhav and Farhan here and move on to our third protagonist- Sanjay and see what destiny has willed for him.

Destiny, providence, fate, luck...whatever you may wish to call it by; seems to be playing some role in our lives. You may disagree, but the instances are far too many to disregard.

Why does a person suddenly decide to cancel a flight ticket and the plane crashes with no survivors? A bus crashes and everybody is killed except a new born baby. A man is thrown out of a train one cold night in South Africa and it triggers a chain of events leading to the end of the British Empire. A meteor deviates from its path and hurtles towards the Earth and wipes out the mighty dinosaurs.

You must also have experienced some of this--some time. It is as if some unseen hand was moving those pieces--you, me in a vast chess board. As if, we were puppets in a grand stage show...

Closer-- in our story; it seemed now that this invisible thing; this unseen hand had brought Madhav and Farhan together, then apart and then together and was now waiting to make its final move and say "Check" and then "Mate".

❀❀❀

Sanjay

Let us now leave Farhan and Madhav- two grown up men, fighting their phantoms and go back in time, more than a decade and a half back. An age when mail still meant what you wrote on pieces of paper and put in postboxes to be delivered by that almost extinct tribe; the postmen. It was not too long ago, but such has been the relentless march of technology that it seems all too long ago. But then, let us not digress from this story.

Let us go back to Sanjay, as he sat on his desk, late in the night, trying to pen a letter to his friend Vivek...

Sanjay tried again and again but the piece of paper in front of him remained blank. The picture of the burning vehicle with those trapped faces haunted him. Those emotions, the turmoil that he was going through, could not be penned. He had to bear this alone.

Life at college went on as usual. Sanjay was affable and friendly and had made lots of friends. He did not belong to any group and was comfortable with everyone.

They had discussed for a few days the terrible happenings in the city, but very soon it disappeared into the background. The annual college festival was around the corner and preparations had begun in earnest. Sanjay was on the organising committee, one of the few freshers, and was kept busy.

By the time the fest ended, Sanjay was exhausted. He felt better after taking a day off and sleeping the whole day. But it had been a good experience- he had enjoyed planning and organising many of the activities as well as participating in many of them. He had made more friends and they had promised to keep in touch.

The day dawned like any other. Sanjay's classes had got over early and he and a couple of friends- Ansari and Pankaj had decided to go to Flora Fountain to look for second hand books. They had stopped for a quick bite at a road side joint. They were in no hurry and they strolled through downtown Mumbai taking in the frenetic pace of the people- people wolfing down their lunches, people talking animatedly, people looking at their watches and rushing...They had taken a detour and were now on Dalal Street, housing the Bombay Stock Exchange.

The Bombay Stock Exchange was established in 1875; the oldest in Asia. The area where it is currently located was acquired nearly fifty years later and a building, housing the exchange came up soon after. It took another fifty years before the BSE moved into the current twenty eight storied building, located at the same site where the old building stood.

It is today the nerve centre of India's growth. Its index - BSE SENSEX has become an indicator of the country's economy and prosperity. Every time, it goes on a downward spiral, the country sits up and gasps. India's leading business lights assure that all is well- panic not; the Finance Minister reiterates the same in more abstruse terms. Financial whiz kids and gurus go in a tizzy trying to explain the phenomenon.Nespapers and televisions go on an overdrive analysing the happening.
Brokers, buyers and sellers go into panic mode.
It becomes the topic of discussion in offices, colleges, shops, parties, homes, buses, trains; even displacing the staple food- cricket.

The SENSEX has become the country's new mantra...

Days later and years later, whenever Sanjay was asked on what he experienced first; his answer would be always the same- it seemed as if the sky had suddenly fallen on his head...

One moment he was walking and the other moment; he was lying flat on the ground as if swatted by a monster. Sanjay lay there on the road, face down. He raised his face and watched the picture unfold before him. People lay scattered all over -some moving, some still, some bloodied and some dismembered. Others were running in a daze...There was smoke and glass all around and a terrible stench; a stench which he was trying hard to forget- the stench of human flesh burning.

The bombs had been in placed in a car in the parking area causing extensive damage in the vicinity of the stock exchange. More than two hundred and fifty people were killed.

The bombs that went off in Bombay signaled the beginning of a new age in the country's violent history. The age of the faceless enemy...An enemy who surfaced time and again, whenever and wherever he/she wanted- Coimbatore, Hyderabad, Varanasi, Delhi, Jaipur, Bangalore, Ahmedabad--in market places,buses,trains,at places of worship, hospitals---leaving the country gasping for breath!

The pictures and sounds and sights of those explosions relentlessly pound us everywhere; in magazines, newspapers, radio, TV... yet we go on as if nothing has happened...
The wise men say that the city, country has shown remarkable courage, resilience in dealing with this new enemy...We shall not be cowed down; we shall go on...
But, this silence--our silence; is this courage or cowardice? Is it resilience or resignation?

Or is it simply indifference...Only time will tell.

Sanjay tried to get up, but he felt as if his feet were weighed down with lead. He managed to crawl and get up. He looked around- there was no sign of his friends. Where were they? They had been beside him. He walked back and saw Ansari walking towards him in shock. And then he noticed Pankaj, lying near the footpath. He bent down and shook him. There was no movement. Ansari joined him and they tried to lift him together when they noticed the speck of blood near his temple. They looked closer; there was a wound- a very small one. A wave of panic surged through them. They lifted Pankaj and started running oblivious to the smoke and noise around them.

He lay there, dressed in white, still, amidst the people milling around. It was time to leave, for good, on life's last journey. They lifted him, tenderly, and laid him on the crudely constructed bed of wood and coir ropes. The professionals got into the act and Sanjay winced as the ropes were wound tightly over Pankaj's body, to keep it from falling off. They lifted the bier and amidst the chanting of *mantras* and the wail of the womenfolk, laid it inside the waiting ambulance. A long line of cars, motorcycles and scooters followed the ambulance as it wound its way to the crematorium. There was a huge mass of people at the crematorium, mostly family and friends. The pyre was getting ready; the body, now covered completely in cloth was kept beside it. There was more chanting from the priest who coaxed Pankaj's father gently to repeat the words.

Sanjay watched the scene with disbelief. It was only yesterday, this time that Pankaj had been joking and laughing along with him. And today, he lay there, ready to be consumed by the flames...shrapnel from the explosion had hit him on the temple; the doctors said that death would have been instantaneous. They were now lifting the body and placing it on the pyre. The crowd surged forward to get a last glimpse and then it was gone, covered by wood. The priest continued his chanting and then turned towards Pankaj's father and gave him the flame to light the pyre. The poor man who had put up a stoic display till now, completely broke down. He was supported by his relatives and the pyre was lit. The pyre caught fire slowly and very soon started blazing, aided by generous doses of ghee and the deft touches of the crematorium staff. The flames leapt into the sky and the smoke streamed bringing in the now familiar stench to Sanjay.

The tears ran down his cheeks, inspite of his best efforts to control them. He tried to wipe them off, but gave up, they kept streaming down...

The clouds were still hanging in there but the rains had stopped. The weather was pleasant and it seemed like old times. They could hear the sound of the horn blaring from the streamer which took the tourists from the Gateway of India to the Elephanta caves and back. The pigeons flew in circles in a pattern of their own and children clapped their hands in glee. Sanjay and Vivek sat there on the ledge overlooking the Arabian Sea and looked at each other. Vivek had managed to squeeze in a week from his holiday to spend time with

Sanjay and his family. It seemed like old times, yet how things had changed. Two years had passed; Vivek was in his third year of college and Sanjay in his second year. Two years, in which they had turned into men from boys.

They had seen death at close quarters-Vivek, his father's and Sanjay...

Sanjay had narrated his story to Vivek after much persuasion. The initial part was difficult but soon the floodgates opened up. Words poured from Sanjay, and Vivek could see his friend's agony in his eyes.

"What was Pankaj's fault? He was a quiet boy, very gentle; he had so many plans...His parents; I went to see them a few days back; they seem to be living in another world. They showed me his photographs and his mother, she went on and on; look how he is smiling, can you not see those dimples. I first noticed those dimples a month after he was born. We were alone; Pankaj's Papa had gone to his office when he smiled suddenly and then I saw those dimples, so sweet they were. He became serious as he grew up and I saw less and less of those dimples. He is, was, such a nice boy; never gave us any trouble. He came up to me one day and said, you have always lived in Bombay so when I get a job, I shall take you and Papa away. He wanted to take us and go far away to some distant land- away from the noise and heat. A place where he could sit and write- poetry. Here, can you see this, he wrote so many of them. We are too simple, we can't understand them. Maybe, you can. Why don't you read them, read them aloud...?"

"And, there I sat in that small room that evening and read aloud Pankaj's poems. Poems of hope, poems of a new dawn, a better future. And,as I sat there and read, tears rolled down the cheeks of those poor souls and I choked and ran away from there."

"I could not bear it anymore, Vivek. I could not sit and see their agony; I ran away like a coward. What did they do, why do they have to suffer?"

Vivek put an arm around his friend's shoulders and held him tightly.

"I sometimes wonder what has happened to that boy," said Sanjay suddenly. "I mean, the boy, whom I took to the hospital. He had seen his family burning; alive...I wonder what has become of him! He was angry at me, the last day, I saw him in the hospital. He was angry that I had saved him and not left him on the roads to die. Do you know, I went back to the hospital again, very soon after that. It seemed he had slipped away from the hospital one day, without telling anybody. The doctors told me he was in a highly distressed condition.

Those men were laughing and gloating when the car was burning and the boy was screaming and sobbing. What was driving them to this heinous act? Their leader, he was barely a boy; he just sat there and egged them on. I wonder where he is today, and how he feels. How could he do this?"

They sat there for a long time, talking, about the past and what the future might hold.

"Let's go home," said Vivek. "Your mother and grandmother will be getting worried."

As they sat at the dinner table that night, it seemed like old times to Vivek. But as he looked at his friend's face; he knew that things had changed and would never be the same again.

Vivek left soon for Kharagpur; his college had reopened.

The year passed by as if in a blur and Sanjay was now in his final year. His father had become restless and wanted him to start preparing for a management course. Sanjay tried to avoid the subject and managed to fend his father every time the topic came up for discussion. But one day, things came to a head.

"You know Rane's son," he went on "the guy who works as an accountant in our bank, his son had got admission in a Management institute last year and this year during the summer, he has been offered a job as a Manager in a multinational even before completing his course. Such is the demand for Management graduates, but you refuse to see any sense and want to join some newspaper and do what? You want to run around and report about this country, about the politicians, where is that going to help you? You can do that when you are young, when we are there to support you. But after that, what happens. You will have a family to feed and take care. And where will you be, running around, any time of the day or night, wherever your bosses send you. Why? Why do you want to do this to yourself? There is nothing in it for you but hardship."

Sanjay tried to argue back but gave up. There was no point, his father would not understand. But he could not listen to his father; he knew this was where he had to go.

Rajni and Pooja tried to reason with both father and son, but failed.

Sanjay passed out from college and joined for a post graduate diploma in journalism. His father after the initial reluctance got resigned to the fact that his son was different and he could do very little about it. But sometimes, he wondered whether his son was a misfit in this age. Whether, his notions of justice and fairplay had any relevance today. He worried whether he could survive in this cut throat world...But, he kept those worries to himself.

Life was back on a high for Sanjay.The assignments in college were exciting and kept Sanjay busy. The images of that eventful year sometimes seemed to him like a dream now. Those faces rarely came to haunt him these days; as they had in those initial days. But, Sanjay was determined not to forget those faces; he had to find answers to the questions, which they seemed to ask. Answers, he hoped to find in the career that lay before him.

The moment of reckoning came soon when he joined as a trainee reporter in the newspaper, where his grandfather had retired as the editor.

That night, they all went for dinner. It was a big group; there were eight of them- Sanjay's grandmother Rajni, at seventy four, was the eldest. She sat at the head of the table, smiling and sprightly as usual. To her right and left, sat her son and daughter- in- law Suresh and Pooja, respectively. Both had aged gracefully. Suresh was an executive director in the same bank where he had joined as a clerk. His hair had become grey which Pooja teasingly said gave him the look of a successful banker. Pooja was her bubbly self and was dressed simply but elegantly. What began as a hobby for her was now keeping her busy. She had become a columnist and was now a regular contributor to a couple of magazines. To her left, sat her sister Archana; a few years older than Pooja but very much a mirror image of her. She and Pooja were talking animatedly with Rajni. Opposite her, sat her husband-Ritesh; now a partner with a leading financial consultant. Both, Ritesh and Suresh were discussing the pros and cons of the country's new Finance Minister- a Management graduate from Harvard. To his right, sat his son-in law Subrojit. His wife Aditi sat facing him next to her mother. They had met while they were doing their post graduation in Princeton and started liking each other. They continued to be in touch after passing out from college; that they both worked in Boston helped. Soon one thing lead to another and they were married. They were in India for a short vacation. At the end of the table sat Sanjay-the guest of honour.

It was a happy family; they sat in a swanky restaurant in downtown, ate, drank and talked.

"It would have been nice if Pradeep and Anjali had been here," said Pooja, referring to her brother and sister-in- law who were based in Bangalore. "But, then, their company is still very much a start up one and I guess they have no time to move out."

"No time for children also," chipped in Ritesh.

"That is not a nice thing to say," retorted Archana. "You know they have gone to all the doctors."

"Oh, I was only joking," said Ritesh.

"I sometimes wonder how Pradeep could quit his comfortable job and start a company at this age," ventured Suresh.

"Oh, come on," said Pooja. "You always want to play it safe..."

"So, when are you going to make Archana a grandmother?" asked Rajni looking at Aditi.

"Oh, *Nani,* come on, we have just started our careers," replied Aditi "and it's too early in the day for kids. Besides, where is the time..."

"Yes, she has no time even to meet up with Kiran who is so close in New Jersey," retorted Archana.

"Come on Mummy!" answered Aditi. "Kiran is busy with his studies; we do get to meet each other once in six months."

"Anyway," continued Archana, "Kiran tells me he has made a lot of friends and he is quite happy."

"That friend of yours," she addressed Sanjay; "What is his name...?"

"Vivek," prompted Pooja.

"Yes, Vivek, he is also with him, isn't he?"

Sanjay nodded his head.

"What do you think of the place, I mean US," asked Suresh, craning his neck to catch Subrojit's attention. "What are your plans for the future?"

Subrojit smiled.

"Well, probably we shall settle down there- we are looking for a house and Boston is nice- you know, very upper-class and all that..."

And so it went on from one topic to another as the evening wore on...

Rajni looked across the table and caught Sanjay's eyes. He seemed to be getting bored. They smiled at each other; a knowing smile.

Within a few months of his induction; Sanjay was assigned to field jobs. His first assignment was to report on a road accident. It was a gruesome accident; in which two kids on their way to school had been mangled by a truck. By the time, Sanjay arrived at the scene, the bodies of the kids had been removed and the truck had been towed away. The police station was not very helpful; all he managed was their names and addresses. All attempts to reach the children's relatives failed, and finally he had to file in a report which had nothing remarkable and never saw the light of the day. His quest to get his article in the newspaper continued and even after six months, there was nothing in what he produced which interested his boss. But; the time spent on the streets of Mumbai exposed him to a seamy side of the city, which he had heard of but had never experienced.

Often, he used to come home and narrate his experiences to his mother and grandmother. They used to listen intently and advised him to take care.

And finally, he got his big break. It was evening and he was getting ready to leave for home when he received the news that a blast had been reported in a bus. The reason was not known but a terror attack could not to be ruled out. Sanjay knew that speed was the essence and within minutes, was at the site of the blast. The bus or what remained of it lay in the middle of the road. The blast was so powerful that it had destroyed the window panes in the surrounding buildings. The police and ambulance had just arrived and the dead and injured were being taken away. He fought the memories of a similar afternoon and tried to concentrate on the job at hand. He noticed a boy- a young man sitting dazed on the footpath. He seemed to be unhurt.Sanjay rushed to him and enquired whether he wanted any help. The boy said he was quite ok and slowly his story came tumbling out. He had been sitting next to a man near a window seat in the bus. The man suddenly got up and started moving towards the exit when the boy noticed that he had left a bag behind. He called out to the man and reminded him to take his bag; at which, the man seemed to panic and rushed towards the exit. The boy found this strange and followed the man upto the exit and confronted him. The man refused to respond and suddenly jumped out of the bus as it was slowing. On a sudden urge, he also jumped out and started to call out to the man; who had now started to run. And then, all of a sudden, the blast occurred and the bus in which he had been travelling was torn apart. He wanted to run after the suspicious stranger but the cries of the wounded drew him closer to the bus. He had helped the police and ambulance to carry the dead and injured and was now sitting there wondering how close he had been to death. He was sure the man who had run away was in some ways responsible for the blast. Sanjay quickly obtained a brief description of the suspicious stranger and rushed back to office to file the story. His story caught the attention of a sub-editor and appeared in the morning newspaper. The sub-editor called him the next day and said he should investigate further. However, his investigations led him nowhere and the trail went cold.

Within the next year, he was assigned to various events and his articles started featuring regularly in the newspapers. On several occasions, at several events, he came face to face with celebrities whom he had seen on television or read about in newspapers or magazines. But the greatest moment of his life came, when he had to cover an event in which, the chief guest was his childhood hero- Kapil Dev. He managed to get Kapil's autograph somewhat sheepishly, but was at a loss of words, when his idol asked him whether he wanted to ask him something. Later, the next day, when he was narrating the incident at home, he berated himself for missing such an opportunity.

He was soon assigned to a desk job, but he requested that he be allowed to continue in his current role, which was granted. Often, in his assignments, when he crisscrossed the city; he would look into those unfamiliar faces and try to find somewhere the faces of those two boys, one of whom he had saved from the other. He was not clear why he did this, but something kept telling him that somewhere, some day, he would meet them again. He did not know what he would do, should he get a chance...

And then one day, the chance arrived.

A body had been discovered on a rail track. It seemed to be a hit and run case - nothing new in the city of Mumbai. By the time he arrived, the body had been removed. A few enquiries at the police station gave him enough to report back. It seemed like the guy had been run over by the train while crossing, it had been dark and it was raining- nothing unusual again. But, something drew him back. He managed to get the dead man's address. He waded through flooded streets to reach the house.

"They have just gone for the burial; you may be able to catch them there," said a forlorn looking lady, who stood near the house.

Sanjay rushed to the burial ground. It was slushy inside and he did not know where to look for. Enquiries with a person, who appeared to be the caretaker, led him to a burial party. He stood at a distance and watched the group perform the last rites. It soon drew to a close and the group started to move away. Sanjay stood there watching them, another family greaving a loved one, torn away from them suddenly. And,then,he noticed him and was surprised that he could recognise him after all these years, so quickly. The features were the same but the face was different- it was that of a man who had seen and experienced everything. It was no longer the face of somebody who was at the mercy of others- this seemed to be a man in charge.

Sanjay's first reaction was to rush and talk to him; but something made him stop. The man appeared to be lost in thought and stressed. Sanjay wondered how the dead man was related to him. The burial party was now moving towards him on their way out and he stepped aside to let them go. Farhan was at the back walking slowly; moving towards Sanjay;who stood rooted to the spot. The man was up close now, at an arms length away; he suddenly looked towards Sanjay and then away and was gone. Sanjay had to do something; he could not let him go again. He started walking towards Farhan.

The party had moved out of the burial ground and was on the road outside now. He saw the man holding an elderly man and talking to him gently. He then moved away from the group and got into an Ambassador that was parked near the gate. Sanjay had to make his move now; or he would be lost again. The car started moving and Sanjay noted the registration number of the car. It would be easy now...

Sanjay got all the information he wanted, very soon. He was surprised that he had not run into this man- Farhan, much earlier, since they lived in the same locality. He was glad to note that Farhan was doing well for himself- at the college and in the business that he had inherited. He did not seem to have many friends but seemed to be comfortable with himself. Although, he felt a great urge to go and meet this man from his past; he restrained himself. The man had not recognised him when they had been face to face and he did not want to embarrass him and open his wounds.

Sanjay felt a great sense of relief; he wanted to share this with somebody and shot off a letter to Vivek, the only person whom he had confided. But, he knew, that he could not rest in peace until the other man was found and Farhan got his justice. He had to continue his search...

The British politician and Prime Minister William Gladstone who lived in the 19th century, is attributed with this famous saying, "Justice delayed is justice denied". This saying has become oft repeated now and has become almost a cliché.

It has become a norm of our times to see cases moving from one date to another, from one court to another, from one judge to another and into the recesses of people's memories...

Most people hope that the system will provide them with justice and wait... Some win, some give up and some others continue to wait...There are yet others, who do not want to wait, who have perhaps no hopes in the system, who are impatient and take it upon themselves to right their wrongs...

Justice delayed leads to frightening consequences; creating a society, groups, who take law into their own hands and mete out justice of their own. Justice delayed creates a society which is disillusioned and wherein, the moral fabric is put to tremendous strain. Justice delayed creates the Farhans and the Madhavs of this world.

"Your father was married at this age. He also kept refusing to marry like you and one day I had to literally force it down upon him."

Rajni looked at Sanjay's father mischievously as she said this. "And if you keep refusing," she turned back to Sanjay. "I will do a fast one on you as well. I am old but am still sharp, you know, and have my contacts. You know Kokilaben; she has a smart grand daughter; she is into designing, fashion or something like that and she is pretty too. And then there is ..." and on and on, she went.

Inspite of his annoyance, Sanjay could not but smile. His grandmother was one feisty lady and would not take no for an answer. He would have to find an answer for her fast or she would take upon herself to do the honours.

"Don't smile," snapped Rajni at Sanjay.

"Why are you both not saying anything?" she turned to Sanjay's parents. "You both seem so disinterested."

"*Ba*, things have changed," replied Pooja. "Let us give Sanjay some time; let him establish himself in his field. He has been working only for two years now and needs time to settle. Let him settle down- give him a year or so and then, we will find a bride for him if he does not find one himself."

Rajni sulked and put up a face.

"C'mon my sweet *Dadi*," said Sanjay. "Don't worry; I will get married soon. Don't put up an act."

"By the time you will get married; I will be long gone," retorted Rajni. "Then, how will I hold my great granddaughter!"

"So, that is the issue," replied Sanjay. "And by the way," he continued, "why do you want a great grand daughter and not a son?"

"So that she does not talk back to me like you do. And besides, she will take care of me better in my old age," replied Rajni.

"In your old age!" exclaimed Sanjay. "So how long are you planning to live?"

Rajni was up in a flash and Sanjay had to quickly get on his feet and run, as his grandmother chased him around the house.

It was a Friday and a national holiday. But, Sanjay had been up in the morning and was busy organising the festivities. Since childhood, Sanjay had always been active in the programmes held at his housing colony and even now, inspite of his busy schedule; he made a point to continue with his involvement. It was the country's 51st Republic Day and there was going to be a flag hoisting ceremony, followed by a cultural programme in the forecourt of the apartment. The flag hoisting was now over and Sanjay was trying to regulate the children for the programme, when he got a message on his pager. His first impulse was to read; but he ignored it and continued his work. There was another message ten minutes later, and this time he could not ignore it. It was a message from his boss- "Rush to office; major earthquake in Gujarat."

He had to leave now; he could not ignore the message. He quickly passed the message to his mother and left. The situation was very grim at the office. The earthquake had been massive and it seemed there had been widespread damage and losses to human life. Ahmedabad had also been hit badly and there was no news from many of the staff residing there,other than that the building housing many of them, had collapsed. People were required there urgently both for reporting and also to address the larger humanitarian issues. A five member team had been constituted to rush to Ahmedabad and Sanjay was one of them.

By the time they reached Ahmedabad, it was dusk. The next few days were defining moments in Sanjay's life. Amidst the death, destruction, misery and chaos, he saw a city rising to a person and reaching out. People; young and old, rich and poor, Hindus and Muslims put aside their personal problems and came together. In those dark moments, Sanjay saw innumerable images of courage, sacrifice, resilience and hope. And in those unending days punctuated by despair and exhilaration; he met his future wife. She was one of the hundreds of nameless and unsung volunteers, who worked tirelessly...Something about her- maybe her smiling eyes, her caring words, her unhurried calmness- drew him to her. By the time, Sanjay returned back home- which was nearly a month later; he knew he had met someone who was going to be somebody special in his life. Her name was Nafisa and she was the only daughter of well to do parents. Her father was a famous surgeon and she herself was a teacher in a school for mentally challenged children. Their initial conversations had been mostly on the relief measures being taken and the way forward. Slowly, as time passed, they got to know each other better and by the time Sanjay was ready to get back; it seemed as if they had known each other for a lifetime. They promised to keep in touch and exchanged telephone numbers and addresses.

Back in Mumbai, Sanjay kept in touch with Nafisa- though not as regularly as he would have liked to. He was now twenty seven and had spent four years at work. He was well liked by his peers and superiors in the office and had grown in his professional life. But even in the midst of it all- Sanjay missed Vivek.He was like a brother whom he never had and the only person whom he could talk to freely. Vivek was now working with a leading consultant company in New York and the job kept him travelling most of the times.

They had last met around two years back when Vivek had come on a brief business trip. The rigours of their work meant that they rarely communicated now.

As he sat in his office on a muggy evening, he realised that he had not spoken to Vivek for more than a year. He had not even told him about Nafisa. She occupied a great deal of his thoughts and he wanted to talk to Vivek about her. He was confused on how he should proceed and hoped Vivek could advise him. He felt an immediate urge to talk to Vivek. He looked at his watch; Vivek should be in office, he thought, if he was in town. He smiled as he remembered Vivek's description of his journey to work in the mornings- they were more than 10000 km apart but it was quite similar to his daily morning tryst with the Mumbai suburban system. He located Vivek's mobile number and called him- the call did not seem to be going anywhere. He tried repeatedly with the same result. Damn it; he said to himself, and got up from his seat. He looked up to see a motley crowd around the television at the end of the hall. The crowd was getting larger. Must be the closing stages of a cricket match, he thought. He remembered how he used to track each match until not too long ago; but if it was a cricket match, the atmosphere would be boisterous; which was not.

"Hey, Sanjay!" cried out somebody. "Come here and watch. Those bastards have hit the Twin Towers."

"What? Where?" cried Sanjay and rushed to the TV screen.

And there he saw those replays being shown again and again- the planes striking the towers one after another and the buildings in flames. He stood there standing and staring and then he remembered. He rushed back to his seat and searched for Vivek's visting card and there it was, clear and bold- 99th Floor, North Tower, World Trade Centre, Manhattan,New York.

He stood there looking at the card and started calling the number again and again...He was so immersed that he failed to notice the loud gasp that had emerged from the crowd. He walked slowly back to the TV set to see the sight of the debris and smoke flying around as people ran helter skelter.

"One of the towers has fallen," said somebody.

"Which one is it?" he cried out.

Nobody seemed to know. He again started calling, frantically...The second tower collapsed and Sanjay sank to the ground. He was in a daze; he could hear and see people crowded near him, enquiring. He went blank.

They never found him. He was one of those who went missing- never to return.

Pieces of information started slowly trickling by.Vivek had been in town and had caught the usual morning train to work. The plane had hit the tower very close to his office- very few there had survived. Death must have been instantaneous.

Sanjay was badly shaken up.Vivek's death left him devastated. Although, he had been in touch with Vivek only intermittently since he left Mumbai nearly ten years ago; he had been there,always,acting as a sounding board. He was filled up with a terrible void...In those moments of despair; Nafisa provided solace to his bruised heart.

Nafisa had come to Mumbai for a training programme. She had repeatedly called him but had got no answer. She had got worried and had come to his house. Sanjay was surprised to see her. So were his parents and grandmother. Sanjay was even more surprised at the ease with which she explained about their meeting in Ahmedabad and their subsequent interactions. She was completely at ease and matter of fact.

They met almost daily, and slowly Sanjay felt his spirits rising. Nafisa was filled with an infectious charm that seemed contagious and slowly she filled the void in his heart. They spent hours talking and walking the streets of Mumbai and shared their past and present. They also talked about the future and what it might hold.

The hours and days passed as if in a jiffy and soon Nafisa was gone as quickly as she had come. A new void replaced the old one in Sanjay's heart.

It was a Sunday and they were at the breakfast table. Sanjay had gone to Shivaji Park for a morning jog and was yet to return.

"Pooja," began Suresh. "This girl..."

"You mean, Nafisa," completed Rajni.

"Yeah, whatever..." said Suresh, "What do you think of her?"

"Funny," replied Pooja. "I also wanted to ask you the same question."

"You know," interrupted, Rajni, "if she belonged to our caste, she would be a good wife for Sanjay."

Suresh and Pooja gave each other knowing looks and nodded. It was the same thought which had struck them also.

"She is smart, charming and very respectful too," said Pooja. "And, Sanjay seems so happy with her."

"Yes," replied Suresh. "That is why I am afraid."

"Afraid?" asked Pooja. "But, why should you be?"

"Maybe Sanjay is becoming too close to her; you know what I mean," answered Suresh. "You would not like to have a Muslim bride, will you?"

"*Hai Ram*!" exclaimed Rajni. "What are you saying?"

"She is a good friend of Sanjay and that's all," said Pooja "and I think you are making a mountain out of a molehill."

A couple of kilometres away, Sanjay jogged gently unaware of the storm that was brewing. He felt good and refreshed. He had not come to Shivaji Park for ages now and it felt good to be back. Everything seemed as usual- there was a cricket match going on; children were running as only they can; young and not so young men and women were jogging,strolling,walking; old men and women sat on chairs, talking and laughing- happy to get away from their children, grandchildren...it was as if time had stood still here. As he jogged, he noticed a figure jogging steadily towards him. Something about him seemed familiar and he gave a quick gasp as the man passed him. It was Farhan. Sanjay stood and watched him as the man jogged in a rhythmic manner without stopping around the periphery. Sanjay gave

Farhan a weak smile as he passed by, the next time but it was met by a steely gaze. Sanjay shrugged and continued his relaxed jog across the park, smiling at the children who passed him by. How innocent they look, he thought. How innocent and cheerful- as if they had no cares in the world...They made him feel happy.

By the time he reached home, he was ravished and ready to pounce on his breakfast.

The family had finished their breakfast but was still at the table.

Pooja kept his breakfast in front of him.

"You look happy," said Rajni interrupting the silence.

Sanjay looked up at his grandmother with raised eyebrows. He knew that tone. His grandmother was leading up to something and he wondered what?

"Yes," replied Sanjay. "It was nice to go back to Shivaji Park after such a long time."

"Hmm!" said Rajni.

"You don't seem to be convinced *Dadi*," said Sanjay. "Out with it, what do you want?"

"You aren't thinking of marrying that girl, are you, the Muslim girl, your friend," blurted Rajni.

The question caught Sanjay by surprise. He looked around. His father was observing him from the top of the newspaper and his mother from the kitchen, where she had gone to get him his tea.

He smiled and replied, "But you wanted me to get married, did you not and Nafisa is a nice girl, is she not?"

He could feel his parents' eyes boring into him as he said this.

"But, she is a Muslim," remarked Rajni.

"So..." retorted Sanjay.

"*Arey*, you can't be serious," said Rajni, her voice raising now. "Why don't you understand? We are Brahmins, vegetarians and they...

Suresh, Pooja, why don't you tell this boy something? That is why I have been after you both to get him married off, but you people did not do anything and now look what it has led to. We will soon have a Muslim girl in our house as Sanjay's wife. My God! Please take me away..."

"Calm down will you," answered Sanjay. "I have no intention of making Nafisa my wife. I was only pulling your leg."

"I do not know," said Rajni getting up.

She pulled the newspaper from Suresh's hand.

"You better find a bride for Sanjay soon, before..."and she stomped off.

There was an uncomfortable silence.Pooja came from the kitchen and gave him his tea.

She touched him gently on the shoulder and said, "You have a wise head on your shoulder, so I trust whatever decision you take, will be good for you and all of us."

Rajni's attempts to find a bride became more vigorous. Sanjay was bombarded with photographs and details of girls... He could no longer postpone the decision.

The thought of marrying Nafisa had never really seriously crossed his mind but as the days progressed, he started thinking more and more about it. He did not know how Nafisa felt about him and was perplexed and confused on what he should do.

And, then fate intervened. A train full of pilgrims caught fire in Godhra. Rumours flew fast and the orgy of violence began in Ahmedabad.

Sanjay tried desperately to call Nafisa but there was no reply. He knew from his Ahmedabad office that the situation was bad. It was Bombay all over again.

And then he made his decision; he would go. His parents and grandmother were upset, but he was not willing to change his decision. His office made the arrangements and Pooja and Rajni watched with a growing sense of unease as they saw the car carrying him turn the corner and go away from sight. All they could do was to pray.

Sanjay arrived at Ahmedabad nearly two years after he had left. The city was in similar condition to what he had seen that evening, when he had arrived earlier- chaos, confusion and misery. But, there was an added dimension this time- fear. The atmosphere was unreal,all around the city; fires were burning, the streets were littered with stones and burnt vehicles. He went straight to the building where Nafisa lived with her parents. The house was locked and nobody was willing to talk. The atmosphere was filled with distrust, hate and fear. The camaraderie he had seen during his last visit was nowhere to be seen. Sanjay felt powerless and lost. He had reached the end of the tunnel and there seemed to be no light at its end. He started to walk out of the building when the watchman came up to him.

"Are you looking for Dr. Ghafoor?" he asked, referring to Nafisa's father

"Yes," said Sanjay eagerly.

"They are good people, Dr. *Saab* has helped so many people but there was nobody willing to help them," said the watchman.

Sanjay's face frowned in worry.

The watchman continued, "There was a rumour that a mob was going to attack the Muslims here - the society had an emergency meeting and told Dr.*Saab* and the other Muslim families, to leave as they did not want trouble in the building. These families pleaded that the children and women be allowed to stay. Some of the members agreed but our secretary and president did not. There were three families; they left in two cars. Dr. *Saab* said he would go to the Old city to the orphanage, where he provides free medical service.

"Do you have the address?" asked Sanjay eagerly.

"I do not have the address," replied the watchman, "but I can tell you where it lies."

He explained the location to Sanjay who noted the details.

"Are you going there?" asked the watchman.

"Yes," replied Sanjay.

“It is a Muslim area. It could be dangerous for you,” he warned him.

Sanjay nodded and moved on. It was now dark and Sanjay decided to suspend his search for the day.

He was up in the morning at daybreak. A few auto rickshaws were plying- after repeated attempts, he managed to get one which would take him close to the orphanage. The driver drove skillfully avoiding the troubled areas and dropped him at the location, he had promised.Sanjay paid the driver and thanked him. Now he was on his own. Sanjay had never felt so much distrust at his fellow human beings as he walked in the shadows of the buildings and shops. There were very few passersby and Sanjay could feel their nervous glances as they passed by. Eventually, he reached the orphanage without any incident.

After repeated knocking, a young man opened the door.

He looked at Sanjay suspiciously and said “What do you want, please go away” and started closing the door.

“Please don’t close,” pleaded Sanjay. “I came to meet Nafisa, she is Dr. Ghafoor’s daughter; we are friends. I want to meet them.”

“No...”said the young man. “We don’t have anybody here. Please go away.”

“Trust me,” said Sanjay and thrust his identity card at the man.

“I am a reporter. Show this to Nafisa, please...”

The young man took a look at the card and said, “Wait here” and shut the door.

Sanjay waited; in the distance, he could hear sounds. The sounds were getting louder- people were running, stones were being thrown. He knocked again at the door,repeatedly.

It seemed like two groups were fighting. He could see the retreating group being followed by another. He had no place to hide, he had to get in quickly, or he would be caught in the crossfire.

The door opened abruptly and he was pulled in.

He blinked his eyes; it was dark and he could hardly see anything. He was led to a small room and told to wait. After about five minutes, Nafisa came in, followed by an elderly gentleman- whom he presumed to be her father. Nafisa smiled weakly at him.

"Nafisa has told me about you," said Dr. Ghafoor as he extended his hand. "But, what brings you here, young man? As you can see, it's not safe..."

"I tried to call up Nafisa many times...I did not get any reply, I became worried and I came..." he concluded lamely.

Nafisa's father smiled.

"The courage or rather the foolishness of youth," he sighed.

They could hear the sounds outside; a battle seemed to be raging.

"Now that you have seen us; you should leave at the earliest. This is not a safe place," said Dr. Ghafoor.

"I came here not to come and look but to take you all to Mumbai," he blurted.

The old man nodded his head.

"Don't be a fool," he said "and why should I come there? It will be all right here in a few days time and we will go home."

The sounds outside had reduced; it seemed as if the mob had passed by.

"I beg of you, to come with me. You can come back after a few days- when it is safe," replied Sanjay.

"But why, should we come with you? Who are you but an acquaintance of Nafisa? Leave us and go away." The old man was getting angry now.

"But why can't we go away with him, *Abba*!" pleaded Nafisa. "He has come this far to save us..."

"But how can he take us to safety?" asked Dr.Ghafoor. "Not only will he get killed, but he will also get us killed."

"Don't worry about that," said Sanjay. "I will manage to get a vehicle from my office..."

"Wait!" Dr.Ghafoor said and went inside.

He came back this time with a lady.

"This is my mother," introduced Nafisa.

The lady smiled "You are a brave man. You have taken lot of trouble to come and meet us; but we don't want to burden you further."

"No, no..." said Sanjay.

"I came so far to meet you and take you; don't disappoint me.," he pleaded.

The discussions went on and on.

"OK..." said the doctor, at last reluctantly.

Sanjay did not know how or why he had made the decision to take them with him to Mumbai. It had been a decision made there and then. As had been his decision that if at all he would marry anyone, it would be Nafisa. He did not know whether she reciprocated his feelings, but then he would cross the bridge later.

The next few hours were extremely trying for Sanjay. He had made a promise and now he had to fulfill it. After repeated telephone calls and anxious hours of waiting, a car was arranged with police escort.

They landed at Mumbai in the early hours of the morning.

The journey through the streets of Ahmedabad had been harrowing; they had seen houses, shops and cars burning everywhere. A mob had even chased them inspite of the police vehicle escorting them. They had felt unsafe in the train also and sat there expecting the worst...

Sanjay ran on the railway platform. The mob was after him- they were getting closer. He was panting and gasping; he had to run faster or they would catch him. He saw an over bridge and started running towards it. He started climbing the stairs and was nearly at the top when he looked up. They were waiting for him there also. He was trapped; he shouted...

The noise grew shriller and shriller and Pooja got up with a jerk from her sleep. The door bell was ringing. She looked at the watch. It was four in the morning. Early morning dreams they said often came true. She folded her hands and prayed. The door bell rang again.

"Who could it be?" she thought.

She went upto the door and opened it. Sanjay stood there with a smile on his face.

She clasped him violently to her chest and cried.

After the initial shock of seeing Sanjay and Nafisa and her family had worn away; Sanjay narrated the happenings of the last two days to his family.

Nafisa and her parents had been apologetic over their sudden appearance but Pooja made them comfortable and made them feel at home. She hurriedly emptied the guest room and took their belongings there.

Over the course of the next two days; they watched, in horror, at the news from Gujarat.

At the end of the third day, Nafisa's father approached Suresh and thanked him for all the help but told them that they would like to move to a hotel as they had caused enough trouble. Suresh refused and said that as long as they remained in Mumbai, the house was theirs.

Days and weeks passed and it seemed normalcy had finally arrived in Ahmedabad. The other Muslim families had returned back to the building where Nafisa and her family lived and Dr. Ghafoor decided it was time to go back home.

Sanjay and Nafisa had drawn closer to each other, even more during these weeks. One evening as they sat in Shivaji Park, watching little children running and playing; Sanjay popped the question. Nafisa seemed a bit surprised, but smiled.

They sat in silence for some time.

"You have not answered my question," said Sanjay.

"If you had not asked the question in a couple of day's time; I would have asked you," replied Nafisa with a smile.

"Then, why did you become so quiet?" asked Sanjay.

"I was thinking," replied Nafisa, "about our families. It will be a shock to my family. My parents have been asking me about you and I have been giving them the slip."

"Yes, that also worries me," replied Sanjay. "I do not know how my family will also react. They have been sounding me out on this and will certainly not be happy. Our families are both educated and modern, but a Hindu-Muslim marriage, that will be the stuff of their nightmares."

Inter-religion marriages are still the exception in India, as elsewhere in the world. So are inter-caste or inter-community marriages. Language, community, caste, region, religion; not in any particular order, continue to be the highest common factors for marriage. Marriage outside these boundaries are still frowned upon and deemed not quite kosher. It's ok as long as you have friends from any community, race, religion, etc;but marriage is still a no-no...Numerous reasons are quoted, depending on which side you are- they eat only grass, their kitchen stinks- they eat only fish, they worship- God knows, how many Gods, they think their God is the greatest, they are un clean, they eat with their hands, they bury their dead, they burn their dead ,they speak in a language which sounds like gibberish, they drink wine all the time, they have loose morals, they are dumb, they are lazy, they are cunning, they keep weapons in their houses, they don't wash their hair... and so on.

How can we live with them? There will be chaos, the children born out of these marriages will have no identity, what will happen to our customs, our traditions and on and on and on...

Us vs. them--the battle rages on...

Sanjay's and Nafisa's families were also watching with concern the growing friendship of their children and their worst fears came true one evening.They were sitting together in the drawing room after dinner finalising travel plans for the departure of Nafisa and her family when

Sanjay said, he had something to announce. As everybody watched in astonishment; he said that he wanted to marry Nafisa.The elders looked at each other in shock. Nafisa nodded her head and said she also agreed with Sanjay.

All hell broke loose. The families spent the entire evening and night trying to threaten, persuade, entreat, and plead with their respective children without much progress.

An uncomfortable silence prevailed in the house the next day, and the Ghafoor family left for Ahmedabad, a day later- leaving many a question unanswered.

Life went on in the Dave family. It was as if nothing had happened, nobody spoke about it. Sanjay bore the reaction stoically, but still kept in touch with Nafisa.The reaction of her family had been similar and the story of their flight from Ahmedabad and return was a closed chapter.

Sanjay still hoped for a change in hearts but as the days progressed; his hopes started fading. Also, there was so much happening in the city and elsewhere making life in office so hectic that he had barely time to think.

Rajni could not bear to see her grandson's face. He seemed to have taken their decision calmly but he had changed and the change had affected the entire household. It was not a change which Rajni liked- everybody seemed to be walking on an emotional tightrope and it was only a matter of time before somebody tipped over. She had to do something to bring the situation back to normal. She broached the subject with Pooja, one evening, as they sat on the balcony watching the setting sun.

"Pooja,"she said, "we are loosing him, he is becoming a stranger."

Pooja looked at her and burst into tears. She could not control herself any longer.

"*Ba*, I want my son to be happy," she said, amidst her sobbing. "It breaks my heart to see him like this."

"We need to talk to him and make him understand," replied Rajni.

"But, he has made up his mind," answered Pooja. "And, I don't want him to change his mind just to please us."

"But..." said Rajni, "Nafisa is a nice girl and understanding; but she is a Muslim! How can we live together- they are so different..."

And, so the conversation went on.

Suresh joined them but mostly sat in silence.

"I think this is not getting us anywhere," said Suresh abruptly. "We have seen, haven't we that Sanjay has been stubborn and unrelenting about certain things in his life- his education, job and we have had to finally give in."

"I think," he paused, "this is again one such instance and we have no other choice."

"But..." began Rajni.

"Enough!" said Suresh. "I do not want any further discussion on it. Pooja, tell Sanjay to fix a date when we can meet Nafisa's parents."

Sanjay hugged his mother as she conveyed the news to him.

"Thank you Mummy," he said.

An hour later he was on the phone with Nafisa; who was overjoyed. Now, she had to convince her parents. Slowly she was able to bring around her mother; but her father remained obstinate. She had always seen her father yielding to her requests and tantrums very easily, and now she was surprised and saddened to see him remain obdurate.

Sanjay was getting impatient and was at his wit's end. His father came to his rescue again.

"Let's go and meet them and let it be a surprise," he said. And then he added with a smile, "It will be very difficult for someone to refuse a guest..."

The late night revellers were still returning home, when the Daves came out of the station.

The *Garba* season in Gujarat had begun.

The word "Garba" originates from the word "garbo," which is an earthen pot with holes and a small lamp inside. For this reason, many traditional garbas are performed around a central lit earthenware lamp. Traditionally, either the lamp or an image of the Goddess is placed in the middle, around which people dance in concentric circles. For nine nights, much of Gujarat becomes a huge dancing arena in which young and old, rich and poor dance to their hearts content. It is also an occasion, when romance is in the air and many a heart is broken when Cupid strikes...

Dr. Ghafoor had just completed his morning prayers when the door bell rang. He walked unhurriedly to the door and opened it. He stood there still, for what seemed like hours but was barely a few seconds. He quickly recovered from his shock and welcomed the Daves and showed them inside. His wife, Lateefa had joined them, in the meantime.

Suresh and Pooja apologised profusely for this sudden intrusion to which they responded by saying, they were hounoured to have them as guests. After some small talk, the conversation started becoming stilted and heavy.

Nafisa's mother went to the kitchen saying she would get some tea followed by Pooja.

"I do not see Nafisa anywhere," began Suresh.

"Oh," replied Dr. Ghafoor, "she has gone for a morning walk, she is very particular about it."

"Yes, yes, I remember, now. " said Suresh.

There was another period of uncomfortable, small talk.

Pooja and Lateefa came in with a tray of biscuits and tea.

"You must be wondering," began Suresh, "why we have suddenly appeared. You must have even guessed. Anyway, I thought it was time to stop playing this cat and mouse game" he paused "with our children. It's their life and let's not play God with them. We have come here to ask for your daughter's hand. Let us assure you we will take good care of her; please do not disappoint us."

Dr. Ghafoor looked at Suresh. He began to say something and then stopped. His wife looked at him with a pleading eye.

At that moment, the door opened and Nafisa walked in. She just stood and stared not believing what she saw.

Pooja broke the silence.

"You look as if you have just seen a ghost," she said. "Come here and sit, we are for real."

Everybody smiled.

"Yes, Dr. *Saab*," began Suresh. "I know how difficult it is for you, but please..."

Sanjay had never seen his father talking in this tone before and felt a great wave of warmth towards him.

"I have nothing against you and your family especially, Sanjay," began Dr. Ghafoor "Infact, I am deeply obliged and grateful to Sanjay for saving our lives. The orphanage in which we had taken shelter was attacked only a few hours after we escaped, and the people there were killed in cold blood. For this, I will remain indebted to Sanjay all my life. And that is why; I do not want this marriage. Our society, our environment is heartless –and I am afraid, Sanjay and Nafisa will face great hardships. I do not want; I cannot bear to see them suffer. How will they, their children survive in an atmosphere of hatred and animosity, where people do not even hesitate to kill their neighbours and friends in the name of religion. I am a religious person; I don't miss my prayers- as you have seen when we were in Mumbai; but violence, murder—this is not what my religion preaches and I am sure this is not what your religion preaches too. I do not want your and my children to be caught in the politics of religion."

There was a period of silence as they all pondered.

Pooja again broke the silence "Dr. *Saab*, I think our wait is going to be long;

Luckily, it's *Garba* time in Ahmedabad and I think its going to be great fun."

And they all burst into laughter.

Over the period of the next two days, they had several discussions. The balance tipped from one side to another and finally, Dr. Ghafoor gave up.

The marriage took place, a month later in Mumbai; it was a quiet affair attended by family and close friends. Nafisa quickly adjusted to her new family, and life in the Dave household returned back to normal.

Mumbai was heating up- summer was setting in, political tempers were on a high as general elections drew close and public anger was seething as the Government seemed unable to identify the culprits or stop the frequent terrorist attacks.

It was back to business for Sanjay.

The General elections got over and now it was the turn of the Assembly elections. Sanjay had been on the campaign trail for the past one month and was getting sick hearing the platitudes of the candidates. It was the last day of the campaign and he was waiting to meet one Madhav Karve- a builder and an upcoming politician. He wanted to complete the interview and get away. He needed a break...

He waited and waited in the hot sun. Madhav was supposed to address a rally and then talk to him for about ten minutes. Soon there was a roar from the crowd- the leader had arrived; albeit two hours late. Sanjay waited near the leader's car, away from the rally ground. The interview was scheduled in the car on their way to the next rally, which was a few kilometres away. The speech began and the crowd slowly started stirring from slumber. At this distance, Sanjay could barely see the man whom he had come to interview. He could hear his voice echoing; he was a young man and seemed to be in fine spirits. The voice rose in a crescendo and the crowd cheered. The crowd cheered several times and after what seemed an eternity, the meeting drew to a close. Dusk was falling as the leader led by his security men, slowly started moving towards the car. A couple of them along with his secretary came upto the car- Sanjay showed his identity card and was told to wait. At last Madhav approached the car and got in. His secretary motioned Sanjay to step inside and get into the front seat. Sanjay got in and the car started moving. The leader was still waving to the milling crowds outside and Sanjay waited patiently.

They soon passed the crowds and into the main road and Madhav finally turned, looked at Sanjay, smiled and said, "You have five minutes."

Sanjay could not remember much of the conversation later; in fact, he could remember nothing of the conversation. All he could remember was that face- it was a face from the recesses of his memory. He was not so sure....It had been so long ago- another age and time...Could it be the same man who had led that murderous attack? He appeared to be; there was something in his swagger and looks which reminded him of that boy. But, again, he was not sure; he needed to find out.

But, first he needed a break; Nafisa and he had not gone for a proper holiday...

They arrived at Ranikhet after a torturous bus ride from the station where the narrow gauge train had deposited them. A sparkling stream had accompanied the train during the end of their journey and Nafisa and Sanjay had felt invigorated by the air. They could see the mountains in the distance and were feeling as excited as a pair of children.However, by the time they arrived at Ranikhet, they felt as if they were dying. It was their first trip upto the mountains and they had been retching and groaning all the way in a bus which looked like dropping into the mountains at every curve. They had been cursing Raj, a colleague of Sanjay, who had suggested the obscure hill station.

Hill Stations, remnants of an era gone by and a legacy of the British Raj. There are today more than sixty of them dotting the hills all across the country. It was here that the British retreated when the plains became too hot to handle and it was here that they built a piece of their motherland. A home away from home...

Today, they are swamped by the great Indian middle class, who rush in noisily at every available occasion and fill in the air with the latest Bollywood songs and the hills and valleys with truckloads of junk food.

Yet, these hill stations survive, and some of them still retain that quaint charm of a bygone age.Ranikhet which literally means Queens meadow was established as the Headquarters of the Kumaon regiment in the late 19th century and is one of those lucky few.

After walking up from an exhausted slumber; Sanjay and Nafisa felt refreshed and famished. They walked upto the restaurant and ordered. The old man there said they would be served in fifteen minutes and suggested they wait in the lawns. They walked out to the lawns and stood there transfixed- the Himalayas loomed there like a picture postcard framed in the horizon. It was the most beautiful sight that they had seen...

They spent their holiday lazing around and reluctantly left a week later back to the heat and dust of Mumbai.

The holiday had recharged Sanjay's batteries and he was back to work with a vengeance.

During the holidays, he had been tempted to tell Nafisa about the incident during the Mumbai riots and his chance meeting with the politician. But somehow he had not. Now, back at work, he was determined to find out more about the politician, Madhav Karve. A couple of weeks of diligent research painted a picture of the man- A powerful builder, a part time politician, a student leader, trouble monger- a man with extreme views on the minority community but with no police records. There were rumours; again only rumours that he had ruthlessly eliminated people who had come in his way; that he had been involved in riots...but there had been no eyewitness.

As he sifted through the life of Madhav; Sanjay was more and more convinced that he was the boy he had been searching for.But, now, it was only his word and his memories against this man; he needed something more tenable in the eyes of the law.

Days, weeks and months passed. Life went on- Sanjay's father had retired, Nafisa had taken up job in a nearby school, his mother continued her social work while his grandmother now clamoured for a great grandchild. Sanjay had also grown up in his professional career and was now a News editor, but something deep within him rankled. All his efforts to find a lead had led him to a blank wall and it appeared that he had come to the end of the road.

And, then one day, suddenly, a new road opened up, or so it seemed....

He had finished a luncheon meeting with an advertising agency and was returning back to his office. As he walked along, he suddenly realised that he was walking past the college where Farhan was a professor and felt a sudden urge to go inside the college. He wanted to see Farhan and talk to him- probably, that would reduce the guilt which had built up deep within him. He walked in slowly, looking at the surroundings. Groups of young men and women were there, everywhere, full of life, talking and laughing animatedly. He suddenly wished he was one of them...He walked up the portico and into the building. The voice came loud and angry- it was that of Farhan and he was talking to a young, smartly dressed man. Snatches of the conversation came to him...

Money, blackmail, secrets.

He was puzzled and then the young man rushed passed him. Sanjay turned and looked back and saw Farhan; he wanted to talk to him, but suddenly saw him also rush out into the street. Sanjay followed in his heels. He seemed to be searching for the young man; Sanjay's eyes followed his as he also started looking for this mystery man. And then he saw somebody whom he least expected, Madhav. He was standing beside the art gallery, opposite the college and was looking agitated; he seemed to be waiting for some body.

Things now happened too fast and Sanjay watched in amazement, trying to assimilate what he was seeing. He saw the animated discussion between the young man and Madhav and the shock and surprise on Farhan's face. He had to take some decisions fast; Farhan had stumbled back inside the college, Madhav stood there undecided not knowing what to do while the mystery man moved away quickly. There was only one course of action; he had to follow this unknown man who seemed to be the link. He crossed the road and started following him. The man was walking very fast and Sanjay had to run to keep pace with him. They hurtled through the seething mass of people and into a bigger cauldron- Churchgate Station. It was now becoming extremely difficult for Sanjay to keep track and he was afraid he would loose his man, any moment. The man was moving fast along one of the platforms and then he suddenly swerved and got into a train .The train started to move and Sanjay started running. The train seemed to be gaining speed but suddenly he found himself in the compartment- unseen hands had pulled him in. He stood there near the doorway, panting and staring at the man who had led him on this chase and who had apparently pulled him in. There was a hint of a smile on his face- Sanjay would remember the smile long after.

"That's not a smart thing to do," said the man. "You could have slipped and fallen. You could have waited, there are so many trains."

Sanjay nodded; he did not know what to say. The train moved on faster.

"Thank you," said Sanjay suddenly, remembering. "I am Sanjay. I am a reporter"

"Oh!" said the other man, "A reporter. That's interesting. What do you report?"

"Anything of interest for the common man, anything that is of concern to society," answered Sanjay.

The other man nodded. They had reached a station and people were getting in.

The train started moving again.

"And, what do the people do; I mean after reading your reports," asked the man.

"Do?" asked Sanjay. "I really don't know, but they are better informed, I guess." He paused and continued, "We, our reports also bring out the wrongs in society and sometimes helps in punishing the guilty."

The other man laughed, aloud.

"Nonsense," he said.

He came closer to Sanjay now; his face hardened. The train was moving fast now and for an instant, Sanjay felt an inexplicable fear.

“You must have reported on the riots, have you not?” he asked harshly.

Sanjay nodded.

“Has anyone been punished?” he asked.

“But, they are trying,” said Sanjay lamely.

“How long will they try?” asked the man. “Are they serious? Do you think the people have any faith? Do you think they will continue to wait hoping for justice? No, they will not. As you said, the guilty have to be punished.”

The man’s face suddenly softened and the smile was back on his face.

“I know a few things, on the riots” he said, “and if you are serious, I can tell you more.”

Sanjay felt his pulse racing; he was onto something now.

“But not today,” smiled the other man. “I am in a hurry. I shall contact you later.”

Sanjay pushed his card into his hand as the train slowed down and the man jumped out at Grant Road Station. The train started moving again; Sanjay was tempted to get down and follow the man. Perhaps, the other man sensed it. He called out, “Don’t try to jump out- there may not be anybody to catch your hand,” and he was gone in a blur.

The next few days were excruciating- as Sanjay waited for a call. And then it came suddenly, when he was at the dinner table. He excused himself and went out.

“Tomorrow at 3 pm at Grant Road Station. I shall be waiting for you,” and the voice went silent.

Sanjay called up again at the number- it was a public call office, the voice at the other end reported that the previous caller had gone immediately.

He waited at the station till ten at night, but nobody turned up. He left with a disappointed heart. He was so close but so far. He waited for the phone call; it never came. A month went by. He grew worried. Had something happened to this man? He scanned the newspapers for any accidents or murders and then something caught his eye. An un identified man's body had been found on the railway tracks. It was the same day he had talked to the man. It seemed like an accident but the police had found some stab wounds. A few enquiries confirmed that the police were investigating, but had no leads; and yes, nobody had claimed the body. It was still lying in the mortuary.

Sanjay had gone to many mortuaries in his reporting career but he still dreaded going into one. The foul mouthed attendant at the mortuary took him along. He seemed to be drunk and did not seem to be sure of where he was going. The doctor had assured him that the man knew his job well and would show him the body. Suddenly, he stopped in front of a table where a body lay covered with a cloth. The man removed the cloth with a flourish. Sanjay looked. It was him, even in death; he seemed to have a smile on his face.

A road had opened but it had lead Sanjay to a blind end. He had now more questions, but very few answers. He started probing further; even going to the extent of tailing Farhan and Madhav, but nothing remarkable emerged. He was becoming desperate and this had started affecting his behaviour; he had started becoming irritated and snappy both at work and home. Nafisa could feel the change and was troubled. Something was affecting her husband but she did not know what. Her repeated attempts to draw him out into conversation, got him more irritated. Sanjay had always been a sound sleeper, but the last few weeks, she had found him tossing and turning and muttering in his sleep. And then one night, she got up suddenly to find her husband screaming in his sleep- he was shouting at someone to let go. She wanted to shake him and wake him up. But something stopped her and she watched her husband's face in the darkness of the room lit by the moonlight, which came streaming in. She could see the agony on that face and amidst the ramblings and screaming- two names kept coming, Madhav and Farhan.And then it stopped, as if nothing had happened. Nafisa could barely sleep that night. She thought about it again and again the whole day and decided she had to confront Sanjay that night.

They had retired to bed around eleven as usual. They usually read for some time before going to sleep. She could feel Sanjay beside her and knew the time had come now.

She asked the question quite innocuously-"Who is this Madhav and Farhan?"

Sanjay turned; she could see the shock on his face. It was as if somebody had seen his mind and soul.

They barely slept that night. Nafisa held him closely and comforted him. After the initial shock and reluctance; Sanjay opened up. Nafisa could feel the pain as he narrated the story. They talked and talked...

Sanjay felt better; it was as if a great burden had been lifted from his shoulders. He was not close to any of the answers but sharing his feelings with Nafisa had made him feel better.

"I want to tell you something," said Nafisa a few days later.

It was morning and they had just got up.

"Yes," said Sanjay.

She blushed.

"What's the matter?" asked Sanjay. "I have never seen you blushing like that."

"Well..." she began.

"Come on, out with it!" said Sanjay.

"You are going to be a father," she blurted.

Sanjay stared; he did not know how to react.

"Does everyone know?" he asked.

"No, I thought you should know first," she replied.

That day and the next few days and weeks went off in a blur, as Sanjay tried to register the news. He was going to be a father...

One night as they were going to bed, Nafisa suddenly asked him.

"Have you found out anything?"

Sanjay blinked.

"Found out what?" he replied.

"You know, those two men..."she said.

Sanjay suddenly felt guilty. He had done nothing these few weeks He had been so overjoyed with the good news, he had nearly forgotten. He had to start again.

Enquiries revealed that the police had still no clue on the death of the man- who seemed to hold the link between Sanjay and Madhav. He had no choice but to wait and watch...

As Sanjay waited and watched; Farhan and Madhav plotted against each other. Nearly twenty years after they had been brought together on a warm February afternoon, they were again being pulled into a net, which seemed to be drawing close.

Dear readers, here, we must pause and look back. Look back at the lives of these men, not very young now, in their mid-thirties; ravaged by time. Born, within a few days of each other and within a stone's throw; but pulled in different directions. Grown up in the same country, in the same city; but they could have been as well living in different planets altogether. Each with a vision of their future, their country; completely different from the other. So divergent, so polarised...

❀❀❀

CHAPTER-IV

The day after

Farhan, Madhav, Sanjay

Farhan smiled again, wiped the sweat from his brow and walked away from the shrill cries of the marching brigade- as he liked to call them.His plan was taking shape very nicely. All that was now needed was to tie up the loose strings. He was doing it alone this time and therefore could not afford to look at the big picture only. He needed to get into the details and he was also discovering now, that the devil was in the details. He missed Salim sorely as he had always delegated all the planning and execution to him but he was learning it the hard way now. He reached home and sat down. And suddenly the tiredness hit him. It came like a huge gust of wind and knocked him over. He felt tired-very,very tired and drained out. He wanted to go into a slumber and not wake up at all. He wanted to end it all. He lay on the sofa and looked around. The photo of his family by the lamp had become smudged with time. He could barely make out the features; it seemed ages back. He had tried to avenge their deaths; destroy the people, the country- which had stood mutely. But, where was it leading to, he thought. He had plotted the death of a few hundreds, created some amount of chaos,fear –but nothing seemed to have changed. He seemed to be fighting a losing battle. He knew there were others like him fighting their own battles. But, a lifetime seemed too less for this battle...

His eyes moved on and fell on the dagger Salim had gifted him- the dagger with which he had killed him. It lay on the same spot. He had not even cleaned the blood which had dried and matted up. It seemed to lie there mocking him. He could now see Salim sitting there, beside the dagger- the smile playing on his lips. He seemed to be nodding his head in disapproval. And then, the image was gone and so was his tiredness. He got up- he had a job to do.

And, then his eyes went onto the card that lay near the dagger. He had emptied Salim's pockets that fateful evening before disposing of the body. He had not got much, except for a card- it seemed to be that of a journalist. He had toyed with the card many times wondering who it was and his connection with Salim. He had felt tempted to find out, but had let it go. He looked at the card; the address was somewhere near his college. The Christmas vacations were on but he had a couple of things to tie up before he embarked on his plan. He decided he would find out more today...

□□□

Madhav walked up and went to the window and looked out. That idiot had tried to tail him but he had not seen him for the past month. But that did not matter; he knew where he lived and it was a matter of time, before he finished him off. He could have easily got it over by now; but he wanted to do it himself and savour the feeling. There was nothing like seeing a man cower and beg for one's life and see the terror on his face when he looked at his impending death. He felt close to God at such times. Infact, he corrected himself; he felt like God-deciding the fates of those puny mortals. But playing God, had to wait for now.

He had other important matters on hand. It was a chance for him to get back into active politics. Since his loss in the elections; he had withdrawn more and more from party affairs to concentrate on his work. He also felt slighted that his party did not offer him any inducement to carry on and seemed to have forgotten his past contributions.

Besides, his party was in the opposition in both the centre and the state. But, Madhav still harboured ambitions of making it big in politics and the ruling party's overtures to him, over the last year, had secretly pleased him. He had been non-committal but the latest offer of fielding him as a candidate for a parliamentary constituency, which had fallen vacant, seemed too good to refuse. An emissary from Delhi was coming and a meeting had been arranged that evening. He had thought about it a great deal- he did not like this party with their constant platitudes and their servile attitude towards Muslims. They were wooing them always and talked as if they were their guardians. He did not like their repeated emphasis on catchwords like communalism and secularism. In fact, he hated them and would have liked to wring the necks of many of the leaders. But he had to play along- he could not wait for his party; he was in a hurry to make it big.

But before that, he was giving a newspaper interview- he had earlier also had interactions with the press –but they were during his campaign, and they were all done in a hurry and were more as a party spokesperson than about himself. This one was about him and him alone and his meteoric rise as one of the city's eminent builders. Madhav smiled- his uncle would have been very proud. He would pay a quick visit to the flat at Worli to pay his respects, before leaving for the interview. His uncle's flat was his temple and his uncle's spirit the presiding deity.

□□□

The interview was scheduled over luncheon at a five star hotel in Marine Drive.

The fish had fallen for the bait. It had not been difficult for Sanjay to entice Madhav for the interview- in fact, it had been too easy.

Sanjay had become tired of waiting and watching,when this brainwave for an interview came to him. But once he had fixed the interview, he suddenly felt panicky. He did not know where the interview would lead him to. What if Madhav discovered that he had witnessed the carnage? What if he blurted out something foolish? So many ifs and buts...

He wanted to discuss with Nafisa but could not. She would get worried and he did not want to let that happen. She had even asked him a couple of times whether he had any leads and each time he had led the conversation in some other direction.

At times, he wondered what he was trying to do and where this would lead to.

The voice, somewhere above, somewhere in his head was telling him to forget about it and get on with life.

"Even the courts of law seemed to have forgotten." it told him; "Why are you bothered? What are you trying to prove? That you are an honest, upright citizen! Do you think the Govt. is going to reward you with a "Param Vir Chakra" or engrave your name in letters of gold. Hey, you have a family to take care- he and his people are powerful, they will simply knock you off? And then what happens to your wife-a widow at this age and your child- your unborn child...C'mon grow up."

The voice was becoming shriller and more insistent.

At these times, he felt that he should stop and simply forget.

But, forget he could not- there was this other voice- a softer one- it seemed to be coming from somewhere inside him-which kept reminding him. Reminding him of that balmy afternoon when he saw a vibrant family getting destroyed and a young boy crying out in pain...

"But!" said the other voice; the shriller one, "even the boy has forgotten so don't be a fool!"

"No, no..." said the softer voice, "Don't you remember that day your grandfather stood before a mob- all alone and defended him. You admired him for that- that gave you courage that day to lift the boy and take him to a hospital while others looked the other way. That still gives you the courage to move on. Do not falter ...Not now."

And the soft but persistent voice had won- at least for now.

□□□

Sanjay had taken a stroll from his office to the coffee shop, at the five star hotel and was there sharp at twelve o' clock waiting for Madhav. He stared outside at the vast expanse of Marine Drive.

Marine Drive, commonly referred as the Netaji Subhash Road is a three kilometre long road overlooking the Arabian sea- with a promenade, beach, cricket-stadium, restaurants, five star hotels and homes for quite a few celebrities.

It is Mumbai's Madison Square, Champ de Elysees and Trafalgar Square rolled into one. It's here where you will find the cities rich and famous- dining, partying and striking business deals; the old and not so old walking, jogging, whiling away on the promenade; the middle class Mumbaite having a gala time eating away with his family on the sands of the Chowpatthy Beach; bus loads of tourists gawking away and taking in the sights incredulously and trying to capture as much as they can on their cameras and mobile phones and couples- so many of them, muttering sweet nothings to each other- as only they can; barely separated from other couples by a couple of feet.

In short, a place which best epitomises the spirit of Mumbai- vibrant, jazzy, attractive and alive. Alive...that is what makes Mumbai tick. And that is what, perhaps, best epitomes this country as a whole...Alive and shouting and kicking away as a new born child inspite of being weighed down by its history and the never ending problems...

Sanjay had not noticed the slightly built bespectacled man following him at a distance; the man who was the reason why he was sitting here.

Farhan had arrived at the newspaper office indicated in the visting card but there his courage failed him. He could not think of any excuse for meeting Sanjay- as the name on the card indicated. He could wait in the lobby till he came out but then, how would he recognise him. And then an idea struck him.

He walked upto the receptionist.

"Yes," she said, looking through him.

"I want to meet Sanjay Dave, I think he works here," he ventured hesitantly.

"Do you have an appointment?" she answered, still disinterested.

"No, no...I mean I want to meet him but not really meet him, you see," ended Farhan tamely.

She looked at him now, a trifle irritated.

"I do not understand what you mean," she snapped.

"I should have explained," began Farhan. "Sanjay and I were classmates in school- we were the best of friends. But, I left Mumbai, when I was in school and I lost touch with him. But, the internet, it's a great thing; it got us back in touch a year back."

He could see from the expression on her face that she was getting bored.

"He does not know I am here," he continued. "I wanted to surprise him- there is only one problem. I will not be able to recognise him- we have not seen each other since we were kids."

"Oh!" said the receptionist as if she suddenly understood everything.

"I have time on my hand," he said "and I will wait till he comes down and then I want to surprise him. The only help I want from you is to point him out to me when he comes out. Can you?"

She smiled and gave him a wink.

"That sounds interesting;" she said. "He usually comes down for lunch. I will help you."

"Thank you," said Farhan and retreated back to the chair where he had been sitting.

He sat there waiting and watching. Suddenly, the lady gave him a signal and he rushed to her.

"There," she said pointing to a young man who was moving towards the exit.

"Thank you so much," he said.

She waved at him with a smile and said, "Have a great reunion."

Farhan walked upto the exit and saw Sanjay walking away. He followed; he did not know where this was going to lead. He did not even know why he was doing this, but he followed. There was something about him, which seemed vaguely familiar and raised memories of a distant past. But; he could not quite place it. They were now crossing the road and for the first time, he saw Sanjay's face. It was that of a young confident man, sure of himself. And, then, the memories came back and he stood there rooted to the spot.

The sound of a blaring horn woke him up from his reverie. He was in the middle of the road; the lights had turned green and vehicles were whizzing past him. Inches away from him was a bus with the driver honking and shouting the choicest of abuses. After what seemed an eternity, he crossed the road and landed on the other side. He looked here and there- he seemed to have lost Sanjay. And then, he spotted him- he was only a few yards ahead of him talking animatedly to someone. He waited, trying to digest his find. He must be mistaken, he thought. But, no, there was something about the way he spoke-which reminded him of those days in the hospital and the boy who had brought him away from the blazing car. But, what was his card doing in Salim's pocket. He moved on, as Sanjay started walking. They reached Marine Drive. Sanjay was now looking at his watch and walking faster. He seemed to be going towards the Hilton Towers which stood majestically, rising upto the sky.Sanjay walked up the stairs and into the hotel. Farhan waited for a second, trying to make up his mind and then followed him. He was in time to see Sanjay disappearing into the coffee shop, adjoining the lobby. Farhan did not want to walk into the coffee shop, it would make him far too conspicous. He took a seat in the lounge away from the coffee shop and waited.

His thoughts went back.

What was the connection between Sanjay and Salim? What would Salim be doing with a newspaper editor? Was Sanjay leading him to Madhav? Yes, he thought. That must be it – that explained his meeting with Madhav that day. Oh! Salim, why did he not tell me? Why was I so foolish? How could I have mistrusted him?

His chain of thoughts was suddenly disrupted. He sat still, gaping. Madhav had walked in, swaggering as usual. He walked upto the reception, said something and laughed aloud. He then strode towards the coffee shop in a hurry.

Sanjay waited. It was now thirty minutes past the appointed hour and there was no sign of Madhav. He was getting impatient. And then in strode Madhav, looking important. Sanjay got up and introduced himself and took him to the table he had reserved. Madhav sat down and looked around.

"I have ordered some sandwiches and soup, is that ok?" asked Sanjay hesitantly.

"Yes," said Madhav, "let's get on with it," he said hurriedly.

Sanjay felt a trace of irritation; the bugger had landed up late and without an apology pretended he was delaying him. Sanjay smiled and showed Madhav his identity card.

Madhav waved it away- "C'mon, I believe you. Let's begin, what do you want to know?"

Later, when he would relive that hour he spent with Madhav; Sanjay would recount the mixed emotions that ran through him. At times, during that interview he had wanted to stand and shout out to everyone the horrible truth about Madhav. At times, he had just wanted to reach out and wring his neck. At times, he just wanted to end the interview and walk out. But he had done nothing of that sort.

"Could we start at the beginning?" said Sanjay. "We want to show the readers the person behind the builder, the politician."

"Well," said Madhav, "Where do I start? I was born in Dadar- in my uncle's hospital. I grew up in my uncle's house. My uncle was a great man."

"But your father..." interrupted Sanjay.

"Oh! He, he was an old man," said Madhav dismissing Sanjay and continuing "As I was saying my uncle played a big role in my life..." And so it went on and on.

A picture emerged of a boy strongly influenced by his uncle who grew upto be a builder- the hard way. A boy, who was affected by the scourge of terrorism and took up politics to banish it from the face of the country. A man, who was ready to give up his life for the country. The mask was complete.

Time was running out and Sanjay wanted the mask to slip. He had to ask some pointed questions.

"What is your opinion on the Babri Masjid demolition and the riots in Mumbai after that?" asked Sanjay suddenly.

The question took Madhav by surprise, but he quickly recovered.

"I thought this was an interview about me- the person," he answered. "But, since you ask, well the demolition of the mosque was unfortunate. Sometimes these things happen- it should not have happened. The riots were even more unfortunate- lots of innocent people died. Terrorism has to be nipped in the bud..."

"But," Sanjay interrupted, "there were lots of rumours, about men from your party, men like you, actively participating in the riots."

The mask fell.

Madhav glared at him. And then he smiled and answered gently.

"Are you accusing me of rioting? That is a serious accusation. You know I can take you to court!"

Sanjay stared back impassively.

"But then, this is an interview and you are after all a reporter- so you are just doing your job I guess," he said. "Listen, I had nothing to do with the riots. I was in college like any other boy of my age...What was your age then? You must have been in college too."

Sanjay smiled and said, "I was nineteen then in my first year of college. I saw a lot of the rioting- we used to live, we still live near Shivaji Park."

Madhav nodded; his face giving nothing away.

He looked at his watch. The interview had been going on well but suddenly it was going in a direction he did not like. He had to close this and get out. This was not leading him anywhere.

"Ok," he interrupted Sanjay. "I think we are running short of time and we should close now."

"Yes, we should," replied Sanjay. "But, since you were asking about me, I wanted to tell you something that I saw during those days which I can still remember."

He stopped; he had caught Madhav's attention. Madhav was looking at him keenly.

"It was at the height of rioting. It was one morning and I was passing by Shivaji Park. I saw a car burning- there seemed to be people inside, who were dying or were already dead. Somebody must have set them ablaze..."

Madhav wriggled in his seat. He was getting uncomfortable.

Who was this guy? What did he want? What did he know? Had he seen them?

Madhav nodded his head sadly "Yes, those were bad times."

"Yes, they were," interrupted Sanjay, "and as I was telling you earlier there were rumours later that some of your party men, men like you who were involved."

Anger rushed to his head; Madhav wanted to strike this guy in front of him. He rose from his seat, pointed a finger at Sanjay and was about to scream when he realised that everybody was looking at him. He controlled himself and sat down.

"If it was some other place- I would have given you a big slap. "Remember," he said, "I shall not forgive you for this. I shall see to it that you are fired from your job. How dare you accuse me?"

He got up and stomped out.

Sanjay smiled.

The mask had completely fallen. But he made an enemy- and that too a powerful one. He had to be careful.

Farhan had been shaken up when he saw Madhav. He was completely lost when he saw Madhav and Sanjay talking animatedly while eating. He sat down; where was this all leading to?

They seemed to know each other well, then why had Sanjay rescued him from the burning vehicle that day. Or had he? Maybe he was mistaken. But, no, the more he had seen of Sanjay, the more he was sure that it was the same person. Had Salim been taken for a ride? How much did they know about Salim? How much did they know about him? Was his game up? Would they come knocking on his door any day? He could not let that happen- he had to complete his mission.

Sanjay paid for the lunch and came out of the coffee shop. He was about to leave, when he saw a man, now familiar, sitting on a sofa. Farhan seemed to be dazed and lost. Sanjay wanted to walk upto him and talk. But, the courage failed him and he walked away.

Somebody was calling him. Farhan stood up startled, his thoughts coming to an abrupt halt.

"Excuse me sir," said a person. "Sorry for bothering. You seem to be waiting for someone, can we help you?"

Farhan stared back at him. It seemed to be somebody from the hotel.

"Yes ...I mean no," he answered. "I was waiting for someone but he did not turn up. I should be going."

It was past two, he had been there for more than a couple of hours. He looked back at the coffee shop; there was no sign of them.

They must have gone, he thought. Had they seen him? He had to speed up his plans.

Sanjay did not want to walk back, he was far too drained. He hailed a taxi and arrived back at the office. He was about to take the lift when the receptionist called out to him.

"Yes, Shanti!" he said.

"Did you have a grand reunion with your friend?" she asked with a big smile.

"Reunion?" he replied. "I went for an interview with a builder and it was not pleasant, believe me."

"But..." she seemed surprised now. "There was this guy..."

She narrated the story.

"I pointed you to him and he went behind you."

Sanjay shrugged. "Maybe, he lost me in the crowd. Anyway thanks! This time if he comes back, send him up and I will surprise him," he said with a laugh.

He stepped into the lift and it started to move up. And then a thought came to him. He stepped out of the lift and came running down stairs.

"Shanti," he said; he was panting.

He needed to get back to his exercising routine, some part of his brain was telling him. He pushed it to his back.

"Yes, Sanjay," said Shanti. "What is the matter?"

Sanjay stopped, catching his breath. "Nothing great- could you just describe this man, so that I can recognise him if we bumped into each other somewhere."

She described him- the description matched Farhan.

"Thank you," he said.

He went back to his office and sat down.

Why had Farhan come looking for him? How did he know he worked here? Did he want help? Then why had he not approached him. He seemed to have followed him upto the hotel. And then it became clear to him, Farhan had somehow located him and wanted his help, perhaps to locate Madhav. And then when he saw them together at lunch; he would have been confused, not knowing what to do. Sanjay could remember the dazed look on his face.

Sanjay sat there thinking. And then the decision was made. He had to meet Farhan today- he had delayed it long enough. He went upto his boss and said," I am leaving; I have a lead- the story could be big."

His boss smiled, "Something to do with the interview you had today?"

"Yes," he said and then he was out of the office.

"Get the child out of here!" shouted Madhav.

He had not gone to the office after his interview and had returned back home.

He was raging mad- how dare that puny reporter ask him such questions, he fumed. Did he really know more or was he fishing?

Whatever it was, he would see that he met an untimely end soon. The interview had really spoiled his day and he really needed some calm for the evening meeting. And now his son was bent on spoiling it further.

What an irritable boy, he thought. Kept coming back at him and asking questions. As if he knew all the answers.

He had threatened and shouted at the boy with dire consequences if he disturbed him further. But the child kept coming back and now he screamed at his wife to take him out of sight. Finally, the boy was removed from his sight; he slammed the door shut and tried to calm himself down.

Farhan reached home- it took him more than an hour. He locked the door and looked at his watch. It was nearly four pm. He sat down and tried to collect his thoughts. He had planned to execute the plan on 12th January; it would be the fifteenth anniversary of his family's ghastly demise. But, it was still a fortnight away. His time was running out. He had to make adjustments and execute the plan today- it was fraught with risks, but now he did not care. He smiled as he went over the plan. It was simple but foolproof. All it needed was a telephone call to set it in motion. He got up and went to the telephone.

Madhav willed himself to calm down- there were bigger things destined for him and he could not afford to be rattled like this. The phone rang. Madhav ignored it. It rang for a few times and then stopped. It again started ringing. Madhav removed the phone from its hook and ended the call. Now, there would be peace.

Farhan was getting panicky. His plan seemed to be going awry. He had presumed Madhav would lift the phone on being called. It had not occurred to him that something else could happen. He swore at himself- if Salim had been there; he would have thought of a back up plan. That is why, he had been so successful. He had a back up plan for everything...

But now— he picked up the phone and again started ringing. The phone was still engaged. He calmed himself down; he had to be patient and keep on trying.

Madhav stared at the phone. What if it had been a call from the party asking him to come early? He should not have disconnected the phone- he was acting like a kid. He put the phone back on the receiver. It began to ring immediately.

"Listen, carefully," said the voice at the other end. "I know what you did with that family fifteen years back near Shivaji Park."

"Shut up!" shouted Madhav. "You bloody reporter; you think you are smart. Your end is near."

"Shut up!" said the voice from the other end. "If you don't listen and act as I tell you, it will be the end of you and your career."

The voice went on- Madhav heard in horror as it recounted in detail his role.

"And that's not the only thing," it went on. "Six years back, in Ahmedabad; you were back; were you not?"

"Stop!" shouted Madhav. "What if it was all true, who is going to believe you and what can you do now?"

"Well," replied the voice calmly. "I killed your parents; I tied them up and burnt them alive. I can do anything."

A chill went through Madhav's spine, as he heard this.

"Bloody swine," he shouted. "I shall kill you."

"Yes," said the voice. "Come and get me. And if you don't come; it will be all there in the morning newspaper. And yes, note down my address- if you are sensible- come alone and meet me in the basement. You have suffered and so have I—so let's make a deal and part."

"A deal with you," shouted Madhav. "Never!"

"It's upto you," said Farhan. "If you don't turn up in an hour's time; then you have to bear the consequences."And, then the phone went dead.

What the bloody heck was the reporter trying? Or was he a reporter at all? But,his voice had appeared different over the phone. And,who was that man who had spoken and met him a couple of years back with a lead? Things were getting murkier.

He swore...

Why was everything happening today? Why did he go for the interview?

He cursed himself. He had put himself into a corner. Now; he had to wriggle out of it and fast. He looked at the address; it was not very far. He looked at it closely, it seemed familiar. He quickly went to his cupboard and took out a file, it was a dossier— a dossier on Farhan Rasool. He smiled. So, that was the game. But then, what was his link with the reporter. He needed to find out. He had planned to finish them off later- perhaps, today was the day. And then there would be no stopping him. He took out a key and opened a drawer and looked inside. There, it lay looking very inviting. He took it in his hand and fondled it. He put it carefully in a leather bag; it was loaded and could shatter a man's head.

Sanjay looked at the building which he knew housed Farhan. He should have done this- a long while ago, he thought to himself. He was about to cross the road and enter the building- when a car drove passed him suddenly; he had to swerve back to the footpath as the car came very close to hitting him. He wanted to catch the driver and give him a dressing down. But, he checked himself. Madhav had got down from the car; he had a bag in his hand. He looked at either side and entered.

Sanjay did not know what to do. Madhav was the last guy he had expected here.

What was he doing with Farhan or had he come to meet somebody else?

Anyway, it was now or never.

Farhan crouched near his car in the basement and waited. It was quite dark and anybody coming there from outside would be disoriented in the beginning. He needed to catch Madhav in that stage. He strained his eyes and watched. And then he saw the silhoutte; there was a man and he held something in his hand. He had to move now. He stopped- there was somebody else behind the first man.

Who was that?

He could not see clearly. But; he had to take his chances.

Sanjay followed Madhav gingerly into the basement. It was quite dark and he could barely see. He walked slowly, not wanting to stumble on something. He saw Madhav removing something from his bag- it seemed like a revolver. Sanjay gasped- he had to stop this somehow. And, then he saw Madhav falling.

Did he stumble?

He waited. The pain was sudden and seared through him like lightning and then his world went black.

He tried to open his eyes- and was blinded. Somebody was shining a torch on his face. He tried to speak. His lips seemed to be sealed- he could not open his mouth. He tried to prise open his lips, but found he could not move his arms. The light went out and he heard a soft voice.

"Welcome, Mr.Sanjay. Sorry to welcome you like this...And, yes, you must be worried about your friend Mr.Madhav. Don't worry, he is also alive- he is lying beside you. But, he will take some more time to come around- I gave him a really solid blow."

Sanjay wanted to say he had nothing to do with Madhav, but nothing came out of his mouth. His head was feeling like a top with innumerable pins sticking in. He lay still- not knowing what to do and trying to focus on the objects nearby. Slowly, his eyes started adjusting to the darkness. And then he saw Farhan; he was sitting on a tyre nearby and looking at him intently. He looked around; a man lay near him, still. It must be Madhav, he thought. He tried to free his arms but failed. He had been trussed up tightly like a chicken. Only his feet was free, but he could do nothing much. A tape was applied across his lips and all his attempts to scream were futile.

Suddenly, he heard a noise. It was the sound of a footstep; he started moving his feet and trying to make some noise. Nothing happened. The sound faded away.

"I am sorry," said Farhan "Nobody comes to this part of the basement. It is pretty damp and broken up-only I keep my car here. Never mind, you don't have to wait here for long. Let your friend get up and then we shall go for a long drive. I know you want to say so many things-but that will have to wait. I will remove the plaster from your lips, once we are inside the car. But one thing I am not clear, I thought that you saved me and took me to the hospital but I must have been mistaken. You seem to be a wolf in sheep's clothing; a journalist and hand in glove with that criminal!"

Sanjay nodded his head desperately trying to clear the air- but gave up.

"Ah!" said Farhan. "Mr.Madhav you have also woken up; your friend here seems to be stronger."

Madhav's head was ringing in pain. He wanted to shout, but could do nothing. He had nicely walked in a trap.

What a fool he had been. Suddenly, he felt afraid; this man had killed his family and now he was also at his mercy. He looked around and was shocked to see the reporter lying next to him in a similar condition. What was he doing here and that too, in a similar condition. And, then he saw Farhan standing above him. He had a dagger in his hand- a long, curved one. Farhan smiled.

"Don't worry," he said. "I will not kill you with this; I could have killed you both, while you were lying in a faint."

"Let's go," he said suddenly. "We are getting late."

He pulled them up one by one and bundled them into the rear seat of the car, standing nearby. He then secured them to the seat by wrapping more ropes around them. It took a long time but finally it was done. Both, Sanjay and Madhav could barely sit as the ropes bit into them sharply.

Farhan got into the driver's seat.

"I am sure you need to talk," he said. "I will give you that opportunity but first, let's go somewhere where there is some light so that we can look at each other clearly."

He started the car and started driving. He drove slowly and Sanjay wondered where it was all leading to. He suddenly wanted to be far away from all this, at home with his family. Suddenly Farhan stopped. Sanjay strained to find out where they were. He was surprised to find that the car had come to a stop adjoining Shivaji Park.

"Well, gentleman," said Farhan turning back. "We have arrived; where it all started."

He got out from the seat, closed the door and went out.

Sanjay and Madhav looked at each other and wondered what was going to happen. They had a common enemy now and they needed each other.

The door on the passenger side at the front opened and Farhan got in. He was now facing them. He suddenly lunged and pulled the tapes from their sealed lips. The pain was intense and they cried out. And, then the shouting began. They screamed and screamed and finally stopped.

Farhan smiled, "Have you had enough? Nobody is going to listen to you. This car is well insulated. And before we talk a few points; I have your mobile phones with me and they are both switched off. Madhav," he said the name with distaste, "your gun is with me."

He pointed it at both of them.

"I believe it's loaded. And yes, I have this nice dagger. I won't hesitate to use either, if you start behaving like naughty children. I also have something else, but we will come to that later. Now, you can ask your questions and I will answer."

There was utter silence as they stared and sized each other.

He looks every inch the professor, thought Sanjay as he looked at Farhan. A far cry from the boy whom he had rescued. Farhan looked distinguished with his grey hair and rimmed glasses. But, he looked far too older than his age, thought Sanjay.The years had taken its toll.

Farhan was looking intently at Madhav. His curly hair was unkempt and his bushy moustache was overgrown. His cheeks were drooping and folds of fat were hanging below his chin. Looks every inch the hooligan, that he is, thought Farhan.

Farhan turned as he saw Sanjay eyeing him. Well, this guy surprised him. He seemed to be gentle and kind but why had he joined with Madhav? His eyes–they were intense and they looked pained. Pained, but why, thought Farhan.

His thoughts were interrupted.

"Why have you brought me here and in this fashion?" shouted Madhav. "I have an important meeting in the evening; I have to go. Let me go and I shall get you whatever money you want- Is that not what you are after?"

"Money," said Farhan, "So ultimately it boils down to money, is it? You want to pay me the price of my family. So, how much is that? What is the price you have fixed?"

"How much do you want?" shouted Madhav "Fifty lakhs, One crore, Two crore, you name the price and I will get you."

Farhan leaned forward and slapped Madhav on the cheek.

"That hurt, did it not?" he asked "If you don't want more of that, do not shout. If at all anybody shouts here, it's me. Where were we, yes money. If only things were so simple..."

He stopped.

There was silence.

"Why did you kill my family?" asked Farhan suddenly. He leaned forward and was inches from Madhav's face. "What did they ever do to you?"

He went back to his seat and continued.

"My sister, she would have been a proud mother by now. Her wedding was fixed but you did not care. My grandmother- poor lady, such a harmless soul. What did she do; what did we do?"

Madhav was glaring angrily now.

"You!" he said, "Your people, they killed my uncle, my cousin. You talk about your sister; what about mine; she was five years old. They were all gunned down in front of my eyes. I escaped. You people- you sit in your cubby holes and plot against us, against the country. You refuse to go away but do nothing for the country. You whine and cry and our government- the incompetent fools, they pamper you. Pump you up with money. Fund your pilgrimages. And what do you do in return; you build more mosques and bomb and kill us. You people have to be taught a lesson—a lesson for good; that, if you live here; you live by our rules. We are a country where we worship Ram, Krishna, Ganapathi, a country with a glorious tradition and we do not want scums like you spoiling our culture. You follow our culture or you might as well get out. Yes, I killed your family and other vermin like you, because you are just that. You are like pests which need to be exterminated and I will not hesitate to do it again."

And so it went on and on...

Sanjay watched in horror at the venom spouting from Madhav's mouth. Madhav was nearly frothing at the mouth as he hurled expletives; one after another. Sanjay could not understand how somebody could have so much hatred. But, perhaps, that explained his actions.

He looked at Farhan who seemed calm. Madhav's litany of hate finally came to an end.

"So," he concluded, "now that you know why, what do you want?"

Farhan looked at him and then turned to Sanjay and said, "And you?"

"Yes, what about me?" said Sanjay, puzzled.

"So, you agree to his views and therefore you joined hands?" asked Farhan.

Sanjay looked more puzzled.

Madhav let out a loud guffaw.

"That is very funny. You think that this reporter fellow is with me. My goodness and I was all the time thinking he was with you and both of you–oh my, this is really funny."

"But, is he not with you?" It was the turn of Farhan to look puzzled.

"But, I saw you both together in the restaurant, laughing and eating."

"My God!" said Madhav, "if you had not tied me like this, I would be rolling in laughter.

He was interviewing me and I, believe me, wanted to twist his neck, still do."

Even Sanjay smiled. Both of them thought that he was with the other and he was now caught in the crossfire.

For the first time, Sanjay saw doubt flickering on Farhan's face. He had to strike now.

"I saw you sitting in the hotel, looking vexed. I returned back to the office and my receptionist mentioned that a person answering to your description had enquired about me. I put two and two together and came to your house to meet you. There, I saw Madhav and I followed him and after that you know the story."

Farhan still looked at him with disbelief. "But, how did you know where I lived and why did you come to meet me?"

Sanjay sighed, "It's a long story and like you said, it started way back, here on this road.

I do not know if you remember, you were like a mad man that day, ready to plunge in the car and die. I did not know what to do; everybody seemed to be looking the other way. I picked you up and carried you to a hospital. You took a long time to recover and then one day you disappeared."

Farhan nodded, "I thought so. I thought you were the same boy who saved me when I followed you that day. But your meeting with this beast" he pointed at Madhav "confused me. And how did you locate my house?"

"Oh! We reporters have our sources," replied Sanjay. "But, I located you long time back; I wanted to meet you and talk to you and share your pain. But, I never had the courage. What do I tell somebody who has seen his family being killed in front of his eyes? I was a coward so I shied away. But, I could not sleep. My conscience pricked me. I had seen Madhav with my own eyes doing this ghastly thing. And here, he was walking scot free and prospering. I had to do something. I fixed up an interview with him; I wanted to provoke him. He got provoked."

"You bastard!" growled Madhav.

"And, then I realised," continued Sanjay, "you wanted to meet me. I sensed you needed help and so I came. But, your actions here surprise me. What do you want?"

"What do I want?" asked Farhan more to himself.

Then he looked from one to the other and said, "I want to kill this man who destroyed my life. I want to destroy this country and its people who looked the other way when my innocent family and many others like them were butchered."

Madhav gave a sardonic grin while Sanjay looked on shocked.

"But..." said Sanjay, "You are educated and a professor; you cannot talk like this. Yes, justice has not come but you cannot hold everybody responsible for it.

This is your own country as it is mine and his."

"Ha!" said Madhav in disgust. "You talk like the government. It is people like you sitting in their glass cubicles, who are encouraging these pests," he said pointing at Farhan.

Farhan said nothing and there was silence. All around them they could see vehicles whizzing past them while Shivaji Park was a buzz of activity.

"I was just like you," Farhan said looking at Sanjay. "I felt I belonged here. My father felt it too; very strongly. He refused to go to Pakistan during Partition, because he truely believed that we belonged here.

I, we never felt different-there were few taunts here and there but nothing much really."

He paused. Sanjay could feel him living those moments.

"We were a happy family," he continued, "just like anybody else. And then one day—everything went crazy. My make belief world crumbled. I suddenly realised that I, my father had been wrong all along. There was no place for me, for us in this society, country.We, Muslims were, are pariahs. I did not believe it at first; my upbringing refused to accept such a situation. But, Salim, he...opened my eyes. He nursed me back and gave me a reason to live and die. I, we decided that we had taken enough; we had to strike back now. But, I did not want to run away, I wanted to live amongst all of you and see you all squirm, in confusion and panic."

"I killed your parents," he said looking at Madhav. "I did that with my own hands. I wanted you to suffer, like I did. But, it did not seem to have any effect on you. We then moved on to bigger things—we engineered blasts one after another. I planned and Salim executed. I loved this dual role; that of a professor and the other of a terrorist; is that the word? Both of you look shocked. But you—your people drove me into this."

"But," said Sanjay, "why are you killing innocent people; children, women. What did they have to do? You cannot penalise the vast majority for the sins of a few."

"The vast majority!" scoffed Farhan. "What were they doing, what do they do when this minority, as you say, kills us- our women, children. They keep silent and look the other way. Everyone, the vast majority as you call it; go about their tasks as if nothing has happened. Of course, they weep in your newspaper columns and now they have a new medium to weep- television. They shed crocodile tears. And, and then they forget. They have better things to do..."

"That's not true," said Sanjay. "Many of us have spoken up, actions are being taken; the guilty will be punished."

"When? When will you punish the guilty?" whispered Farhan. "When everything becomes a faint memory? When everybody is dead and gone? When it's far too late that it does not matter anymore?"

He continued ... "Look at this man—he has prospered, he has become rich. Has he been punished? No. He never will be. After all he is one of you. How many of those who burnt and killed innocents have been punished? Speak from the bottom of your heart, Sanjay. You know the truth, you can count them on your fingers."

"Don't pretend to be holier than thou," shouted Madhav. "You talk as if you and your people are saints while we are the guilty? Who was it who started the killings? Who was it that burnt the train?"

And so it went on. Each trading allegations. The split was complete. Sanjay watched in horror. Tears rolled down his eyes. Tears for a country gone horribly wrong somewhere...

"Shut up, will you, both of you!" shouted Sanjay.

And the car fell silent.

"What is the matter with you people? Have you both lost your senses? Do you want a civil war?" asked Sanjay

"Yes," replied Madhav and Farhan in unison.

"Ah!" said Sanjay, "there is at least something you both agree upon."

"Yes," replied Madhav, "we have to finish the unfinished task of Partition. They cannot have the cake and eat it too."

"Yes," agreed Farhan, "let it be a battle to the finish—It is either us or you."

"But, I, we, will not let this happen," replied Sanjay. "We will not let this country be taken over by people like you. We will resist and we will win..."

"Enough of this for now!" said Madhav. "I am getting late now, I need to go."

"And," he said pointing at Farhan, "I will personally ensure that you are hanged for your crimes against the people of this country."

"Oh!" replied Farhan, "the pot calling the kettle black, is it? And what about your dark deeds?"

Sanjay sat and watched as they began all over again. Sitting there, they looked like animals growling and raging, ready to pounce at each other.

He felt a sadness seeping through him; where, why had everything turned out like this? Was there nothing to be done? Had we not paid enough for the sins of our forefathers? Why did we need to carry their prejudices forward? When will we ever learn the lessons of history? Could we not break those shackles and move ahead and rewrite history? Could we not create a new dawn for our children and our grandchildren?

"Stop..." he whispered.

But, it had the effect. The car went silent.

"Yes, there have been mistakes from both sides. But killing and blaming each other is not going to erase those mistakes. It will only keep the cycle going on and on. And perhaps that is what you want. But, it is time now to stop, reflect and start again. Both of you can start this process of healing. I know hundreds will join you. Let us join hands—let us forgive and forget; let us give future generations a chance to start afresh."

Sanjay stopped. He did not know from where those words came; but they had come out of him like a torrent.

There was silence again. Sanjay looked out. He could see the street lights now; it was the time of the day before dusk. The light was fading...

"It's too late Sanjay," said Farhan, breaking the silence. "I used to think like you once upon a time." He nodded his head. "It's too late."

"Yes," said Madhav. "It's either we or they—there can be no way in between."

Sanjay shook his head; he had tried, but had lost.

"I think we have talked enough," said Farhan. "We now understand each other; I mean we now know why we are driven to take these actions. We may not agree, but then that's the way it is. And, now, its getting late. It's been a long day and I am tired. It's been a long time since I have rested—–fifteen long years. Fifteen long years since I put my lap on my *Dadi jaan*'s lap and listened to her story. Fifteen long years since I felt my *Abba's* breath as he clasped me to his chest. Fifteen long years since I heard Mumtaz chattering away. Fifteen long years since I felt the reassuring gaze of my *Ammi*." He paused.

The others were watching him.

"I want to join them, touch them, talk to them; I have waited enough. I have killed, destroyed many families.But, I cannot go now, I cannot rest in peace, not until I take him along," he pointed out at Madhav. "Maybe he will also find peace there..."

"What are you talking?" asked Sanjay.

"This car is loaded with explosives," continued Farhan. "It was not difficult to get them and assemble. I have a device here," he pointed at something which looked like small TV remote to Sanjay. "I press this and boom goes this car. Not only will this destroy this car, but also create havoc to everything within fifty metres of it."

"No...No..." shouted Madhav. "Don't do this. I won't tell about you to anybody. I will give you money." He was now pleading. "I will get you a new identity, a ticket so that you can go away from this country. Far away- where nobody can reach you. Believe me, I have contacts. Please don't kill me. I want to live."

Madhav was now whimpering and crying.

"And you Sanjay, you look calm, what do you have to say?" said Farhan.

Sanjay had felt a strange calmness as he heard Farhan speak.

"It's you against Madhav, isn't it; so blow up the car or do whatever you want, but not here. What have all these people; women, kids, old people done to you? Leave them alone."

"No!" nodded Farhan. "They have to pay a price for the deeds of their forefathers, their relatives or uncles or whatever. They have to pay a price for being born and living in this society. They have to pay a price like me and Madhav here..."

He turned back and got into the driver's seat. "Time to set the wheels in motion. Tell your prayers to whichever God you worship and prepare yourself."

Madhav squirmed and shouted and pleaded. Sanjay desperately looked for signs of escape, but there was none.

He could see the street full of vehicles- people on the way back home. The park was full of people- enjoying the pleasant evening. He could visualise his parents, wife, and his grandmother waiting, at home, for him. His mind went back to the visit he had paid to the gynecologist with his wife, a week back. They had done an ultrasound and there he had the first glimpses of his unborn child.

He could not sit there and let this happen. He had to do something. For himself, for the people around, for his family, for his child- who waited in the comfort of the womb.

The car started moving.

"You cannot harm me," said Sanjay to Farhan. "I did no harm to you, in fact I saved you."

The car stopped and again started moving.

"Why did you save me?" said Farhan, behind the wheel of the car. "You could have left me to die there. You saved me so that I had to wallow in this miserable life. You did no favour to me, Sanjay.You harmed me more than anyone else. Besides, I did not seek you out, you came on your own and so you die."

Madhav was now screaming in terror and anger. "The police will catch you and hang you. They must be on their way now. I informed them to come looking after me; if I did not come back."

"Do not bluff!" said Farhan.

The car was gaining speed; it turned left and started moving along the eastern periphery of the park.

"And I don't care if the police are coming; this will be over in a few moments."

"No, no..." pleaded Madhav.

Farhan turned back and smiled.

"You seem to be calm, Sanjay; you seem to have accepted your fate. You are a brave man and I admire your courage. You remind me of what I could have been, if not for..." the words trailed away.

The car had reached the north east corner of the Park. It turned left again and started moving.

What was he doing, thought Sanjay.Why was he going in circles? He could now only sit and pray. He had never been one for praying. He participated in all the festivals and also accompanied his parents and grandmother to the temple without demur. He even recited some *mantras-* which had been taught to him as a child, as a matter of routine when he went to temples or at the *Ganapati puja* festival. But, he had never really prayed in that sense. But today, he prayed and the happy moments of his life flashed by. He could see his grandfather smiling; Vivek was with him and they were all playing cricket on the terrace. He could see his father hugging him when he won his first prize; it was for an essay competition. He could see his grandmother fussing over him as he rushed through his breakfast. He could see his mother's approving glance as he wed his wife Nafisa. He could see Nafisa and himself smiling...

And then, the car stopped and Farhan got out. Farhan must have bluffed, thought Sanjay. He must be getting away from the car leaving them to die. He resigned himself for the explosion. The door at his side opened a fraction. Sanjay could see a little bit outside; it was dark now. He suddenly felt Farhan leaning over him and cutting the ropes that tied him to the car. He felt himself being pulled out of the car and pushed onto the footpath. Passers-by looked startled.

Farhan looked at him and smiled.

"Go home, Sanjay and tell the world our story..."

And then he was gone and the car started moving again.

For a second, Sanjay did not know what to do and then he began to scream.

"There is a bomb in that vehicle; it will explode any time. Call the police."

He desperately rolled on the footpath trying to attract passers-by.

The car gained speed again and moved on.

"I let him go," said Farhan to Madhav. "I wanted him to write about us. I do not know why?"

Why do men, humanity tend to leave signs of themselves wherever they go? You can see signs of that in those caves where prehistoric men lived, in those paintings and sculptures that adorn our houses and museums, in those photographs that live on in those albums and walls and now in pen drives. You can see more signs when you go visting ancient monuments or the cities- graffiti. You can see signs of those again in those writings and poems and books and magazines. Man wants to leave a trace of himself back in this world before he fades away into oblivion. He wants to make some statement---it may be small like the scribble on the wall by the child, learning to write or it maybe big, really big like the Taj Mahal. It maybe man's eternal quest for immortality...

"Please leave me!" begged Madhav. "I have wronged you. I have made mistakes but what could I do? What would you have done in my place? Tell me, Farhan."

People had gathered around Sanjay now. An eatery owner located by the roadside had got hold of a knife and cut him free. He got up and ran shouting at others to get away. The car had now turned the corner and was on the main arterial road abutting the western periphery of the park- Veer Savarkar Marg. A policeman was now running towards him.

"There is a car, Ambassador, black; it is going to blow up. Do something."

The explosion was so intense that it shook the ground on which Sanjay stood. He could see flames rising in the distance. Smoke was billowing, people were screaming and the smell of burnt flesh wafted in.

❀❀❀

Epilogue

The car bomb killed many and maimed others for life—men, women, children, Hindus, Muslims, Christian, Marathis, Gujarathis, Punjabis, Malayalees, rich, poor, pedestrians, people travelling by cycles, bikes, taxis, cars, buses...It tore apart many lives. It cut short many a dream and left people unhinged for life. It ended Farhan and Madhav's brief sojourn in this world.

The police went into action; citizen groups rallied; there were discussions and articles, there were protests, there were accusations and counter accusations, there were condolences and condemnations from parties and world leaders and there were arrests.

Slowly, the blast faded away from public memory and remained only in the minds and lives of a few hundred people who had been there at the time of the blast or whose loved ones had perished or escaped providentially.

A series of articles appeared in a newspaper. It told the story of two men—one Hindu and another Muslim. The identity of the two men was not revealed. It was penned by Sanjay Dave. The article raised many questions but there were very few answers.

The police traced back the ownership of the car to Farhan.They raided the house. There was nothing. They were up against a blank wall. News that their apartment complex housed a terrorist, sent shockwaves amongst Farhan's neighbours.They heaved a sigh of relief that they had escaped without harm. His students and co-teachers refused to believe the reports. They held condolence meetings and prayed for his soul. Farhan's sisters did not know what to believe. They had moved far away from Farhan when he was alive and in death, they completely disassociated from him not wanting his spirit to prey on their lives. In private, they cried and prayed for his troubled soul.

Reena, Madhav's wife was distraught. They could barely get any of his body parts. She had never been happy when Madhav was alive but even in death; he cast a shadow over her life. The rumours of his violent past came thick and strong. Her father was completely broken. They sold off all their properties and business and went back to their ancestral village.

A girl was born to Sanjay and Nafisa. Rajni held the baby in her hands and wept tears of joy.

They named her 'Sana'. Rajni had coined the name for her great granddaughter from the names of her grandson and his wife—it meant 'Brilliance' in Arabic. The entire family came together for the naming ceremony. It was a low key but happy occasion.

And there ends this story of three men, drawn towards each other by a quirk of fate.

We...all of you out there and me have seen their lives up close, unknown to them.

We have cried and laughed with them. But now its time to move on...It was a story after all.

Time to get on with our lives. Time to do, whatever we have been doing.

I know you are in a hurry, the story is over and the curtain has fallen.

But, wait! For one last time...

I can hear this sound more and more now---it is louder and clearer. And it frightens me. It wakes me up from my sleep. It gives me nightmares. Sometimes; I feel I must be imagining it. Maybe, I am going insane. Nobody really seems to be affected by it.

But sometimes, I see a few souls who also seem to be haunted by it. But they are few and far. They also know not what to do. I can see them trying their best, but they seem to be fighting a loosing battle.

I am terrified that one day this sound will ring in the death knell of our society. Yes; I am terrified by the sound of silence---our silence. It is all pervading and all encompassing. It can be heard clearly---as our society gets torn apart, as people die on the streets, as bombs explode, as our cities burn...We, choose to be silent, maybe because we believe, perhaps naively that it will not affect us; sitting in our comfortable homes and colleges and offices and clubs and cinema houses and hotels and restaurants....We believe we are insulated, perhaps we want to be insulated.

But, I fear we are living in a fantasy world...a world which can come crashing down any time.

But this fear is also tinged with hope. For man lives on hope. 'Hope' that one day, not too far away, we will speak. 'Hope', that we will all speak together and its reverberation will shatter this deafening sound that I hear today. 'Hope' that these reverberations will echo throughout our society and stop this madness. 'Hope' that future generations will be wiser and learn from our follies. 'Hope' that our children and their grandchildren and their children will one day see and live the dream of a frail old man who had defied the odds and had dared to speak out...

❀❀❀

Reviews of Murali's debut novel, Dreams Die Young

Murali has woven a veiled commentary on the present seething turmoil. Murali's lucid prose, efficacious trenchant realism, an insightful mode of characterisation, psychological overtones has enabled him to unravel a theme of timeless human significance –relationship of the individual and the society, raising the book to the stature of a sociological document.

— The Tribune

Intense and intricate, it is hard to believe that this is C V Murali's debut novel. Unlike a few writers who just claim to guide the genre of contemporary English literature to glory, C V Murali effectively does the job.

— The Free Press Journal

C.V. Murali has gone into the subject with a quiverful of questions. Murali prefers a crisp, matter-of-fact-style... The twist in the climax is well-produced.

— The Hindu

There are lots of pearls one could gather-the style, gripping narrative and the classy opening. The hallmark of the book is its excellent narrative.

— The Week

There is a freshness about this slim, nostalgic first novel which should sustain the interest of the reader to the end. As a first novel, Dreams Die Young shows promise, and this will, no doubt, be realised in future works as the author matures in craftsmanship.

— Indian Literature (Sahitya Akademi's Bi-monthly journal)